The Lioness and the Spellspinners

Cheryl Mahoney

Stonehenge Circle Press

Stonehenge Circle Press

ISBN-13: 978-1-68012-631-0
ISBN-10: 1-68012-631-8

First Edition

Cover images courtesy of CaptBlack76/Shutterstock

This book is a work of fiction. Resemblance to any persons living or dead is purely coincidental.

Dedication

For Karen

Thank you for listening to me ramble on the day I started writing this story (and on many other days!) and for asking all the right questions. This would be a very different book without you!

This story is set two centuries before *The Storyteller and Her Sisters*, ten years before the curse that strikes the country of Marileigh and its twelve princes.

Book One

~ ♦ ~

Chapter One

Forrest set down his bucket of cracked seed on the barn floor and called, "I know you're up there, so you may as well come down."

The gentle drift of hay from the loft overhead stopped abruptly, likely as the person above froze in place. Whoever was up there was being impressively silent, but hadn't counted on the gaps between the wide wooden slats. Probably one of the kids from a nearby farm, snuck out for the night. He could sympathize; it was only a few years since he'd done that kind of thing himself.

"It's too late to pretend you're not there, and there's only the one ladder so—" He broke off as the fall of hay flakes redoubled, with the accompanying sound of wooden slats creaking. The scrape of shutters opening made him realize that the person above was not heading towards the ladder.

"Now wait, you can't go out that way!" He set down the lantern too and started for the ladder himself, hadn't even touched it yet before he heard a thud from outside. He shook his head and pivoted on one heel to change direction, to the barn doors into the yard. What idiot jumped out of a window fifteen feet off the ground?

He stepped out in time to see a slight figure pick itself up, so at least no necks had been broken. The figure seemed intent on making a run out of the yard, but Forrest caught up in a few long strides, reached out to catch one slender shoulder.

"Just a minute, there's no need to—"

"Don't touch me!" a female voice snarled, whirling around as Forrest's fingers barely grazed her shoulder. She backed off a few paces then stumbled, face creasing in a grimace. She halted, reaching out with one hand to press against the rough stone wall of the barn.

Definitely not one of the kids from a nearby farm. The sun was only just beginning to cast rays over the horizon, but even in the dim light and long shadows of early dawn, it was still easy to see that much. She was small enough, but the narrowness of her face and the curves of her body both marked her as over sixteen, and her clothes marked her as, well, *not* a neighbor. Her black cloak hung open to show a leather vest over a deep purple shirt, dark pants and high leather boots. Not exactly the latest word in fashion among the local girls.

Clearly she was from somewhere very different from his small island. Maybe some place where jumping out a window to get away from a stranger who didn't mean any harm made sense, as unimaginable as that seemed.

Forrest spread his hands to the sides, and employed the tone he usually reserved for skittish sheep. "Nobody's going to hurt you. Will you tell me who you are? What you're doing here?"

"I'm not doing anything except leaving," the girl snapped, started to take a step and flinched, pressing her hand harder against the wall again.

He instinctively reached out to offer her help, but caught himself. Clearly that wasn't going to be welcome. "You hurt your ankle landing, didn't you?"

"It'll be fine in a minute." She reached down to rub her right ankle, mouth pulling into a scowl, gaze still on Forrest. He couldn't tell if her eyes were really gray, or if it was just the pale light.

"You could have just taken the ladder," he said, trying a smile that was not mirrored.

"I've jumped from higher windows," she said, eyes narrowing. "And I was hoping to avoid a stupid conversation like this. So how about you just go back inside and forget I was here, hmm?"

First she jumped out a window, now she seemed determined to hobble off on a twisted ankle. Where had she come from, and what kind of trouble was she in that made her so desperate to get away? "There's no reason you have to sneak off," he said, keeping his voice soft. "My name's Forrest, and this is my family's barn you were sleeping in."

She just stared at him, unmoving.

"And your name is?" he prompted.

"I can't imagine any reason you would need to know." She exhaled, blowing air upwards and making the loose strands of hair lying across her forehead flutter. "Just spare me the attempts to be friendly or helpful or whatever it is you think you're doing, all right?"

"I'm only trying—"

"And what kind of name is that anyway?" she interrupted. "Forest like the trees?"

He blinked, taken aback. Basic politeness couldn't be that different wherever she came from. "No, my name has two R's in it," he said, a little edge entering his voice. He hadn't had to field this question for years. Everyone around here knew his name.

"So?"

"So…forest like the trees only has one—"

"Why are you imagining I care about this?" She reached down to rub her ankle again, shrugging her cloak back as she did. His gaze followed down to her leg, and this time he noticed something he hadn't before—something that looked a lot like the hilt of a knife, just visible protruding up out of her boot.

It was growing easier to decide that, however curious he felt about who she was and why she was here, sometimes satisfying curiosity just wasn't worth it. "Perhaps you had better just go."

She rolled her eyes. "*Perhaps* that's exactly what I've been saying." She took a few steps, and though the corner of her mouth deepened into a frown, she nodded in apparent satisfaction and didn't reach for the wall again. She started across the yard, at a steady if not very fast pace.

He stood by the barn and watched her go. It was better this way. The girl might be *in* trouble, but she clearly *was* trouble too. Better that she just go on her way, and—he blinked, as it suddenly occurred to him which direction she was walking. He took a few hurried steps after her, reached for her shoulder again.

She jerked away, turned just as quickly as before, maybe faster, and suddenly she had a glint of metal in one hand. "What did I tell you," she hissed, "about coming up behind me?"

Forrest swallowed and backed up a step, gaze on the small knife in her hand as it caught the brightening rays of sunlight. He raised his own hands, empty and palms out. "Nothing, actually, you just said not to touch you."

Her forehead crinkled momentarily. She took a breath and shifted into a glower. "Close enough."

With an effort he found his soothing tone again. "I was only going to say, it would be better if you took the path the other direction." His gaze shifted down to her boot. He didn't think she had reached down—no, the hilt-edge was still visible. So that was two knives. At least.

"I know where I'm going. The shore is this way."

The shore was every way. It wasn't that big of an island. "Still, it's better to circle around the other way—"

"Do I really have to keep saying I don't want your help?"

He wasn't trying to help her. He was trying to get her out of here without going past his family's house. "Yeah, that was clear. But I still think you should go the other way to—"

"I don't care what you think, and I did not ask for your advice!"

"All right, fine. Then just keep walking." He could hear her voice getting louder; a few more words like that, and it wasn't going to matter which direction she went. "But be quiet."

She glared at him, and resumed her limping pace. Quietly.

He couldn't let her go past the house alone. A stranger who didn't want to be seen was bad enough, but one carrying weapons she knew how to use... Who knew what else she was hiding, or what she might take it into her head to do? He grabbed the long pitchfork leaning up against the barn, caught up to her again maybe a hundred yards away from the gray cottage.

She didn't say anything, but her glance at the pitchfork was eloquent enough.

"I know how to use it," he said, lifting it a few inches.

"To do what, toss hay?"

His fingers tightened on the wooden shaft. "If you want to get out of here so badly, just stay quiet."

"You're talking more than I am...tree-boy."

"I'm older than you are," he snapped without thinking. If she really was sixteen, then he had three years on her.

She smirked. "Only in years."

His mouth clamped shut. Trouble. She was definitely trouble. But it didn't matter, because she was going to walk right by the house and, for all he cared, right on into the sea, and the point was that it didn't matter what she said or thought because she was *leaving*.

In theory, at least. He really should have known better, known that walking quietly past the house wouldn't be enough. He had never understood exactly how his mother could make porridge, braid one daughter's hair, chide two others to get ready *and* see everything out the window. He could almost believe it was magic, except that he knew his mother's magic didn't work that way. All the same, he should have expected that she'd be on the doorstep before they even came opposite the house.

She stood with her hands on her hips, sunlight gleaming on the gray streaks in her brown hair, and smiled benevolently at the cloaked girl. "Hello, dear, you're just in time for breakfast. Forrest, do introduce us."

"She's not staying for breakfast," he said, quickly taking up a position beside his mother, half a step in front of her.

"I'm just...passing by," the girl said, looking confused. "I'll just—"

"Nonsense, dear, you look hungry, and I wouldn't dream of letting you go on without eating something first. There's plenty of porridge. Forrest, go in and dish out an extra bowl."

He could have predicted what she'd say almost word for word. If he had just got the girl past unseen and on her way—but too late for that easy solution. He still didn't make a move to go inside. "She was sleeping in the barn, Mother. And she won't tell me her name."

Mother's lips pursed in disapproval. "Sleeping in the barn? That's terrible. You should have knocked at the door. We can always find a spare bed when someone needs it. Now come along inside."

She reached out to take the stranger by the arm, and Forrest took a step forward, because so help him, if she drew that knife again—but the girl just let herself be steered inside, confused expression still on her face. He let out a breath, and followed them in. He left the pitchfork leaning up against the outside wall, not without regret. But Mother felt strongly about farming implements in her kitchen. And it wasn't suitable for a close fight inside anyway.

Mother took the stranger straight to the kitchen, of course. The background chatter of voices, so familiar Forrest barely heard it anymore, went abruptly silent as they entered the room. He halted on the threshold and leaned against the doorway, crossing his arms and trying to look imposing.

All three of his sisters were already in the kitchen, all watching silently as Mother brought the strange girl in. Clara, thirteen, was sitting at the table, bowl of porridge in front of her and hair neatly pinned up. Elena, eleven, was kneeling over the bucket of water in one corner, halted in the middle of scrubbing at a stain on one sleeve. Rosie, eight, was sitting by the fire, one hand holding the end of her braid, while the other half of her hair spilled loose over one shoulder.

The stranger took one darting glance around the room, then looked down at her feet while Mother ushered her over to the table. "Now sit right there, that should be fine."

The girl looked at the chair, then limped around the corner of the table to take a different one, facing the doorway. Fine, Forrest preferred being able to keep an eye on her expression anyway, in case it gave warning before she did something threatening.

Mother didn't even blink, just continued, "Call me Lynette, everyone does, and let me take your cloak."

"No," the stranger said flatly, hand reaching up to close around the metal clasp at her throat.

"As you prefer. Clara, get a bowl of porridge for our guest, and Elena, I already told you that scrubbing will only spread the ink, just let it soak for a few minutes." She sat down in the wooden chair behind Rosie, gathered up her loose hair, and began braiding. "After I'm done here, I want to take a look at your ankle," she directed at the stranger, "and we'll have to call you something, you know. It doesn't have to be your real name."

For a moment, the still picture held. Then Clara slid off her chair to go to the pot of porridge hanging over the fire, Elena dunked her arm into the water bucket, and Forrest glared at the stranger, just daring her to say something nasty so he'd have an excuse to throw her out before the situation got any worse.

The stranger bit her lower lip, slowly lowered her hand to the tabletop, and said, "Karina. You can call me Karina."

Disappointingly, that wasn't nasty at all.

Mother nodded approvingly. "Now that's a lovely name."

Karina's mouth twisted in a frown. "I know."

"I like it," Rosie piped in. "My name's Rosaliana, but nobody calls me it."

"Because it's bigger than you are," Elena remarked.

Rosie stuck her tongue out, then resumed, "You're not from here, are you? We know everybody from Daygeor, so you must be from another island, right? That's *so* exciting, we hardly ever see anyone from anywhere else and it's awfully small here."

"I noticed," Karina muttered, and Rosie chattered on. You didn't have to contribute much to a conversation to keep Rosie talking.

Forrest stopped listening in favor of thinking about how he was going to get the girl—Karina—out of here. Because no one carrying two knives and a truly nasty attitude should be sitting with his family.

Chapter Two

Karina was half-inclined to believe she'd been cursed. In some ways it would be easier to believe that, rather than to accept what was clearly the actual truth—that she'd simply been supremely stupid.

She should have checked where the ship was *going* before she snuck aboard, in case she managed to choose what was surely the only ship in the entire harbor going towards this benighted, isolated pile of rock. Any other ship would have sailed along the coast, where she could get off, light out and run. You can't run far on an island before you wind up back where you started.

And she should have found somewhere else to sleep, somewhere she wouldn't be found immediately. She had meant to leave at dawn. Who knew farmers would be out and about before the sun even showed above the horizon? People in the city didn't get up at such ungodly hours.

And she definitely, absolutely, unquestionably should have *landed right*. A meagre fifteen-foot drop, she should have been able to land and roll and be off before the lumbering farmer even got out of the barn, but no, she had to land all wrong and twist her ankle like the rankest amateur. The boys would laugh themselves sick over that.

Or they would have. If they were still alive to laugh about anything.

The stupid decisions stretched back before getting on that ship, that was clear enough. Although it hadn't been *all* her fault.

But she wasn't going to think about that. That would be a stupid thing to do too. She couldn't change what had been done, so she'd just have to deal with the situation as it was. And try not to continue being stupid.

So she sat in the warm kitchen and ate the bowl of porridge the oldest girl had passed to her. It was the first hot meal she'd had in three days. It would also be stupid to miss free food. While she ate the thick porridge, she tried to surreptitiously assess the situation.

This was an almost dangerously comfortable place. With a high-beamed ceiling, clean white walls, a flagstone floor and a roaring fire, the room was both airy and warm, a welcome change from a damp ship's hold or a smelly barn. Not that the city smelled like a rose garden, but she was used to *those* smells. Country smells were different. Though at least the smell of hay had mostly masked the smell of chickens.

She scratched irritably under her collar with one finger. She had bits of hay clinging all over her. How could something so soft in a pile be so itchy in individual pieces?

This room was all full of soft cloth over the seats of the wooden chairs, and woven tapestries on the walls, and if she wasn't careful she was going to relax. And that would also be stupid.

She couldn't afford to relax, even if there didn't appear to be immediate danger. Unless the woman or the girls were hiding powerful magical ability (unlikely) they weren't a threat. The farmboy might be. He was standing in the doorway, glaring at her. The message was perfectly clear: try anything, hurt anyone or even move too fast, and I'll destroy you.

Well, he'd try to. He was filling the doorway, both tall and muscular, but she had years of experience fighting larger opponents. More importantly, he didn't move like a fighter, so while he could be a threat, he was probably a minor one at most. She was a Black Lion; she could handle Farmboy.

All right. Suppose she did relax, just a little. Maybe she could get some supplies, let her wretched twisted ankle rest a bit, find out something about the area—and then figure out how to get off this island. It had to be a minor risk, to stay just through breakfast.

The one advantage of a benighted, isolated rock was that surely no one had followed her. Not yet, at least.

It was easy to think while the little girl was chattering at her, especially since she didn't appear to expect any real response. Lynette was much harder to ignore.

"I'm all finished here, let me look at that ankle, Karina," she said, settling into the next chair over at the table.

"It's fine," Karina said automatically, drawing it back under her chair. She tried to ignore both the painful twinge in her ankle, and the emotional twinge as the woman used her name. Add 'giving her real name' to the list of stupid decisions. Maybe. Maybe not entirely stupid. No one back home knew it, not since her mother died years ago, so no one would be asking about a girl with her name. And fake names have a way of being awkwardly forgotten. She'd know who they were calling if they used this name.

Lynette was looking at her through narrowed eyes, lips pursed. "Nonsense, the way you were limping was definitely not fine at all, and that sort of thing only gets worse if you ignore it. Now take that boot off and let me look. I have plenty of experience, I assure you."

Reluctantly, Karina leaned down and started unlacing her boot. It was easier than arguing, and anyway, the woman had a point. Hobbling about on a bad ankle wouldn't let her move fast enough when she needed it. Better to get it wrapped up or splinted or something so she could move. She just didn't like people poking at her.

The youngest girl—what had she said her name was? Rosali-something?—went bouncing over towards the farmboy, a braid clutched in each chubby fist. "Forrest, you have to tie off my braids!"

Farmboy took half a step back through the doorway, then stopped, gaze on Karina again, eyes narrowed.

She smiled, sweetly and provokingly, just because it was so *easy*. And because she needed a distraction from how much it hurt easing her boot off.

His glower darkened, then smoothed out when he looked at his sister again. "Go get the basket of scraps for me, all right, Rosie?"

Her lower lip stuck out. "But I can't!" She bobbed her braids up and down. "My hair'll unravel if I let it go!"

Karina wondered if he'd risk leaving her alone with his family— just how dangerous did he believe she was?—but the middle sister, the one with the stained sleeve, solved the problem for him. "I'll get it," she said, standing up from the bucket and patting her damp sleeve with a cloth. "You can tie up mine too."

Lynette tutted softly as she lifted Karina's foot up onto her lap and examined the swollen ankle with firm but careful hands. It still hurt. She'd felt worse, but the pain combined with the unease of letting a stranger touch her made her want to look away, to think of absolutely anything else.

Her gaze landed on the middle sister as she went by the table, and noticed her single braid was already tied with a bit of string. But she wanted her brother to tie up her hair? Perhaps he was going to do something fancier…

Baiting Farmboy, that was better than thinking about her ankle. "So do you have a talent for tying bows?" Karina asked, smirking at him.

His frown deepened, but all he said was, "Yes."

Disappointing.

"They work better when Forrest does it," Rosie said, apparently unaware the question had been in any way sarcastic. And apparently equally unaware that her answer didn't make any sense. Bows didn't *do* anything but hold hair together, and that hardly seemed worth being impressed about.

Karina might have asked, or might not have bothered, but her ankle chose that moment to give another throb. She couldn't quite stop her sharp inhale, but she managed not to curse. It would probably shock the country family.

"I'm sorry, dear, it looks like that spot's sensitive," Lynette said, fingers moving lightly over Karina's ankle.

"It's not that bad," Karina muttered through gritted teeth, glaring at her own traitorous leg. How the boys would have *laughed…*

"I've certainly seen worse," Lynette agreed. "It's not broken, but it is a nasty twist. Elena, get the bandages too."

"All right," the girl said, ducking past her brother and out of the room. Forrest just went on watching Karina.

"If you're not from our island," Rosie said, cheerfully picking up that thread again, "where are you from? Somewhere else in Marileigh? The capital?"

Karina almost said yes. It was obviously a story they would believe, and perhaps would relegate her to the status of not so unusual after all. But when she couldn't even remember the capital of Marileigh, she couldn't possibly sustain that lie. She could feel Farmboy staring at her, waiting for her to trip up and give him a reason to get rid of her. Like lying about her origins. "No, not the capital," she said, looking down at her bowl, and scraped at a bit of remaining porridge with her metal spoon.

"Oh," Rosie said, nose crinkling as she tugged on one braid. "Are you from Ronley? Marmeer? Dizahl?"

What were these, other towns? Other islands? Why couldn't she have ended up on a ship going to a country she knew anything at all about? She had a vague picture in her head of a map she'd seen once, of a country made up of a cluster of islands, but she certainly didn't remember names or details. "I'm not from Marileigh," she said finally, because she'd never be able to convince them she was. "I'm from the continent." There, honest answer but thoroughly vague. That would have to do.

The little girl's eyes went round. "Oooh, I've never met anyone from the continent before!"

And so much for being inconspicuous and blending in.

Thankfully, before Rosie could start in on even more questions, Elena interrupted by returning with a bundle of rolled green cloth and a basket filled with a multi-colored jumble of yarn. She handed the basket to Forrest and put the cloth on the table next to her mother.

Karina still didn't want to think about her ankle, and she had hit the bottom of her bowl of porridge, so she watched Forrest fold himself to sit down in the doorway, basket in front of him, and stir one hand through the pile of loose yarn. "What'll it be today, Rosie?" he asked as the little girl crouched next to him.

Rosie's expression turned tragically mournful. "Luck. Definitely luck," she said, making absolutely no sense to Karina. "We have a test about the royal family, and I can never remember the names of all the princes. Twelve is just too *many*."

A test implied school. This family could be wealthier than she had thought, if they were sending their girls to school. Might be some money around she could get her hands on, that could make getting out of here much easier. Once she was able to walk again.

It was strange, though; nothing about the place looked wealthy. A butter churn stood in one corner of the kitchen, and braids of onions, fishing nets and coils of rope all hung from the ceiling. Those didn't suggest a family that used coins for every need.

But plenty of onions were up there, the porridge pot had leftovers after everyone appeared to have eaten, and they must have milk and cream from somewhere to need the butter churn. Comfortable, but not rich. Maybe you didn't have to be rich for an education in this country. Karina hadn't even known there were twelve princes, so it wasn't as if she knew what their schooling was like. Or what it meant to want a hair tie for luck.

The request must have made sense to Farmboy, since he just nodded and pulled a strand of purple yarn out of the pile, a piece maybe six inches long. He joined it with a white strand and a lavender one, tied a knot at one end and began quickly braiding them together. So he was a farmboy who knew how to braid and tie bows. How cute.

"I don't think you need a splint, Karina," Lynette announced, reaching for the roll of cloth her daughter had brought. "A good tight wrapping should be enough."

Karina turned her attention back that way, getting her first good look at the cloth as it unrolled. It was a strip of very close knitting, weaving together three shades of green. "Oh no," she protested without thinking, "that's much too nice for a bandage."

"Nonsense, dear," Lynette said with a smile, passing one end of the strip under Karina's ankle. "That's what it was made for."

"But any cloth could be a bandage." Who went to the trouble of knitting something to use for a purpose like that? Any decently-clean rag would do. Maybe they were rich after all, to be this wasteful.

"Perhaps, but I think you'll find the injury will heal faster with the proper knit to support it." She had already wrapped the strip of knitting around Karina's ankle twice, and now she held up the loose end. "I've used a basic Moss Stitch here. I find the interlocking pattern is especially good for strengthening injured muscles, and then of course the three shades of green were all chosen to promote health. The intertwining of multiple shades is also good for additional support."

Karina stared at her. Absolutely none of that had made any sense.

Rosie's chatter was finally helpful as she piped up with, "Mother knits the most powerful healing bandages on the whole island. Everyone says so."

"Yes, well," Lynette said with a slight smile, "it's not a very large island."

"Powerful healing?" Karina repeated. "What, you mean like magic?"

She had to be wrong about this. The question had to be springing from mere paranoia. And so, she fully expected another modest disclaimer. She did not expect Lynette to say, "Yes, you could certainly call it that."

Magic healing bandages. Karina looked around at the other faces. The oldest girl was still finishing her porridge, the middle one was waiting to have her hair tied next, and Farmboy was tying his bit of yarn around the end of Rosie's braid. There wasn't so much as a grin to suggest that this was all a joke, or a story they told their youngest family member.

Marvelous. Not only had she fallen into a family that, Farmboy aside, was weirdly and unnervingly friendly. They were superstitious too.

She believed in magic, of course. Some people said it was all just sleight of hand, but after the things she had seen…no, magic was real enough. But *this*? Magic was something fine magicians with loads of schooling and loads of money did. These people might be educated, but nothing suggested they had the kind of money or knowledge that magicians had. And who could really believe that ordinary people, knitting together ordinary bits of yarn and string, could possibly make anything magical?

They had to be wrong about this. They couldn't really be capable of magic. And she was going to cling to that disbelief for just as long as she could. Without it, she was likely to lose her head entirely and do something else stupid.

Chapter Three

Forrest was glad his hands knew how to tie knots and weave braids without much input from his head. It let him continue keeping an eye on the stranger while he dealt with Rosie's hair, and he didn't miss the expression of disdain that flashed across Karina's face when the subject of magical knitting came up.

"Don't you believe in magic?" he asked, trying to sound as imposing as possible while sitting in a doorway.

"Sure I believe magic exists," she said, with a roll of her eyes that was becoming both familiar and annoying in equal measure. "Never seen it do much good for anyone though. Or seen anyone knit a spell."

"It's a rare talent." He was pleased to know something she didn't—and irritated by her immediate disregard for that knowledge.

Rosie twisted her head around to look at him, a pucker on her forehead. "Is something wrong?" she asked in a whisper that no doubt carried to every corner of the room.

Great. He had no idea if his hostile tone had any effect on Karina, but it was worrying Rosie. He made himself smile at her and said, "No, honey, everything's fine."

He gave her tied-up braid a tweak, and reached into the basket to find the right yarn for the next one. Once a smile came back onto Rosie's face, he returned to watching the strange girl. He didn't look at his hands as they pulled out three strands by instinct. He couldn't have explained how he knew they were the right ones; he just knew they were, and that they would match the previous three.

While he lined up the new pieces of yarn, Mother finished securing Karina's bandage. "There, that should be much better. I wouldn't recommend walking on it for some while though, so obviously you'll have to stay with us until tomorrow."

"*What?*" Forrest spoke, hearing the word echoed from Karina. "She's not staying here."

"He's right, I need to go."

"But I wanted to hear more about the continent!" Rosie complained, and Forrest noticed that he had dropped the next pieces of yarn for her. He reached back into the basket to find them again.

"Wherever you think you need to go, it will have to wait," Mother said, in the tone that had brooked no argument for all of Forrest's life. That didn't mean he wasn't mentally marshaling arguments. "Walk too soon on that leg and you could cause worse damage."

"I have to leave," Karina said, with an edge in her voice that made Forrest stop mid-knot. He didn't like *her* tone at all.

Mother seemed utterly unperturbed, putting her hands on her hips and continuing in much the same manner. "If it's a ship you're wanting, you'll only be able to get one in town, and that's five miles away. That is not a walk for a twisted ankle. It's a pity you didn't knock on the door sooner. You might have taken a ride into town with my husband. He left before dawn with our only cart."

Karina's glance shifted away, and Forrest wondered if she had slept through his father getting the horse out of the barn, or if she had just managed to stay still and not give her presence away. He wished Father *had* caught her. He could have taken her to town and out of the way—or stayed behind, which would make Forrest feel better about this whole situation.

"He'll be back some time tonight," Mother continued, "and we'll be able to arrange a ride into town tomorrow, which I'm sure will be quite soon enough."

Forrest repressed a groan, and began tying up Rosie's second braid. Once Mother was sure of something—well, that was it, whether you liked it or not. Though he still had those arguments ready.

Even Karina must have sensed a certain inevitability in the situation. She kept her gaze on her bowl of porridge and just muttered, "I guess I can stay for a while."

And then somehow everything picked up into a flurry of activity to get the three girls out the door and off to the schoolhouse. Elena wanted a bow on her hair for courage, to help with a recitation that afternoon, while Clara declined any magic, and Rosie rushed about looking for her lost sweater and finally ran out behind the rest, pausing only to give Forrest a hug good-bye and to throw over her shoulder to Karina, "Don't leave before we get back—I want to hear your stories about the continent!"

And then, like the calm after a departing windstorm, the room grew quiet. Forrest noticed Karina was gazing in the direction the girls had gone, and shifted in the doorway to move into her line of sight. Whoever this girl was, she did not need to be thinking about his sisters.

"So," he said into the silence. "Do you have any stories about the continent?"

"No," she said, and looked away.

Mother stepped past him into the next room, remarking, "Are you going to stand in that doorway all day, or are you going to fix that broken fence around my vegetable garden?"

Right. That had been the plan for the day, a whole…twenty minutes ago, before everything had turned upside down. "I'm not going to—" He broke off. Karina was smirking again, and he was sure she knew exactly what he was thinking. He shot her a glare and went after his mother, who had continued on into the parlor.

He stopped by the long couch below the window and folded his arms, even while knowing that trying to look imposing with his mother would be useless. "I am not going to leave you here alone with her."

Mother paused in rummaging through the tall wooden cabinet in the far corner and turned to face him, hands on her hips again. "Now really, dear, what do you think is going to happen?"

"I don't *know*." He might feel better if he knew. He wasn't used to meeting someone this unpredictable; he knew everyone on the island, and not one of them seemed as unique as Karina. "She's a complete stranger, she has trouble written all over her, and she's definitely hiding something. Including a knife in her boot." He ended with that deliberately, feeling sure it would be conclusive.

He was not prepared for his mother to just nod and say, "She's not hiding it very well."

He blinked, feeling as though the thick woven rug on the floor had slipped beneath his feet. "You knew?"

"I could hardly miss it when she was taking her boot off," Mother said, and turned back to the cabinet.

"She has one in her sleeve too," he added, in a desperate attempt to rally.

"Quite a sensible precaution for a young woman alone in a strange place." She shifted a stack of blankets onto a nearby table, and he had a horrible realization she was planning to make up the spare bed in the next room.

"But you can see how unfriendly she is!"

"Considering the way you've been glowering at her, it's not surprising."

He barely bit back a defensive, "She started it." That hadn't ever worked when he was fighting with one of his sisters—years and *years* ago, when he was *much* younger.

She didn't wait for a defense or even a reply. "The poor girl is lost and scared, and the least we can do is be kind to her."

"Scared," he said. "Really." That seemed wildly unlikely, and even if it was true that didn't prove that they shouldn't be plenty scared too. He nearly kicked at the nearest leg of the couch, but stopped himself in time. It would just make her scold more.

"Yes, scared," Mother said firmly, then her expression softened. "If it will make you feel better, fix the fence tomorrow and stay around the house today. Finish that scarf for Clara's birthday."

Scarf-knitting wasn't usually an occupation for sunny days, much better suited to storms and evenings, but this was a strange day. And a better option than being off over a hill in the vegetable garden, while any disaster could be happening here. "Fine. Good," he said, knowing his voice was grudging. This was not ideal.

"Good," she agreed, turned and reached into the cupboard again to hand him the half-finished scarf and ball of yarn, needles sticking out of the wound-up ball. She headed back towards the kitchen. "You already fed the chickens, so at least that's done."

The chickens. "Um…" He had taken the grain to the barn. But he hadn't actually done anything beyond that.

She stopped, looked back. "The chickens weren't fed?"

"I kind of…got distracted."

She sighed, but smiled slightly too. "Fine. I'll do it while you stand guard here. I can collect the eggs at the same time."

She went upstairs for a shawl and Forrest went back to the kitchen. He could see Karina through the doorway, and he found himself stopping on the threshold to look at her. Alone, she had let her shoulders slump. She clutched the clasp of her cloak with one hand and played with her spoon with the other, tracing patterns in the bottom of her emptied bowl. She was staring down, expression…sad? Forlorn? Some emotion he hadn't seen on her face previously.

All right. Maybe she was lost and scared. *Maybe.*

He deliberately stepped audibly on the wooden floor as he came into the room. In an eyeblink her shoulders were straight again and her face had wiped smooth of any expression at all except faint disinterest.

"There's more porridge in the pot if you want it," he said, even though he doubted that was why she'd been staring into the empty bowl.

Her gaze flicked to the pot hanging over the fire. "I can see that for myself."

Maybe lost and scared, but still unfriendly. "Right," he said, pulling out a chair at the opposite side of the table with possibly more force than necessary. He sat down and unrolled the half-made scarf, concentrating his attention on untangling the loose end of the yarn and lining up the last row of stitches on the needle.

"So you don't just tie bows," Karina drawled, "you also knit?"

Everything about how she said it, even the way her head was leaning on her hand, made it clear this was meant to be provoking. But...well, even if she *had* started it, he could still try to be friendly. And he had no idea why he was supposed to be provoked anyway. "Yes, I also knit. It's common enough. Most people around here do."

"Most...*people*."

That provoking tone again, but he still didn't know what she was trying to get at. "Yes. So?"

She shrugged and looked away. "Where I'm from, men don't knit."

His eyebrows rose. "Why not?"

"Because it's something women do."

He considered that, stitched three stitches, and said, "That's not an explanation, that's just restating the same thing from the other direction."

She turned to face him again and said slowly and clearly, "It's not men's work."

"Yes, I understood that to begin with, but it's still just a restatement. And not making any sense." He raised one hand, spread his fingers. "It's not like male and female hands are significantly different."

"Yes, but..." She trailed off and frowned. "It's just what is."

"Not here. Where did you say you were from again?"

The frown deepened. "I didn't."

"I know."

Before he could push that one any farther, Mother leaned in the doorway to say, "I'm going out to feed the chickens. I'll be back in a few minutes. Try not to kill each other while I'm gone."

Forrest winced, but noticed Karina flush and felt a little better.

No one said anything for the length of three rows of knitting, until finally Karina asked, "So are you knitting a magic scarf?"

He'd had enough time to take enough deep breaths to be able to answer civilly. "Just a variation on a basic Luck scarf."

"Oh. A *lucky* scarf."

Lost and scared, and he was trying to be friendly. Right. But sometimes he got very tired of being nice. All the same, he nicely, politely, with all sorts of friendly overtones, said, "It's for Clara's birthday, so it's 28 stitches wide because her birthday is on the 28th day of the month. Each purple stripe is seven rows, because seven is traditionally the best number for luck and purple the best color for invoking luck, and each blue stripe is six rows wide because there are six of us in the family, and invoking familial power is always a good idea when knitting something intended to provide both luck and general protection. Assuming you actually like your family, of course."

She was staring at him. "Of course."

"You asked," he said with a smile. And he didn't mind demonstrating that this at least was something he knew much more about than she did.

Assuming she believed his explanation. "And how much of that did you just make up?"

"None of it."

"Uh-huh. So everyone around here would know that six stitches is for luck—"

"Seven rows," he corrected, "although it could be seven stitches, except that's too narrow to be much use for most projects." She was still staring, with an unnervingly blank expression. He took a breath, finished a row with a final two stitches and swapped needles between his hands to begin on the next. "This kind of magic is a specialty of our island, although you'll find magical knitting in other parts of Marileigh, just less of it. And apparently it's not done at all in that unspecified place you're from."

"No. So are you a powerful...stitch magician?" She was drawling again, and even with his gaze on his knitting he could see that her head was back at that provoking tilt.

He gritted his teeth. "That's not a term." They rarely called it anything. It was common enough to not need a name; everyone knew what it was. Some old stories called it spellspinning. He thought of trying to explain that, when knitting wasn't the same thing as spinning, although the spinning was part of it too and of course it was all connected—but he thought of Karina's inevitable mocking gaze and decided to just not even mention that. What was her actual question? Right, about his ability. "No, I'm just average."

"But Rosie likes how you tie bows?" she asked, her tone sweet and sarcastic and scornful of the whole idea.

At that he looked up from his stitches to lock gazes. "Yes," he said evenly, and kept staring until she looked away. Mocking his island's magical tradition or even mocking him was one thing. Taking a jab at his youngest sister was something else, and if she thought Rosie was silly to believe in this, she could just keep her mouth shut about it.

To her credit, she looked abashed. "Sorry about that one," she muttered, gaze lowering.

Maybe the small victory made him feel generous. He grinned and said, "But not about the rest?"

"Not at all," she said, with the closest thing to a genuine smile he'd seen from her yet.

Chapter Four

All in all, it was a strange day. Karina spent most of it sitting in the kitchen, avoiding questions about her past and trying not to say or do anything too stupid. Farmboy got friendlier, which was good in terms of dangers—though since he'd been the only one showing a reasonable, healthy level of suspicion, it was disconcerting too. His mother invited her to help chop vegetables, and then handed her a knife, for heaven's sake. Did she really seem *that* non-threatening? Or maybe these people just weren't used to threats like her.

The boys hadn't thought she was dangerous to them either, but…no, still not a smart thing to think about.

Farmboy's sisters came back late afternoon, and all three happily followed their mother's lead and viewed Karina without suspicion. Only Rosie proved to be a problem. She was just so…*friendly*. Karina found it harder not to reveal anything to a little girl who had five million questions, and who did not view taciturn non-answers as a reason to go away or end a conversation.

All this warm welcome wouldn't last. Either these people would reveal ulterior motives behind all this cheerfulness, or she'd slip up, tell them too much and they'd change their minds about all this trust and kindness.

Or whatever had been going wrong in her life would catch up to her, and maybe them too.

So really it would be best to put an absolute stop to this strange interlude here, as soon as possible. She even knew how she could do it. It was so obvious. All she'd have to do would be to say one really nasty thing to Rosie. Not just a non-answer, but something actually mean and hateful. She could verbally jab at Forrest all day and not do any real damage, but try that on Rosie and…

She almost did it. She saw a dozen easy openings. But she couldn't quite make herself say the right words in the right tone and put an end to the little girl's bright smile.

By suppertime she was still there, sitting on a couch in the parlor, somehow roped into helping Rosie roll a big loop of yarn into a ball. And maybe that was just as well, for now. The stew simmering over the fire smelled amazing.

As though it was timed, Lynette's husband came home just before supper was ready. Rosie dropped her ball of yarn and dashed off into the kitchen to meet him. Karina carefully eased the loop off of her hands, set it down on the couch, then went to the kitchen at a slower pace. Not limping much. She must not have really twisted her ankle all that badly, despite the pain in the morning.

She studied the new arrival from the kitchen doorway, and could see where Forrest got his height.

The whole family had gathered, the three girls crowded around their father. Lynette stirred her stew (although if the rumpled hair she was smoothing back was any indication, she'd already greeted her husband), and Forrest stood near the table, watching the flurry of welcoming.

As Karina glanced at Forrest, she realized something had changed. A kind of…stiffness had disappeared, from his face and his posture. She hadn't been able to tell until right now just how tense he'd been all day, because she'd had no point of comparison. She looked back at the man who gravely nodded as his youngest daughter told him about her royalty test. So his father came home, and Forrest clearly felt a burden had lifted.

What was that like, to feel that way about someone?

Not likely she'd ever find out, so it wasn't much use thinking about it. Or being bothered that, obviously, *she* was the burden that had just been lifted.

Perhaps Forrest felt relieved because he expected his father to throw her out. But she only briefly guessed that and it didn't seem to be the answer. Lynette and Rosie between them introduced and explained her, and then she was shaking hands with the smiling man who told her to call him Richard, and only minutes after that they were all sitting down to supper and seemed to find it perfectly reasonable that she sat down too. Forrest still eyed her surreptitiously and it was very tempting to make a production of cutting up chunks of meat with her knife, but she managed to resist. Mostly.

She managed to behave too. Mostly. She didn't really want to be tossed out now, when it was dark outside and getting colder. Better to just bide until morning, and take steps then. Whatever steps she could think of, when the morning came.

She listened hard to Richard's news from town, trying to pick up something useful. She only learned that the town was small enough that her arrival would undoubtedly be gossip should anyone glimpse her, and that ships back to the continent were disappointingly infrequent. Of course she had to be on the only ship from home that came this way in a month. Though that might stymie any pursuit too. And she ought to be able to get a ship to another island, and take a longer passage from there. How exactly she was going to get onto either of those ships, considering her current funds stood at zero…well, she'd think about that tomorrow too.

Richard didn't get to the really interesting news until well into his third helping of stew, and if she judged the gleam in his eye correctly, he'd been holding it back deliberately. As he dished out that third helping, he casually remarked, "The royal ship from the capital came in yesterday."

Instant flurry of questions, of which Karina only managed to decipher Clara's, "Did they bring news about the latest fashions?"

Neither that one nor any others were answered, as Richard went imperturbably on. "And the ship brought three of the young princes to spend the summer."

"Oh goody, they haven't come here in years and *years*!" Rosie exclaimed.

"It's only been four years," Elena remarked.

"I can't remember that far back!" Rosie countered. "Which ones came, Father? I know all their names!" Her nose scrunched and she tugged on one braid, still tied up with Forrest's lucky yarn. "Well, most of them. Ten, at least."

Richard leaned back in his chair. "I'm not sure if I heard the names…"

Forrest was grinning into his bowl of stew. "Because of course no one at all would be mentioning names."

His father grinned back at him. "They do run together though."

"Let me guess!" This, of course, from Rosie. "Let's see, is it…Damek? He's the youngest. Or Dallon, he's my age so I can remember him. Or…"

Elena groaned. "Just tell us so we don't have to listen to her try to remember all of them."

Clara cleared her throat. "It's Daemyn, Danton, Dacien, Dathan, Daylin, Dagan, Dastan, Darshan, Darnell, Darius, Dallon and Damek. That's all twelve." Rosie stared at her, and she shrugged. "I had to learn it when I was your age too."

Twelve princes who all had names starting with D? That settled it for Karina. Clearly she had landed in a country that was utterly mad, complete with a strangely trusting populace, superstitious local practices, and a royal family with no apparent creativity in naming their offspring.

"I do believe," Richard said finally, "that it was Dathan, Dastan and Daemyn."

"Ooh, Daemyn's the crown prince, that makes it even more exciting!" Rosie announced.

"They sent their *crown prince* out *here*?" Karina said without thinking, realized belatedly that maybe she'd put too much scorn on that *here*.

Forrest frowned at her, predictably enough, but Lynette smoothly replied, "The royal family believes it's wise for the princes to spend time in all parts of the country, the crown prince especially. After all, a king needs to know the people he is ruling. Being a series of islands as we are, it would be all too easy for remote areas to become cut off from the rest of the country."

"The royalty takes a different view where you're from?" Richard asked, with no apparent ulterior motives to the question.

"You could say that," Karina muttered. Did the royalty ever even come out of their castles? Maybe sometimes, but they certainly never came to her streets, or mixed with her kind of people. Or gave much sign that they ever even thought about that part of their populace.

She applied herself to her stew, and let the continued chatter wash past her. There was *one* reason to be glad about members of the royal family turning up here. With that kind of gossip, no one would be talking about one random girl who'd landed ashore too. So anyone looking for her would have to hunt. Hopefully.

Chapter Five

If anyone had asked, Forrest would have predicted that the day Karina came falling out of the barn was about as strange as days ever got, and the next day couldn't possibly contain anything stranger. That day began fine and comparatively normal, with everyone still alive and nothing stolen (not that there was much to steal). He had half-expected Karina to simply vanish (on foot or by more unusual means) but she was still there when he came into the kitchen for breakfast.

He tried not to watch her while he filled a bowl of porridge from the pot; it wasn't like she was doing anything very interesting anyway, just sitting there at the table eating breakfast. She wasn't watching him.

He had just sat down at the table himself when Elena banged in through the outside door. She set the basket used for egg collecting down on the table with a degree of drama that eggs didn't usually warrant. She looked around the room, cheeks flushed, and announced, "I think something has happened to the chickens!"

Forrest glanced immediately at Karina, who was going right along with eating. This time she noticed his gaze, raised one eyebrow, and dug her spoon into her porridge again. Not exactly an expression of guilt. But what did he really imagine she might have done to the chickens?

Mother looked up from stirring the pot over the fire with an expression that did not bode well for anyone. "If Andrew's dog got into the barn again, I have *warned* him what would happen."

"No, not anything like *that*." Elena gestured to the basket with a great deal of flourish. "Look at *this*!"

Forrest leaned over his bowl to look into the basket, and blinked twice at the sight. Nestled amongst a bed of hay, twelve eggs gleamed a rich metallic gold. "Oh. Well, that's...unusual." Anything unusual occurring was, well, unusual. Though surely golden eggs were a *good* unusual. A simpler, better unusual than a mysterious girl with uncertain motivations, for instance.

"What is?" Rosie asked as she bounced into the room. With everyone looking at the basket, she came over too and peered in. "Ooh! Golden eggs!"

Elena put a hand on the basket handle again. "I found all the ones I could! Does this make us rich?"

"Can I have my own horse now?" Rosie asked, voice rising to an excited pitch. "A white one? Or maybe a beautiful brown one, with a white star on his forehead and—"

"Let's not get ahead of ourselves," Mother said, a voice of calm amidst the growing excitement. "We're not quite sure what's happening yet."

If it *did* mean they were rich, Rosie could get her horse, and maybe they could hire someone to do things like repairing fences and chasing after lost sheep on cold nights, and he could buy all sorts of yarns that were beyond their ability to spin, and he could go visiting other islands or even the continent and see what life was like there and...

"So just to be clear," Karina said, waving her spoon towards the basket, "this isn't normal?"

"Is it normal where *you're* from?" Forrest asked.

"No, but neither are lucky scarves," she shot back.

He had to reluctantly, privately concede that point. Although he had *said* the eggs were unusual; she'd know that if she'd been listening to him.

Elena sighed, a delighted sigh. "Magic is *so* exciting. I've always wanted to see real magic."

"You *have*," Forrest pointed out, slightly nettled, not sure if it was because of Elena or Karina or the utter unexpectedness of golden eggs at breakfast throwing his world off-balance. "What do you think all that knitting we do is?"

Elena waved a hand at him, the blatant dismissal of a younger sister. "Oh, that's not the same. That's ordinary magic. This is *different*."

"It's magic too," Forrest muttered, not appreciating a dismissal of his abilities—and right in front of Karina too. Though Elena was right in one way. Knitting was normal. If this was real, it was magic on a much more dramatic, far more unnatural level.

He stared at the eggs, brow furrowed. Magic that nudged the world, he was used to that. This was magic that *changed* the world, changed it into things it wasn't supposed to be and...a small hand reached into his vision, reaching out towards the eggs, and he automatically grabbed Rosie's wrist. "Don't touch them. We don't know what they might do."

She pouted at him. "They didn't hurt Elena."

Right. Obviously. He felt a twist of embarrassment. He hadn't thought of that, he'd just reacted instinctively.

"Gold very rarely bites," Karina drawled, reached out and picked up an egg. She rolled it between her palms. "See? Harmless."

It was as good as a challenge. Forrest picked up an egg himself, was surprised by how light it was. "Gold should be heavier than this..." He weighed it in his palm. It felt about like a normal egg, in fact. He squeezed slightly—and with a crack, egg guts were dripping through his fingers.

It was all right when Rosie giggled, less all right when Karina snorted. He told himself that after all, that was unrefined of her and therefore he shouldn't be feeling even more embarrassed. Mother, to his supreme gratitude, offered a towel, a bowl for the egg shell and no comments.

While Forrest wiped his hand off, Mother picked up another egg. "I'm not sure this is really gold." She reached for another bowl, gave the egg a brisk tap against the edge. Like the egg on Forrest's hand, a normal-looking yolk and white dropped into the bowl. "We appear to have chickens that are laying gilded eggs," she said, inspecting the broken egg shell.

"I don't think we should eat that," Forrest said, looking dubiously into the bowl. Who knew what enchanted eggs would do to a person?

"Are golden egg shells valuable enough to buy me a horse?" Rosie asked, looking at the cracked shells. "I *promise* I'd take care of it. I'd brush it, and braid flowers into its mane, and feed it, and it would be *wonderful*."

"I don't know how much these are worth, dear," Mother said, cracking another egg, "although even a small amount of gold is valuable."

"Or you could hardboil the eggs," Karina said. "It might stop anyone buying them from realizing at first that they're not solid gold, so you could sell them for a lot more."

Everyone turned to look at her for a silent moment before Rosie scrunched up her nose and said, "Wouldn't that be lying?"

Karina looked around at everyone else, and her cheeks turned just faintly pinker. "Um...yes. Which is...bad, so obviously you wouldn't do that, I was just...it was just a thought."

Just a thought, and one that made Forrest wonder all over again where she'd come from and, more importantly, what she'd done there.

"I'm not sure it really is gold at all," Mother said, turning over the second egg shell. "It's just a thin coating on the outside, with normal shell beneath."

"So it could be a prank, not actual magic," Forrest suggested. That would make the world normal again. It would be less interesting, but it would be simpler. "Someone could have snuck in and planted eggs painted to look like gold." He picked up another egg, carefully. He didn't see brush strokes, but that didn't prove anything.

"Why would anyone paint eggs gold?" Karina asked with her head at that provoking tilt she did.

"As a joke, obviously," he said, with possibly more edge than he'd intended. "It's more likely than a magic spell, because why would anyone bother enchanting a bunch of chickens? Paint would be easier." It had to be easier than this kind of world-twisting magic.

"But magicians don't think like other people," Karina said in a low voice. "And the strange things they do always have a reason."

Forrest watched her staring down at the egg in her hand. She didn't seem to find this exciting or funny or even entertaining. Maybe she knew something—or maybe she just had instincts the rest of them didn't. "I think I'll check if anything else strange is going on in the barn." Whether it was a prank or a spell, there could be more trouble, and it might not be as benign as gilded eggs.

"Good idea," Mother said. "Girls, you still need to get to school, so sit down and eat your breakfasts."

"We don't get to miss school because of weird magic?" Elena complained.

"You do not, if it even is magic." Mother pointed toward the table. "Now sit and eat."

Forrest took two steps towards the door before he remembered. His father was already out checking on the sheep in the north pasture, and if he went out to the barn now... He halted, looked back towards Karina. She was rolling an egg between her fingers and it was a moment before she lifted her head and noticed his gaze. She raised an eyebrow at him, but it was only a few seconds before she caught on, judging by the way her expression shifted towards irritated. She frowned at him while he kept up a steady stare back, and finally she exhaled dramatically.

"I think I'll go to the barn too," she announced loudly, setting the egg back in the basket and rising to her feet.

"There's no need for that, dear," Mother said, "and I still think you should be resting that ankle."

"No, no, I am *deeply curious* about chickens laying gilded eggs," she said, lifting her cloak from where it hung over the back of her chair.

Forrest bit back a grin and pushed open the door. "After you." It was only then that he noticed he was still holding the second gilded egg he'd picked up.

He let Karina step past him, then quickly set the egg back into the basket and followed her out. She was walking towards the barn with what was probably supposed to be a haughty attitude, but was somewhat spoiled by her continuing limp. She was walking better than the day before, though. Not that he was paying any special attention to her legs in those trousers. They weren't tight, but they hid less than an ankle-length skirt.

"You know," she said once they were away from the house, "I'm really not planning to kill anyone, so you can just stop worrying. Somehow you got this idea into your head..."

"Possibly when you pulled a knife on me yesterday," Forrest suggested, letting the grin come more easily.

"You grabbed me from behind!"

"I did not," he countered, "I barely touched your shoulder."

She turned to glower at him, then rolled her eyes. "You took me by surprise, and I reacted as seemed appropriate in the moment."

"And if someone else takes you by surprise?"

"I do not accidentally kill people by losing control and stabbing them, all right?"

"You just accidentally kill people other ways?"

As soon as he said it, he knew it was a mistake. It was supposed to be a *joke*, a play on how she had happened to phrase that sentence, because sure, he was still cautious but he didn't *really* think it likely that she was going to hurt someone. So it was just a joke, just another line in the rapid-fire exchange of friendly argument. But she flinched back as though he'd hit her, her face went cold and hard, and she turned away to continue walking down the path at a faster pace.

"I didn't...mean anything," he said, knowing it was a feeble defense. But what in her past had prompted *that* reaction to *that* remark?

She didn't say anything in response. She didn't say anything at all on the way to the barn. Inside, she didn't even glance at the chickens, just walked over and sat on a bale of hay near the horse's stall. Silently, and without looking at Forrest.

He rubbed the back of his neck and had a guilty feeling he ought to fix this. Except he didn't know what he had done to begin with, and anyway, if some utterly irrational girl who had dropped out of nowhere and inexplicably made herself at home in the middle of his life decided to get upset about a perfectly harmless comment, how was that his problem anyway? Right then.

The chickens. He was supposed to be looking at enchanted chickens. Elena had left them in their pen, so he went that way.

They didn't look enchanted. But what did enchanted chickens look like? Maybe they should have gold feathers and shoot sparks. As it was, the chickens were still white, and they still bobbed and fluttered and clucked the exact same way they always had. If *they* were worrying about this new development in egg production, they weren't showing it.

Of course, chickens were pretty dumb. They'd probably try to hatch solid gold eggs, if the situation came to it.

Now there was a thought. Could they hatch gilded eggs? The inside of the egg seemed normal enough...but if they tried it, what was going to break out of the shell? Maybe they should experiment. Carefully.

When he had done all the staring at chickens that seemed reasonable, he glanced over towards Karina. She was still very determinedly not looking at him.

Right. Any other stray magic floating about? He poked around amongst the usual barn clutter and climbed up into the hayloft, just in case, but everything seemed normal. He came down from the hayloft—by the ladder, not the window—and halted near the door. "So, I'll just…check around outside."

No answer. Not even a flicker of movement. He stared for a moment at the long black cloak and dark braid that was all he could see of Karina from this angle. Then he gave up and went outside.

Possibly he spent more time than was strictly necessary poking around outside, especially since absolutely nothing unusual was happening. No golden songbirds, no magician hiding in a tree. Whatever had happened to the chickens seemed to be an isolated incident.

He headed reluctantly back into the barn. He'd just tell Karina he was returning to the house to finish breakfast and she could do whatever she wanted with the information. She didn't even have to talk if she'd rather sit and sulk.

She wasn't sitting on the hay bale anymore. She was standing by the horse's stall, and Millie had thrust her head over the low wall to be patted. Millie liked absolutely everyone so that wasn't surprising. It took him more by surprise that Karina was apparently being friendly back. She had her face close to Millie's and was rubbing the soft spot on her nose. The defiant set of her shoulders had relaxed.

He watched for a long moment before he noticed he was doing it. When he noticed, he cleared his throat and said, "Nothing to see out here, so I'm going back inside."

She looked away slowly, blinked at him once, and then her shoulders squared again. Maybe less adamantly than before though. "I always liked horses," she said, reaching up to rub once between Millie's ears. Then the corner of her mouth quirked up just the tiniest bit. "They don't say stupid things."

"They might if they could talk," he pointed out, more relieved than he liked to contemplate that she was speaking again.

"Maybe so," she agreed, gave Millie's nose one more pat, and walked across the barn. "I hear you're fixing a fence around the vegetable garden today," she remarked as she passed.

"I might be."

"Suppose I'd better come, then." She looked over her shoulder at him with a smirk. "Can't risk terrors and mayhem happening while you're gone."

Apparently he had been forgiven.

Chapter Six

Karina didn't really *mind* going out to the vegetable garden with Forrest. Honestly, it sounded better than sitting inside and chopping vegetables or unsnarling yarn.

She ought to be getting into town, finding out how to get away from this rock. But everyone had work they needed to do this morning, Richard had promised her a ride in the afternoon and that was soon enough. She'd get there earlier walking, but her ankle still felt tender and it would be easier to find out about a ship with someone local to help. She still wasn't entirely clear on how she was going to pay for passage, but…she'd work that out. Or she'd find out about the ship with Richard, and then sneak aboard later when neither he nor the ship's captain was looking. That would serve too.

In the meantime, it wasn't so bad sitting in the warm sunlight, leaned up against a convenient rock. There hadn't been many sunny meadows in her past. None at all, in fact.

The quiet was new too. It wasn't silent, with the distant murmur of waves, bird cries and occasional scurrying of small animals through the grass. Repairing a fence involved some knocking together of wood and other sounds. But behind all that was a deep *quiet*, a quiet of empty land with far fewer people on it than she was used to.

It wasn't quiet like this at home. At home people were all jammed in on top of each other and someone was always making noise. Shouts and conversation and creaking carts and a hundred other sounds. Except maybe in the very deepest, darkest part of the night. And that was a wary quiet, not a peaceful one. That wasn't a quiet you lingered in. That was a time to get your work done and get gone, quick, before anyone else found you out in the dark.

No, it wasn't bad sitting out here. She had pulled the hood of her cloak down over her face, with an announced intention to take a nap. She did doze a little…and she also spent some time watching Forrest work on the fence, under the cover of her hood's shadow. It was a good view.

Arm muscles like that, she had known Farmboy had to be good at something besides knitting.

Forrest was knocking the last fence post into place when a new arrival came into view around a fold of hill. Karina kept her hood pulled down and studied him covertly, an automatic habit and safeguard—though probably unnecessary here, since the stranger looked to be all of ten years old.

On the other hand, she had met some dangerous ten year olds. She had been one.

This one was a boy with a shock of thick dark hair, and nicer clothes than Forrest's family. Nicer clothes than anyone she knew back home wore too. She didn't know or care much about fashion, but she could recognize expensive when she saw it. The tunic was good material, and the embroidered pattern around the hem was either gold thread or a convincing imitation. As he came closer, she observed the smudges on the knees of his trousers, and mentally raised his social class even higher. Poor people with one grand outfit didn't get smudges on it.

"Hello there," Forrest called as the boy wandered up. "New to the area?"

"Does it show?" the boy asked with a cheeky grin.

Yes, Karina decided. It was in the clothes.

"Not really," Forrest said, although if his family really dealt in knitting and cloth as much as seemed evident, he probably had noticed the clothing too. "I just know everyone from around here."

"Good, then you'll be able to tell me how to get back to town," the boy said, with an easy confidence that marked him as someone who usually led a comfortable life where people were helpful and polite.

"About three miles that way," Forrest said, pointing.

The boy wheeled and looked that direction, though the hills hid this town Karina hadn't seen yet. "Really? I thought this island was too small to get lost on, but I guess I was wrong."

"It happens. I'm Forrest, by the way."

The boy hesitated, kicked a bit at the dirt with one very well-made leather boot. "Dastan, and yes, the royal one. But I'm only seventh in line, so don't start bowing or anything, all right?"

Forrest grinned. "If you say so. Welcome to Daygeor. Sleeping Beauty over there is—"

"—wide awake, thank you," Karina said, straightening up and pushing her hood back. "Is there going to be a search party out looking for you?"

"I don't think so," Dastan said, scratching behind one ear. "Not until dark, anyway."

"So you're actually encouraged to just wander off alone?" Mad. Completely mad.

"I don't know if I'm *encouraged* exactly," Dastan said with a thoughtful tilt of his head. "But that's kind of the point of coming here. We're supposed to meet people. And anyway, our governess is back at home and nobody else watches as closely."

Maybe if you had twelve princes, you figured you could afford to lose a couple to, oh, kidnapping or assassination or the like. Or did they really consider this island to be that safe?

"She's not as unfriendly as she seems," Forrest said in a loud whisper to Dastan.

Karina glared at him. "I am *exactly* as unfriendly as I seem. Maybe more so."

Forrest gave a 'what can you do?' shrug to Dastan, which was intensely irritating, and said, "I was just finishing here. If you come up to the house, we can give you a ride back to town."

"Thanks, but you don't have to do that," Dastan said with a shake of his head. "I got here; I can get back."

"And we can give you something to eat," Forrest added.

The prince's face lit up. "Now that you mention it, breakfast was *ages* ago."

"I'm sure Mother's got something cooked up for the midday meal, and we can always put another plate out."

Yes, that much was obvious. You couldn't get past that woman's door without having food pushed at you. Though just at the moment, Karina didn't object so much. Breakfast did feel like it had been ages ago. She'd been eyeing the vegetable patch, but it was too early in the season. Every vegetable she liked didn't look ready for picking yet.

They walked back to the house, Forrest and Dastan talking agreeably about the island and Karina minding her own thoughts. When they arrived, Lynette treated the appearance of a strange young prince much the same way she'd treated the appearance of a strange young woman. There was welcome and food, and a good deal less formality on all sides than Karina would have expected. Marileigh's royalty was definitely not like the royalty at home.

Chapter Seven

Forrest was just chewing the last bite of his fish pie when his father pushed his own plate away and said, "I'll go hitch up the cart and see about that trip into town."

Forrest swallowed hurriedly, managed not to cough, and said, "I could do it. I wouldn't mind," with surprising alacrity for not being entirely sure why he was volunteering. "I finished the fence this morning. And you just drove in yesterday." That was it, he was being a considerate son.

Father frowned thoughtfully. "Well, I would like to keep an eye on those lambs up in the north pasture. There's one of the ewes I don't quite—"

"Good, perfect," Forrest said, rising to his feet.

"I really can walk it," Dastan said, around his last mouthful of pie crust. "No one has to go to any trouble."

"It's no trouble," Forrest said. "Karina wanted to go into town this afternoon anyway."

"Now, you're not to just get on a ship and vanish," Mother said, somehow keeping her gaze on Karina even while she cleared the table. "Find out what's putting out to sea in the next few days, but I expect you back again. The girls would never get over it if you left without saying good-bye, and besides, I'll put together a bundle for you of things you might need."

"Of course," Karina said with a bright smile. "I'll just see what the options are."

Forrest studied her narrowly. That smile was *too* bright, and he'd bet money she was planning to slip away on a ship at once if the opportunity presented. Which meant he'd have to keep a close eye out and make sure she didn't have the chance. Purely so that he wouldn't have to come home and explain Karina's disappearance to his mother, of course.

If they'd been alone while walking out to the barn, he might have brought the subject up. But Karina probably wouldn't appreciate discussing her plans in front of the prince—and he wasn't certain that easy back and forth of argument was going to happen with an audience anyway. He wasn't sure how it happened when they were alone. It had never happened with anyone else.

So he didn't say anything until he was inside the barn, and then he just walked over to Millie's stall and said, "Hello there, old girl, how are you today?"

Millie stuck her head over the low wall, shook it once and then, clear as life, said, "The hay is fine, there isn't rain, but I'd like some oats and grain."

Forrest's head jerked back and he stared at Millie, who stared back quite placidly, as though she hadn't noticed anything unusual.

"You didn't tell me your horse talks!" Dastan exclaimed. "That's amazing!" He bounded up closer to the stall to peer in at the new wonder.

Forrest felt more like edging away, but stopped himself. Karina was watching.

"She doesn't usually talk," Forrest said, staring at Millie, who just blinked innocently back at him. That shiver of uncertain excitement was stronger about Millie than it had been about the chickens. The chickens might have been a trick. This? This had to be magic. He was *used* to magic woven into a scarf or a sweater, but he didn't know how to feel about *this*.

"So this isn't normal either?" Karina remarked, hands on her hips.

"No, of course not," Forrest said automatically, rubbing the back of his neck and trying to think this through. They'd had Millie since she was a filly, and in six years she'd never done anything remotely exciting or noteworthy.

Until right now, as she casually remarked, "There are no clouds, the sun is bright. I'd like a walk, if I might."

"Why is she talking in rhymes?" Karina asked.

"Why is she talking *at all*?" Forrest countered.

"A magician came to our castle once with a talking bird," Dastan volunteered, hanging onto the edge of the stall. "The bird could sing songs. You know, with lyrics. Did a magician come by lately?"

"Not that we know of," Forrest said. "We don't get a lot of visitors here…but we do have one." He turned his baffled stare away from Millie to Karina. She seemed as surprised by this as everyone else, and he couldn't imagine why she would want to make the chickens lay gilded eggs, or to make Millie talk. But she was the new factor in the situation.

She raised her hands, spreading her fingers. "Don't look at me like that. I can't do magic. And why would I make your horse spout poetry?"

"Grass and grain and oats," Millie muttered, "I wonder which I like the most?"

"That wasn't a very good rhyme," Dastan told her.

Maybe she didn't have a reason to make Millie talk—but this still wasn't an entirely new idea. "You *were* talking about the horse talking this morning," Forrest pointed out.

"I was not," she countered, "I said I appreciated that horses *didn't* talk. *You* brought up the idea that they might."

"Not exactly. I just said they might say stupid things if they could."

"And now the horse is saying stupid things!" Karina said, pointing with a flourish at the horse. "Sorry, Millie."

Forrest shook his head, rubbed his palms on his trousers. "All right, never mind how this started." Because tying it to their conversation—no, that didn't really make sense, he'd never seen magic work that way. "The question is what we're going to do about it now."

"Why do you have to do anything?" Dastan asked, patting Millie's nose. "I think it would be fun to have a talking horse."

"A sugar lump, an apple core?" Millie said in hopeful tones. "Something sweet, a little more?"

"The problem isn't that she's talking," Forrest said, "it's that we don't know why or *how* she's talking." Golden eggs were a good thing, and a talking horse wasn't exactly a bad thing, but where was it all coming from? It would be much easier to find this fun and exciting if he knew why it was happening. Or maybe if he was still ten years old, not old enough that he had to take the responsible, calm and cautious view of things.

"Listen to enough of those rhymes and the talking could start to feel like a problem," Karina remarked, leaning an elbow on Millie's stall to peer in closer. "You're sure there are no magicians on this island? Other than, you know, stitch witches."

"That's *not* a term, and yes, I'm sure," Forrest snapped, and almost but not quite didn't notice an odd tone in her voice. She'd buried that question about magicians in between two provoking, joking comments—but *that* question hadn't sounded like a joke.

"Oh wait, I know what to do!" Dastan said. "Let's ask *her*." He took Millie's head firmly between his hands and stared into her eyes. "Did someone strange come into the barn today?"

"A man I knew, one boy and girls two." Millie's poetry did not seem to be improving with practice.

"That's just the three of us and Clara this morning," Forrest said.

"Anybody else?" Dastan persisted. "Did anything *magical* happen?"

"Chickens squawk, hay goes crunch. Flies buzz, I munch."

"On the hay, not the flies, right?" Karina asked with a smirk.

"Don't distract her," Forrest protested.

Karina rolled her eyes. She did that a lot. "She's not saying anything useful."

Dastan grinned. "Sure she is. She just told us nothing strange happened. Except the talking, I mean. Could we find a magician to ask about it?"

"There aren't any here," Karina said, voice coming out cold enough that Forrest looked at her sharply.

Dastan didn't seem to notice, just scratched behind one ear. "Yeah, that's a problem with that plan. It's strange not being at home. I forget other islands are farther away. Could we send a message?"

"Not quickly," Forrest said, still watching Karina.

She flashed a suddenly brilliant smile, which probably meant she knew he'd been studying her, and clapped her hands together. "Oh, I know! You could knit the horse a muzzle!"

Either her mood was swinging wildly or she was trying to cover a lot more unease than she was admitting to. If it was anyone else, he would have asked her what it was all about. But he already knew that wasn't a reasonable plan with her. "In the realm of *useful* suggestions," Forrest said evenly, "whatever's going on with the horse, the prince still needs to get back to town today."

Dastan sighed loudly. "Nothing will be happening that's as interesting as a talking horse."

"I'm sure a hunt for a missing prince would be very interesting, but still better to avoid," Forrest said. Someone had to be the responsible one. "I don't think we should bring a talking horse into town…"

"But a mob of curious bystanders would be interesting too," Karina murmured.

"…at least not until we know more about what's happening. And even though no magicians live here, I do have a friend in town who might have some ideas. So if you don't mind walking, Dastan, I'll walk in with you."

"Yeah, I can walk," he said without enthusiasm. "But riding a talking horse would be much more exciting."

Forrest glanced at Karina, and looked away. "You shouldn't be walking on that ankle, so—"

"I can still come. My ankle's fine," she said, and frowned when he raised his eyebrows. "I really mean it this time."

Forrest shrugged. If she wanted to reinjure her ankle and wind up forced to stay here even longer, he wasn't going to risk his skin arguing with her. "If you insist. Just don't expect me to carry you."

"Don't expect me to let you!"

They went back into the house to report about Millie, and then the walking to town plan carried, although Mother insisted on inspecting Karina's ankle before she'd let them try it. Forrest watched Karina as they set off on the road, Dastan trotting along with them, and she really didn't seem to be limping. He decided he could feel smug about this. She might not believe in magical bandages, but it's a funny thing about magic. You don't have to believe in it for it to work.

If she was actually just hiding the pain well, and he did end up having to carry her back—well, she probably wasn't that heavy.

Except, obviously, it would be incredibly awkward and unfortunate on many, *many* levels. Obviously. So. Best to hope the bandage really had worked.

Chapter Eight

The town seemed laughably small to Karina, compared to home. From the hill overlooking it, you could actually see *all* of it. And not in a vague, hazy sort of way where the edges of the horizon got blurry with rooftops, but really, definitely all of it, every building distinct. All three dozen thatched stone buildings, clustered together with the harbor at one side, a couple of boats bobbing off the dock. She hadn't come in this way when she landed, and while she had expected the town to be small, she hadn't expected this. There weren't even proper roads, just winding pathways.

Where did people *hide* in a place like that? How did anyone go unnoticed, ever?

She was still staring at the paltry collection of roofs when Dastan pointed towards one larger, multistory building set a little apart. "That's the summer house over there, where we stay when we're here."

It was the largest building in sight, although hardly huge. Was the proper castle bigger, more impressive, back at the capital? Probably. If nothing else, they needed space for twelve princes. She was still studying the summer house when it occurred to her that it wasn't on the same path as the dock. They were in the same general direction—the whole town was in the same general direction—but the summer house was off to one side.

"I can see the dock from here," she said with deliberate cheerfulness, "so why don't you two get the prince home, and I'll see about a ship."

She was bound to stand out in a town that small, but she could at least reduce the effect by *not* walking in accompanying royalty. And it would be much easier to sneak aboard a boat and be away if Forrest wasn't on the dock with her. The boats looked small, but all she needed was one going to a larger island. They ought to be big enough for that.

"You don't want to go down to the dock," Forrest said, and was he studying her a little too closely? That fake cheerfulness didn't work very well on him. "You're better off going to The Wool and Spindle. It's the tavern and inn, and the best place to find out about any ships in port or ones expected."

"The Wool and Spindle?" she repeated, because it was irresistible. "Really?"

He shrugged, irritatingly unruffled. "Cloth and thread are kind of important around here. Anyway, the friend I want to see is staying there too, so—"

"—so you should both go there," Dastan interrupted, "and I can get home by myself."

Forrest hesitated. "I don't know..."

The prince sighed loudly. "I know you're trying to be responsible and everything, but if I come back on my own, it'll help me convince my older brothers they don't have to look after me."

Karina had an unexpected pang as, for the first time, she thought about twelve brothers as something more than a ridiculously too-high number of princes. What was it like having such a crowd of people wanting to look after you? Probably intensely irritating.

Most of the time.

No one else seemed to notice her sudden reverie, still fixated on the immediate question. "Your brothers already let you wander off today," Forrest pointed out.

Dastan scratched the back of his neck. "Yeah..."

"They do know you're gone, right?" Forrest asked, in a suspicious tone.

"They know by now," Dastan said with a cheeky grin. "And it's not like I'm not allowed to wander off, just that Daemyn thinks it's his job to watch us all."

"He's the oldest?" Karina asked.

She regretted it when Dastan blinked in obvious surprise. "Yeah, of course."

And no doubt everyone from this country already knew their crown prince's name. Or maybe it was just typical royal assumption that they were so important everyone knew about them. She felt a prick of guilt over that thought, though. Dastan was much less arrogant than she would have expected a prince to be.

He was more open to argument too, but in the end, he still won the debate. He set off alone while Karina and Forrest walked towards The Wool and Spindle. Which, while not as convenient for slipping away as walking in alone would be, still had to be less conspicuous than walking into town with the prince.

Maybe. Theoretically.

The first building they passed was unmistakably a blacksmith's shop, based on the forge. The man sitting by the forge was unmistakably the blacksmith, based on his enormous size. He grinned and raised a hand as they approached. "Forrest, good to see you. Tell your mother those bandages she knitted for me are the best I've ever had for burns."

"Glad to hear it," Forrest said with a smile.

And then the blacksmith's gaze drifted to Karina, and she *knew* a question was coming. She ducked her head and kept walking, picking up her pace. Somewhere behind her she heard Forrest say something about seeing someone at the tavern, and in a few paces he had caught up again. It was those long legs.

"In a hurry?" he asked.

"Yes."

That was pretty much how it went all through town. Forrest knew *everyone*, they all wanted to say hello, and they were all curious about the girl with him. She might as well have come into town with

Dastan after all. Maybe the prince would have been a distraction. As it was, she only managed to dodge being introduced half the time.

They weren't unfriendly. But they looked at her with such interest. Back home, she was invisible most of the time. And when she wasn't, she knew how to deal with the kind of attention she did get; it wasn't this kind of friendly. But most of the time she was invisible, and she liked it that way. She needed it to be that way right now. Because if anyone came to this island on the trail of a dark-haired young woman, the entire town was going to be able to report on her.

She should have refused to come into town with Forrest, should have snuck out in the middle of the night and found her way by herself. She'd been lulled by his family's calm assurance that this was the best way to do things, that giving and accepting help was perfectly normal.

For such a small town, it seemed to take a long time to get through, but at last they reached The Wool and Spindle. It was the second largest building in town, after the royalty's house. Two stories, a thickly thatched roof and a wooden sign hanging above the door. Karina glanced up at the sign as they passed under it. It showed, predictably, a sheep and a spinning wheel.

Inside, she let out a relieved breath to find herself on more familiar footing. Taverns are taverns the world over. It was a little cleaner and more light shone than in most of the places she frequented back home, but the scattering of tables, big fireplace, and long counter at the back were familiar enough. And it was blessedly empty, apparently too early in the day for hard-working, respectable townsfolk to be at the tavern. Which meant no one to stare.

She had started to relax when a woman approximately her own age walked into the room, from a doorway probably leading to the kitchen. The girl's face broke into a wide smile as soon as she caught sight of her visitors. "Oh, Forrest!" she trilled. "You haven't been to visit in ages!"

Karina sighed inwardly. He really did know everyone. And she wouldn't be able to avoid an introduction here.

Forrest ducked his head slightly, rubbing the back of his neck. "I was just in last week."

"Well, it feels like forever," the girl insisted, hands on her hips. "I was beginning to think you forgot the way to town."

"It's not like it's a complicated route," Karina said unthinkingly, and could have kicked herself the moment the words were out. The first person who *hadn't* shown any interest in her, and she had to draw attention. What had made her do that? Sure, it was a stupid thing for the girl to say, but she could have let it go by.

The girl turned her head to face Karina, and though the smile stayed fixed on her face, it went brittle around the edges. "And who's your friend, Forrest?"

"This is Karina, she's…visiting. Karina, this is Dahlia. Her father owns The Wool and Spindle."

Of course she was named after a flower. She was a tall, willowy blond wearing a lavender dress that showed off her figure and had just the right number of flounces in the skirt. Karina might not care much about fashion, but she could tell when someone had found a dress that worked for her. She had already realized that her own clothes were not remotely in the local style, but the contrast between that lavender dress and her own vest and trousers could hardly be more dramatic. And…yes, she could see the tips of matching lavender slippers peeping out from under the skirt. Figured.

"So lovely to meet you," Dahlia said, voice ever so sweet. Her smile definitely didn't reach her eyes anymore. "Any friend of Forrest's, you know."

"How very kind of you to welcome me to your lovely establishment," Karina replied, and smiled with too many teeth. Two could play this game.

"And will you be visiting long?" Dahlia asked.

Would Dahlia's smile crack if she said she was staying permanently? Tempting, but hardly practical. "No, I'm afraid not. In fact, I'm here to find out about any ships leaving the island."

"Oh, what a pity! It would have been delightful to get to know you."

"I'm sure we would have had *so* much in common," Karina returned, and watched as Dahlia's eyes flickered. They likely had nothing at all in common, but they did at least understand each other.

"So…" Forrest said, looking faintly puzzled as though he wasn't quite sure about what had just been said, "are there any ships setting out in the next day or two?"

Dahlia hesitated, and said with a frown, "I'm sorry to say there aren't. At least, none of the ships here are setting out, and we aren't expecting any. The princes' ship left this morning, and the two at the dock have business that won't be settled for a few days."

Karina would bet she really was sorry about that, and it gave her a totally irrational satisfaction to set against her own sharp pang of disappointment. Three or four more days here? *Anything* could happen in three days. With regard to pursuit, probably it was good they weren't expecting a ship. But that didn't mean ships couldn't arrive unexpectedly. And she was stuck here.

Could she steal a boat? No, that was idiotic. She could probably steal one, but she couldn't sail it, so what good would that do her?

She hated being on an island. There was nowhere to *run*.

"Surely that's not the only reason you came in today?" Dahlia asked, plainly taking advantage of Karina's momentary silence to try to regain control of the conversation.

"No, I was hoping to see Master Aurum," Forrest said. "Do you know if he's in?"

Dahlia blinked once, and the melodic tone of her voice went flatter. "Yes, he's upstairs. You know which room."

Oh, was that not the answer she had been hoping for? How very sad.

"Thanks, Dahlia," Forrest said cheerfully, and headed for the stairs.

"It was *so* nice to meet you," Karina said, because how could she pass the moment up?

Dahlia's mouth compressed into a straight line. "Yes, of course," she said, turned, and swept back towards the kitchen in a flurry of skirts and a flash of lavender slippers.

Those slippers would probably wear out in a month, and the skirt would get in the way of—well, practically anything useful. Karina thumped up the stairs after Forrest, leather boots landing firmly on the wooden steps, bottom edge of her black cloak swirling about her ankles. Although…just now and then it might be nice to be the kind of person who wore clothes that were beautiful and impractical. Just now and then. Not most of the time, not even often, but… She shook her head. Sure, and it would also be nice to have a pocketful of gold.

She followed Forrest down the narrow hallway, to where he knocked on a heavy wooden door.

"Yes, what is it?" a muffled voice from within came back.

"It's Forrest, Master Aurum, I was hoping to speak with you."

"Ah, yes, of course!" And the door was being pulled open practically before the words were finished. He really did know *everyone*.

What kind of person did you have to be for everyone to like you? It was not a talent Karina had ever possessed. Just witness how well she had got on with Dahlia.

The person behind the door proved to be a hunched old man with wisps of white hair, ink stains on his shirt and a beaming smile. Karina was beginning to wonder if anyone in this town wasn't friendly. Besides Dahlia.

"Always good to see you, my boy, and…" Master Aurum trailed off, turning his head to look at Karina. "And who are you, my dear?"

She wanted to say that who she was not was *his dear*, but…she gritted her teeth and said, "I'm Karina, I'm just visiting for a few days." Introduction done, move on.

But he kept looking at her, still smiling, his eyes very intent. "I thought you must be new to the area. I'd certainly remember you," he said, gaze traveling up and down over her.

Everyone in town had been looking, but no one had been so obvious about it. She had been looked over often enough back home, but…Master Aurum's smile hadn't quite turned into a leer, which was all that saved him from being punched in the nose.

"I was hoping to talk to you about a magical problem," Forrest said, apparently oblivious to this interplay too. "We've had some…strange things happening."

"Of course, of course," Master Aurum said, nodding without taking his attention off Karina. "Do come in."

She hesitated on the threshold. Maybe she should beg off, say she'd wait downstairs. Except then she'd probably have to talk to Dahlia again. The other girl might have her claws out openly if Forrest wasn't in the room—and Karina didn't really relish the thought of explaining why she had hit Dahlia in her pretty little rosebud mouth. If it came to confronting anyone, it would be easier to explain hitting Master Aurum.

She stepped into the small parlor. Three chairs clustered around a fireplace and mountains of books and papers covered every flat space, with stacks of books reaching to precarious heights on the floor in two corners. Another door was closed, but likely led to a bedroom.

"Sit down, sit down," Master Aurum said, moving a pile of papers off of one seat, and dumping it on the ground next to the chair. He came towards Karina with one hand outstretched. "And let me take your cloak."

She backed up a step just before his reaching fingers would have touched her shoulder. "No, thank you." She gathered her cloak around her, black cloth in her clenched fingers, and sat down in the emptied chair. The room was perfectly warm, but she didn't know this man, she didn't trust him, and she would prefer to keep her belongings to herself. She had few enough of them.

"Ah. No matter," Master Aurum said, sitting down in another chair as Forrest took the third. "Now then, what can I be of help with? I'm always glad to provide my magical expertise. It is my profession, after all."

"You're a magician?" Karina said sharply, hands tightening on the edges of her cloak, heart jumping up to a faster pace before she remembered that Forrest had said no magicians lived on the island. He *had* said that, hadn't he? She hadn't misunderstood? Magicians were dangerous, unstable, untrustworthy—

"Oh no, no!" Master Aurum protested. "I am merely a scholar of all things magical. I do not, alas, have any ability myself."

"You're not missing anything," Karina muttered, but relaxed a little. She could handle someone who just knew *about* magic, but who couldn't actually turn anyone into a toad. Or say a few words and tear someone's life apart in a flash of magical power.

"I've made a lifelong study of all varieties of magic," Master Aurum continued. "A fascinating subject, and there are so many unpredictable elements!"

"You might say we've been having some unpredictable elements lately at home," Forrest said, and went on to describe the gilded eggs and talking horse.

"Speaking in *rhymes*, you say?" Master Aurum tapped the end of his quill pen against his chin, then scribbled a note on the papers he had seized as Forrest told the story. "It sounds very much like Good Fairy magic."

"You think a fairy enchanted the horse?" Karina said, arms folded across her chest. "Why would one bother?"

"That would be the question, yes." He nodded and scribbled some more. "It has all the characteristics of a Good Fairy type-spell. Any number of magic practitioners have been known to enchant animals to speak, but Good Fairies are the most likely to make an animal start speaking in rhyming couplets. Has the horse been saying proverbs?"

"Only if they're proverbs about hay," Forrest said with a half-grin. He was leaning back in his seat, looking perfectly at ease with the situation and the conversation. Naturally.

"Hmm. The gilded eggs are an interesting feature. Solid gold would be much more in line with tradition, but perhaps it isn't a very good Good Fairy." Master Aurum frowned, tapping his quill again. "That is to say, not a very *capable* Good Fairy."

"So an inept fairy is casting spells, but *why*?" Karina repeated. One magic user or another, who cared, the important point was what it meant and how to stop it before anything horrible happened. Or at least, that would be the important point if this whole discussion mattered to her. But since she would be leaving very soon, probably before they even solved the mystery, she had no reason to get invested in the question.

Master Aurum waved his hand, quill pen looping through the air and a few ink drops spattering on nearby papers. "Oh, Good Fairies can have quite varied motivations, but usually they're trying to reward the worthy. You might view all of this as rather a compliment. Now let's see, the magic began this morning..." His eyes slid sideways to Karina. "And when did you arrive, my dear?"

She lifted her chin and made sure to meet his gaze solidly. "Yesterday. But this has nothing to do with me. I'm not enchanting anything, and I don't know any fairies."

"Mm-hmm, mm-hmm. So you're quite sure you're not a princess?" Master Aurum asked.

Karina stared at him. He might as well have asked if she was sure she wasn't purple. "...yes." Princesses were all beautiful and blond and useless. At least, all the ones she'd ever heard of.

"Hmm. Magic tends to happen most often around royalty." Master Aurum turned back to Forrest. "Now, no one in your family has a Fairy Godmother? Or has anyone helped a mysterious old woman in the last few days?"

Forrest shook his head. "No, neither." He grinned. "Not a mysterious *old* woman, anyway."

Karina just glared at him, because that didn't deserve a verbal response.

He ignored the glare, with no apparent dent in his overall good cheer. "So if a Good Fairy enchanted our animals, what do we do about it?"

"I don't know that you need to do anything," Master Aurum said. "The effects sound harmless. Even beneficial, in the case of golden egg shells."

Forrest nodded slowly. "I guess that makes sense. Millie might get pretty annoying spouting poetry about hay and flies, but it's not dangerous."

Karina leaned forward, hands tightening on the arms of her chair. "Maybe *this* isn't dangerous, but if things keep happening, they'll turn that way eventually." Was he really going to just dismiss this?

Apparently yes, since Forrest simply shrugged and looked at her with an expression so reasonable it was infuriating. "But why should the spells turn bad? I mean, if a Good Fairy is doing it, the spells ought to stay good."

The naïveté was appalling. Maybe it came of being from a trusting family—or a tiny island. "You can't trust any magic doers," she said, jaw tight. "Ever."

Forrest's eyebrows rose. "None at all?"

Or maybe it came of believing that he could knit magical scarves, which was obviously harmless. She rolled her eyes. "Magic doers who can do things this dramatic. And unpredictable."

"I understand magic can be a bit scary, but I hardly think there's any reason to panic," Master Aurum said, with a patronizing smile that made Karina want to smack him with his own quill pen. "I've never yet heard of a modest Good Fairy, so I expect the responsible party will make herself known if you're simply patient. Although..." He started tapping the quill again, a tic which did not calm Karina at all. "...if it would make you feel better, I could come out to investigate a bit more. I could go back with you now."

The clench in her stomach confirmed that it would *not* make Karina feel better, and she was relieved when Forrest said, "No, it'll be dark by the time we get back. I couldn't ask you to come tonight. Since the magic has been harmless anyway, you should wait and come tomorrow morning."

"Yes, well...perhaps." Master Aurum's gaze shifted to Karina again, and she felt her spine stiffen instinctively. "And are you visiting long, my dear?"

"No," she said flatly. "Just a few days."

"Ah. Such a pity. This is really a fascinating place. I myself am a visitor, having only come two months ago."

She glanced around at the stacks of books. He clearly didn't believe in traveling light.

"Of course it was the magic that drew me here. The culture of textile enchantment is quite unparalleled in my experience."

Karina raised an eyebrow. "You mean that lucky scarf stuff?" So he believed in it too.

Forrest sighed. "I told you, it's more complicated than that."

"Yes, very much so," Master Aurum said with a nod. "The complex interplay of technique, numeracy and chromatism is most intriguing."

"Right," Karina said. Whatever that meant. Even *if* she was intrigued, she still wouldn't ask him about it.

"Perhaps it doesn't interest everyone," Master Aurum said, with that patronizing smile again. "Forrest, I do look forward to seeing that scarf you're working on. How is it coming?"

Forrest was staring at Karina, a stare that made her shrug uncomfortably. What did he *want*? After a moment he blinked and said, "The scarf's good. It's almost finished. So we'll see you tomorrow, then?"

"Absolutely. I'll be there just after breakfast." His glance shifted to Karina again. "I look forward to it."

Maybe she should have stayed downstairs after all. As it was, they managed to get out of The Wool and Spindle without seeing Dahlia again, which unquestionably meant they avoided any amount of trouble. She had fewer introductions to face going out of town, since it was mostly the same people waving. Forrest seemed less friendly too, more inclined to stay quiet and keep walking. Karina didn't understand that, but wasn't going to question it.

Relatively quickly, they were going up the hill back towards the farm. Karina shoved her hands into her pockets and frowned at the path beneath her feet. Now that no one was around to listen, she could ask something she'd been stewing over. "How long have you known that Master Aurum?"

"Since he came to the island. Couple of months."

"Hmm. Are you sure you trust him?"

Forrest turned to frown at her. "What's that supposed to mean?"

She shrugged, her spine prickling uncomfortably. "I didn't like the way he stared at me."

"Oh—sorry, I should have warned you," Forrest said, though his voice was still colder than normal. "He stares at everyone when he first meets them. He's trying to see their magical aura. If they have one."

"So…he can't do magic, but he can see other people's magic?" Karina scrunched up her forehead, thinking this through. "That doesn't sound right."

"There's a complicated theory and technique involved. He explained it once. I didn't understand it."

"Yeah, he seems to really like complicated theories," Karina muttered.

"And what's *that* supposed to mean?"

"Nothing."

Disapproval was positively radiating off of him. His shoulders were too tense as he kept striding forward too quickly, staring straight ahead. "You're thinking of when he started talking about knitting, aren't you? When you could have at least *pretended* to be interested. Just to be polite."

Karina pushed her hands deeper into her pockets. "Yeah, I could have, but I told you, I didn't like him. I wasn't going to smile and nod and pretend I wanted to listen to him explain about spinning magic."

"*Knitting*, he was talking about knitting, not spinning."

She smirked, knowing it would annoy him. "So if you don't spin, where does the yarn come from?"

His voice was more heated than she could ever remember hearing it. "We *do* spin, that's part of the magic too, but—that's not the point, the point is you wouldn't even listen to him about it and—no, the point is you have no reason to dislike him. He's a perfectly nice old man—"

"Who you've only known a couple of months."

"I've only known *you* a couple of *days*!"

"Am I asking you to trust me?"

"You're sleeping in my *house*."

"I didn't ask for that, I was dragged in."

He glared at her, and she glared back, and there was silence until they reached the crest of the hill.

"You know," Karina said quietly, "I could sleep in the hay loft again. Or I could just find somewhere else entirely, I can take care of myself—"

"You don't have to do that." He wasn't looking at her as they walked, but his shoulders weren't as tense as they'd been a few minutes before.

Karina waited until they had gone up another hill and the tension had relaxed further, and then remarked, "So—you and Dahlia, huh?"

"Me and Dahlia what?" he asked, but sounded more puzzled than irritated.

"Are you courting her?"

His head swung around to stare at her. "What? No!"

"Well, she wants you to," Karina said complacently. "Why aren't you?"

"I don't know, I—I mean, she's nice, but...we've known each other forever, I just never..." He shook his head, eyes narrowing. "Never mind that, why do you think she wants me to?"

"Why do you think she hated me on sight?" Karina countered.

He shook his head again, but this time it was perplexed. "She didn't hate you. She was friendly."

Karina studied him for a moment with her eyebrows raised, then nodded once. "Oh, I see. You only heard what she said out loud. Believe me, all that honey she was spreading around was heavily laced with poison."

"Assuming that's even true—and I'm not saying it is—what does that have to do with anything?"

Karina sighed dramatically. "Because I came in with *you*. That makes me competition." She walked another three paces before she properly thought that one through, and felt her cheeks turn hot. "That is...it makes me *look* like competition. If you see what I mean."

"Sure," Forrest said, gaze on the horizon and a slight smile on his face. "That much makes perfect sense."

Which, aggravatingly, didn't make any sense at all.

Chapter Nine

Dusk was making the shadows long by the time Forrest and Karina got back to the house. The walk had not been long enough for Forrest to stop being privately, quietly, secretly amused that Karina thought Dahlia was interested in him romantically.

Not that he was going to do anything about the information, if it was even true. Dahlia was nice enough, but she was somehow…predictable. He knew just what every conversation with her would be like, before ever having them. This idea that she wanted him to court her was the first surprise she'd ever provided. If it was true, and not just Karina's imagination.

It might have been nice to know how exactly Karina felt about the idea. She had brought the subject up, but that didn't clarify much. Not that it mattered. She was leaving in a few days. But it would have been nice to know.

And he wasn't sorry that no ships had been leaving today.

They were still a hundred yards from the house when Rosie came running out the front door to bounce around them. "How could you let the prince leave before I got to meet him?" she demanded. "And he was even one of the ones I remembered for my test!"

"He had to be home before dark," Forrest said. "You wouldn't want his family to worry, right?"

Her lower lip stuck out. "But I wanted to *meet* him!"

"And I'm sure you will. He'll be here all summer." He caught her by the waist and whirled her around. "Maybe he'll come back tomorrow."

"Really?" she asked, starting to dissolve into giggles already.

"Maybe." He swung her up onto his back and carried her towards the house. "Did you see what happened to Millie?"

"Yes! Isn't it funny?"

"Is she still speaking in rhymes?" Karina asked.

"Yes. Mostly about hay."

They went into the house, where supper was ready and everyone agreed it was a good idea for Master Aurum to come the next day to look at Millie and the chickens. Karina didn't comment, which probably required a heroic amount of self-control.

Maybe everyone else's approval had convinced her to change her opinion, but Forrest wouldn't bet on that. She was just being paranoid about Master Aurum, and about this magic business. Master Aurum was a nice old man who knew about magic and said they had no reason to worry, and if Karina was going to persist in worrying, well, that was her energy to waste.

After supper, and after the girls had gone up to bed, Forrest got out Clara's scarf again. He needed to weave in some loose ends where he had changed colors, and wanted to do that before Master Aurum looked at it. He sat near the fire, where the light was best. After a while, Karina sat down on a footstool nearby. Not that he was paying attention to her or anything. He carefully didn't look at her, focused on his work. It suddenly seemed to require more concentration than usual to *not* stab his fingers with a needle.

She watched for a minute or two, then said, "So it's the number of rows that makes it lucky?"

"Partially." He cut off a loose end and dropped it into the basket of scraps by his feet. "You don't have to pretend to be interested."

She rolled her eyes. "What makes you think I would bother pretending?"

He shrugged, went on working…and watched her covertly too. She was watching his hands. She seemed smaller somehow, without that black cloak swirling around her. He finished weaving in ends and had resumed knitting before either of them said anything again.

"So what is it besides the number of rows?" she asked finally.

If she was going to ask... "It's the color too. Purple is traditionally a good color for luck, and it's also naturally attuned to young girls. It's not just about creating the right components for luck, it's about creating a garment that will be especially powerful for the individual who'll be wearing it. I mean, if you want to go beyond a basic level."

"So what you're making is more advanced?"

"I'm not a master or anything, but it is more complex." He glanced across the room at his parents, but they appeared to be engrossed in their chess game and not listening to the conversation. "Seven rows for luck is basic knowledge, and pretty much everyone in town has something knitted in sets of seven. Using purple, which makes sense for Clara, means it should be luckier for her than if someone else wore it."

Her forehead wrinkled. "Is that what your Master Aurum was saying? Something about technique and numbers and chra...whatever else he said."

"Chromatism," Forrest said with a grin. "It's just a fancy word for colors. I thought you didn't want to pretend to him that you were interested?"

"I wasn't *not* interested, I just didn't want to ask *him*." She drew one knee up and wrapped her hands around it. "So does the blue mean something?"

"Mostly it's because of Clara's birthday. Blue is good for protection but also for summer birthdays, and it's stronger because I'm using 28 stitches to each row, because—"

"—that's the date of her birthday, I remember."

He would have sworn she hadn't actually been listening when he told her that. "Um, right. And then it's blue stripes of six rows, because there's six of us in the immediate family, which ties in with birth, heritage, and so on." He hesitated, then added, as a kind of concession, "It's called spellspinning. Sometimes. In old legends."

Her lips curved in a positively wicked smile. "But you got all upset when I called it—"

"You didn't know what you were talking about." He wasn't going to concede everything. "And that wasn't the point anyway."

"Fair enough." She reached out and picked up the trailing end of the scarf, smoothing it between her fingers. "So what about this stripe on the end? It's a different shade of blue."

"You can't really see it properly in this light." He knew what it looked like in sunlight—a deep blue, shining with hints of green when the light struck it just right. "That's Marileigh Blue. It's sort of a national secret—the dye comes from fish that are only found near our islands. We spin the yarn and dye it ourselves, and no one outside of the country knows the exact technique to achieve the right shade."

Surely this would now prompt a snide comment about how the deep secret of a shade of yarn couldn't be that important.

Instead, she ran her fingers over the stripe again and said, "I like it. I've never seen it before."

"It's rare outside of Marileigh. And expensive, even inside of the country. That's why I'm only doing one stripe of it, at either end."

"What does it do magically?"

That was, perhaps, why it was so expensive, even beyond its rarity. "It connects people, bonds them together." He hesitated. Did she really want to hear this? But this was a softer side than he'd seen yet, very different from the scornful, hostile front she usually showed. "The legend has it that Marileigh Blue reflects the color of the ocean around our islands. And that it connects people together the way the water connects the different pieces of land."

"Hmm." She let the scarf end go, and it swung back to rest against his leg again. She folded her hands over her up-drawn knee and laid her cheek against her fingers. "That would be nice," she said softly. "If some yarn could connect people. Keep anyone from getting lost."

The depth and solemnity in her tone surprised him. The memory of the morning drifted into his mind, and that comment about people being accidentally killed...but he didn't want to think about that, wasn't sure he liked where that thread would take him. "It's not like a love spell or anything," he said quickly, with a forced heartiness. "It doesn't create connections, or force anybody to feel anything. It just...helps, if a connection is already there."

She just nodded, and went on watching as his hands followed the familiar rhythm of loop and cross and tug.

Chapter Ten

Karina knew where she was when she woke up, before she even opened her eyes. Extra bed in the tiny little room off the parlor, in this absurdly hospitable family's house, on this tiny little island, out in the middle of an enormous sea.

She hadn't remembered immediately when she woke up the day before, had had to look around to get her bearings back. She was used to that. That split-second of dislocation was as familiar as…well, as waking up in familiar surroundings would be.

Today she lay with her eyes closed for a moment, not needing to check where she was, recognizing the weight of the heavy knit blanket over her feet, the smell of cinnamon from the morning's porridge.

After a drowsy minute or two, her brain stirred itself properly awake, and her instincts came back with it. She sat up, feeling a pang of guilt. After just two days, she was growing careless. It didn't matter if it was nice here, she couldn't get drowsy and comfortable. She knew better than that.

Tomorrow or the next day or sometime *soon*, she'd be leaving. She'd be taking the first ship out of here. And that would be that.

She sat up, swinging her legs over the side of the bed. She leaned forward, putting weight on her feet, and was pleased to find her injured ankle not even sore. It had been all right walking yesterday, and she didn't seem to have strained it again. Maybe those magic bandages did work. Maybe.

Lynette had loaned her a nightgown. Karina pulled the soft cotton garment over her head, and quickly changed into her own clothing, black trousers and dark purple shirt. She always wore dark clothes. The better to blend in. She sat on the edge of the bed again to quickly braid her hair. It wasn't the perfect plait Lynette would do for her daughters, but good enough to keep hair out of her eyes. She tied it off with a bit of black string, and found herself thinking of Forrest's scraps of yarn and the bows he tied for his sisters.

She shook her head, trying to shake the thought away. She didn't need anything like that. And some gaudy, brightly colored bow would look ridiculous on her.

She leaned over, one elbow pressing into the blankets, to reach around the foot of the bed with her other hand. She had left her boots sitting on the floor. Once she had pulled those on, she'd be ready and... Her fingers brushed something in the right place, but it didn't feel like leather. She frowned, pulled herself along the bed to look over the edge.

It took a moment to recognize what she was seeing. The wooden floorboards, but in one patch they looked distorted. Then, as her hand brushed again against something cool and smooth, she blinked and it became clear. She was seeing the floor through glass objects.

She grasped one and sat up, pulling it onto her lap. It was—her boot. Every lacing, every strap, perfect and complete and familiar, even the knife in its sheath and the notch missing from one flap where she'd caught it on a nail once. Her boot, except it was made of glass. The knife, the lacings, all of it turned to glass. She grabbed for the other boot too, stared at them side-by-side in disbelief.

What could be more utterly useless than *glass shoes*?

And she had *liked* these boots. She'd only had them a year, they were still good and sturdy, but worn-in and comfortable. She felt the most ridiculous lump in her throat. She had run with nothing but the clothes on her back and the boots on her feet, and now even that... She felt a new flicker of panic. How could she run now without boots? How could she do anything?

She took a deep breath. Panicking wouldn't help. She'd just have to get new shoes. That was all. Or go without. She was getting soft if she really thought she couldn't make do barefoot. It had been good enough for enough years.

Or maybe Master Aurum would know how to turn them back into leather. This had to be connected to the other magic that had been happening; it was as stupid as the rest. Maybe he'd know if there was a way to reverse it. If she asked him. She grimaced at that thought. It didn't matter what Forrest said, she just didn't like the man. Still...it was an option. Not an option she had to pursue, just something to keep in mind.

She set the boots down and slid a hand under the pillow for her second knife in its sheath. That, at least, was unchanged. She strapped it on her forearm, dropped the sleeve over it, and reached for her leather vest on the nearby chair. She'd just lace that and go out to breakfast and deal with the boots later. As she lifted the vest, a fall of powder spilled over her hands and out onto the chair. She shook her hand and looked more closely at the vest. One of the pockets bulged. She tipped it over her cupped hand, and studied the mound of dust that piled on her palm. Vaguely yellow, but it sparkled and shone in the light. It almost looked like gold dust, but wasn't the right color. Close, but not actual gold. She couldn't be that lucky, of course. Whatever it was, how had she wound up with a pocketful of...

Her heart beat harder as pieces began falling together into a very disturbing picture.

Yesterday, at The Wool and Spindle. She had been looking at stupid Dahlia's stupid lavender shoes, and she had been thinking that it would be nice to have pretty clothes and a pocketful of gold. Today her boots had turned into glass and golden dust was spilling out of her pocket.

She had been thinking about horses talking yesterday, and then Millie started talking. As to the eggs...she'd considered stealing them, back when she was lying up in that hayloft. And hadn't she had a fleeting thought that it was too bad she couldn't find something more valuable to steal? Could that be enough? It had to be, because all the evidence was pointing one direction.

She was causing it. Somehow, she was causing the strange magic to happen.

She pressed her palms against her temples, swallowing hard against a sudden roll of nausea. How could this be possible? How could she be behind all this? Master Aurum thought the spells were the work of a Good Fairy. But that didn't make sense, she didn't have a Fairy Godmother—or if she did, the woman had been astoundingly ineffective for the past sixteen years. Still was, based on these absurd spells.

The Good Fairy theory was only Master Aurum's *theory*, he could be wrong. It could be a curse. It could be something happening inside of her. What if it kept happening? What if it stopped being small, silly things? What if she thought about the wrong thing at the wrong time and... She hadn't meant to do anything, and that was maybe the worst part. How could she control something, when she didn't know how she was doing it?

And it would hardly be the first time she hadn't meant to do any harm, and everything had still gone hideously, horribly awry.

Maybe she should talk to Forrest; he knew a little about magic—about how the knitting worked anyway, which probably didn't have anything at all to do with what was happening to her. But still, she'd like to talk to him about this...except he'd tell Master Aurum. That would be the first thing he'd say, that they should talk to the supposed expert.

She clenched her hands into fists, fingernails digging into her palms. She *didn't* trust that man, and she *didn't* want him to know she was somehow responsible for this. He was already too interested in her, he didn't need more reasons. Maybe it was an irrational dislike, but she didn't care.

She wouldn't let him know. So she couldn't let anyone know.

Chapter Eleven

Forrest tied bows in Rosie's hair, and hoped it wasn't obvious that he was watching for Karina. He tried not to stare at the doorway—but she was late coming into the kitchen for breakfast this morning.

He had finished with Rosie's hair, and with Elena's, before Karina walked in. He made himself wait a breath before saying, "Good morning."

"Morning," she said without making eye contact, walked directly over to the table and sat down. Same chair she'd sat in the first day.

"Karina, look!" Rosie exclaimed, running up to the table and holding up her braids. "Purple today, like your shirt."

She glanced briefly. "Very nice."

Forrest frowned slightly. He had been all ready with an explanation about what Rosie's bows meant today. If she had asked. She had been interested the night before, so it hadn't seemed too unreasonable.

"And we don't have school today," Rosie chattered on, plopping into another chair, "so if the prince comes back, I can meet him! *And* see if any new magic happens!"

"Maybe nothing will happen," Karina said, looking down at the table. "Maybe that's all over."

"I hope not, it's exciting," Rosie said. "Nothing exciting happens usually."

Something about Karina looked different today. He tried to covertly study her out of the corner of his eye. The usual clothes, same braid as ever. She wasn't wearing her cloak, but she'd had that off other times, so that wasn't it. His gaze traveled down over her legs, pressed against the legs of the chair.

That was it. Bare feet. He sat down in the next chair over and asked, "Forget something today?"

"No," she said, without even asking what he meant. One of her feet crossed behind the other, as though hiding.

And now would be the snide comment about how it was none of his business what she wore, or that she didn't comment on *his* clothes…right?

Wrong. This felt disappointing to an entirely unreasonable degree. The rest of breakfast featured about the usual amount of conversation from everyone else, but was silent from Karina's direction.

Yesterday he had started to think…but now they might as well be back to the first day, when he had still seriously suspected her of being a danger or a madwoman. Actually, she'd been more talkative then.

They had nearly finished with breakfast, and Forrest was still trying not to stare at Karina too obviously, when the outer door swung open.

"Good morning," Dastan said cheerfully, came several paces in, then paused with a slightly guilty expression. "Uh, may I come in?"

"Of course," Mother said, and gestured towards the fire. "Take a bowl, there's more porridge in the pot."

"Thanks!" Dastan said, picking up a bowl. "I mean, they fed me at home and everything, but it smells really good."

Rosie was sitting straighter in her chair, studying the prince, and Forrest smiled in spite of himself at her obvious delight. "Are you Dastan? I'm Rosie. I got your name right on my test two days ago."

"Good!" Dastan said, dishing out porridge. "Did they make you memorize our ages? Even I mix that up. I have to stop and count to remember how old everyone is. It keeps changing, you know."

"No, just the order. Is that a lute?"

"Yeah," Dastan said, setting his bowl of porridge on the table and pulling the wooden instrument off his back, where it had been hanging on a strap. "I've been learning to play it." He leaned it against his chair as he sat down.

"I thought princes learned things like sword fighting."

"I'm learning that too," Dastan said, digging a spoon into his bowl, "but I like music better."

Between Rosie and Dastan, there was almost enough talk for Forrest to forget Karina was still being quiet. Almost.

"Is Millie still talking?" Dastan asked.

"Yes!" Rosie said gleefully. "And the chickens are still laying gilded eggs. I checked this morning."

"So you've been to the vegetable garden too, right?"

"No...why?"

Dastan paused with a spoonful of porridge in the air. "Oh. No one's been out there? I walked past on the way here and I just thought..."

"What happened to the vegetable garden?" Karina asked sharply, making Forrest forget to pretend not to be looking at her.

If the prince noticed her tone, he didn't show it. He just grinned at her. "There's going to be a *really* good harvest."

So more magic had popped up. Maybe a Good Fairy really was taking an interest in them. He wondered suddenly if a fairy could have sent Karina here too. Was that the kind of thing Good Fairies did? And could her arrival even be considered a gift?

Well...she wasn't a curse.

Karina herself didn't seem to share that attitude about this new magical happening. Her lips tightened and she stood up from the table. "I'm going to go see."

"You might want your boots," Forrest pointed out.

"I might not," she snapped.

"If you aren't wearing shoes," Mother said, "at least take your cloak, dear. It's cold out."

She opened her mouth—closed it again, went into the next room and came out again with the cloak over one arm. Fine, so *Mother* could make harmless suggestions about her wardrobe.

"What's the rush?" Forrest asked, rising to his feet. He was curious too, but this kind of urgency felt like more than curiosity, and it entirely lacked any enjoyment in the strange happenings. "I doubt the garden's going anywhere."

"Don't joke about it!" she said, and pushed out the door.

"Wait for me, I want to see too!" Rosie said, sliding off her chair.

"Have you finished your breakfast?" Mother asked.

"*Yes*, Mother," Rosie said, snatched up her cloak hanging near the door, and scampered out the door after Karina.

That did at least give Forrest a good excuse for following too, which he'd been intending to do anyway.

"Wait for me too," Dastan said, carrying his bowl with him.

Forrest caught up to Karina, while Rosie and Dastan trailed a little way behind. Karina was walking with a single-minded purpose that seemed all out of proportion to how exciting this was likely to be. And which far exceeded her previous interest in magical happenings.

"Is something wrong?" he asked finally.

"Other than magic running amok? No."

But something had seemed wrong before the prince came in, so the magic couldn't really explain it. "Are you sure?" he persisted.

"*Yes.*"

He waited a beat. No further response. "Something must be wrong," he said, aiming for a light tone, "you didn't make a sarcastic remark and tell me to stop bothering you."

It didn't lighten the mood the way he had hoped. She came to an abrupt stop, wheeled to face him and said, "I wish—" Her forehead scrunched and she clamped her mouth closed as though she could physically halt the next words. "Never mind, I don't."

"You didn't even say anything."

"Never mind, I just *don't*." She resumed walking, possibly even faster.

He slowed his own pace, let her get ahead, and watched her black cloak flutter on the path in front of him. Why was he kidding himself into thinking he knew this girl? They hadn't even known each other for three days, and the relationship had started with her pulling a knife on him. Not that there even *was* a relationship, of any kind. It was just that, yesterday...especially in the evening, when they had started talking about magic and Marileigh Blue, he had thought he saw something. He had thought he understood something.

But why should he imagine he had any insights? He had known Dahlia for *years*, and according to Karina, he didn't have the slightest idea where she was concerned. Why imagine he knew anything about this baffling woman who could be friendly one minute and snapping the next and then the minute after that...still be snapping, but be friendly at the same time.

Right now, things were just silent—aside from Dastan and Rosie's chatter behind them. Apparently they were getting along wonderfully.

Up ahead, Karina passed the last fold of hill hiding the garden. A faint, "Oh..." drifted back to Forrest, who hurried the final few steps to see for himself.

He stopped short next to Karina, standing by the garden gate. It was one of the few pieces of fence still standing.

The garden had overflowed its neat rows and beds and knocked down the fence wherever it stood in the way. Tomatoes the size of cabbages had dragged their vines right over into the cabbages, which had swelled to the size of pumpkins. A pumpkin the size of a carriage loomed in one corner. Bean stalks stretched twenty feet up into the air, heavily hung with pods. Zucchinis had grown to the size of swords, and he was a little afraid to pull up a carrot, based on the size of their feathery tops.

"Most of this shouldn't even be in season," he said at last.

"Is that really what seems most important?" Karina demanded, whirling to glare at him.

"I was also thinking I shouldn't have bothered with the fence yesterday."

"How can you be so *calm*?"

He shrugged. Giant vegetables felt much less unsettling than, say, Karina's wild swings in friendliness. Maybe he was getting inured to strange magic, but wildly growing vegetables didn't feel as far outside the realm of normal as golden eggs. This was just a more dramatic version of the way the plants tended to grow by leaps and bounds anyway. "It's not like bad things are happening. Strange things, but a good harvest isn't a bad thing. Master Aurum is probably right about a Good Fairy being behind it all. And anyway, he'll probably have an idea when he gets here about what we should do."

"Oh yes, I'm sure your good friend will just solve everything!"

She stalked off to go prod at the enormous pumpkin, while Forrest tried to decide if this was the friendly kind of argument or not. He was leaning towards not, but wasn't sure he should trust his instincts anymore.

Dastan and Rosie caught up then, and the prince said, "See, I told you. A *really* good harvest."

"Isn't it exciting?" Rosie said, tugging on Forrest's sleeve. "You could make a *house* out of that pumpkin!"

"Mm-hmm," he said, watching as Karina nudged the pumpkin with one foot. Why was this bothering her so much more today than it had yesterday? Yes, she'd raised some warnings about the dangers of magic, but today she seemed much more emotional about it.

"Oh wait," Rosie said with a frown, "do you think Mother will make us eat all of this? She *already* makes us eat too many vegetables."

"Maybe you can convince her magical vegetables would be dangerous," Dastan suggested, leaning against the gate and digging into his bowl of porridge. "Might turn you into a rabbit. Shouldn't take the chance."

This was silly enough to catch even Forrest's attention. "Why would enchanted vegetables turn anyone into a rabbit?"

The prince grinned. "Why not?"

It was probably as likely as anything else that had happened.

Chapter Twelve

All Karina had done was regret that more of the vegetables weren't in season. She hadn't even said it out loud, she'd just *thought* it, and an entire garden had gone mad. She sat outside the range of the most trailing plant and stared at the evidence, while Rosie and the prince went poking about through it all.

She wrapped her arms around her knees and tried to breathe evenly. Magic was *dangerous*, magic was something to be *avoided*, a crutch and a snare for the foolish who wouldn't do things the hard way and always paid the price in the end. Now she was somehow causing spells to flare up all around her and she didn't know how to stop it.

She had come so close already this morning, to telling Forrest she wished he'd just leave her alone. What disaster could magic spin out of that? Was it enough already that she had thought it, even though she hadn't said it?

How many dozens or hundreds of thoughts did she have every day that she didn't really mean, or that magic could twist up and make come out all wrong? So far, the worst thing that had happened was to turn her boots into glass, but the *possible* catastrophes were…limitless.

If she had cast a spell on Forrest with that half-wish, it hadn't taken effect yet. After standing at the gate for a while, he came and sat down on the grass next to her. Even if he didn't say anything, that could hardly be defined as leaving her alone. Especially since she could see out of the corner of her eye that he was watching her out of the corner of *his* eye, and not hiding it very well.

She felt a very confusing mixture of relief and irritation.

When he cleared his throat, obviously in preparation for saying something, she snapped out, "If you ask me again if something is wrong, I will scream." Just because she didn't want him to be magically compelled to never come near her again, that didn't mean she wanted him to talk to her either.

He tipped his head to one side, considering. "No, you won't. You wouldn't want to scare Rosie."

She opened her mouth to contradict him—but he was right. "I'll scream quietly."

To which he had the nerve to chuckle. But he didn't actually ask her anything, so she just rolled her eyes and they continued in a slightly more companionable silence.

He probably would have asked again what was wrong. He was obviously someone who would keep asking until she actually told him, and then he'd feel obliged to do something about it, except there was nothing he could do. And the thing he *would* do, telling Master Aurum, was exactly what she didn't want to do.

Fortunately or not, depending on how you looked at it, Master Aurum himself came walking up the path before Forrest attempted any more questions.

"I assume this is the most recent development?" he asked, studying the garden with an interested eye.

"So far," Forrest said, getting to his feet and walking over towards Master Aurum. Karina did not get up. "We discovered it this morning. Actually, Dastan did."

Master Aurum looked away from the giant pumpkin to look with equal interest at the boy trying to pull up a carrot. "Prince Dastan?"

Dastan grimaced. "Yeah, but—" The carrot came suddenly loose from the earth and he went tumbling backwards to sit on the dirt. "But it's not a big deal," he concluded, clutching a carrot as long as his arm.

"A pleasure to make your acquaintance," Master Aurum said, with a nod that stopped just short of the formality of a bow. Good. Karina could only hope a prince would distract the old scholar and keep him from paying attention to her.

"So does an overgrown vegetable garden still seem like Good Fairy magic?" Forrest asked.

"Oh, unquestionably," Master Aurum said, tapping his fingers against the gate. "They're very fond of giant pumpkins especially. I couldn't tell you why, but there are numerous examples. Do you have any idea when this particular spell was cast?"

"Not really," Forrest said, and glanced towards Karina. "Some time since yesterday afternoon. It was normal then."

"Of course, sudden plant growth overnight is characteristic of the spell," Master Aurum said, nodding sagely.

Forrest glanced at Karina again, raising an eyebrow this time.

If he thought she was going to come join the conversation, he was wrong. She raised her eyebrows back and stayed where she was, hopefully thoroughly out of anyone's attention. She would have made an excuse to go back to the house, except that she'd have to draw attention to herself to do it.

"Do you have a Fairy Godmother, your highness?" Master Aurum asked.

"No, Father says they're more trouble than they're worth. And you can just call me Dastan."

Master Aurum tapped his chin in what Karina judged as an exaggerated effort to look wise, and began to poke about the garden. He asked some questions about planting and recent activity, and made a lot of lofty pronouncements about the size and variety of the vegetables, and didn't actually say anything useful or even all that insightful. He didn't make any conclusions about how to stop this kind of thing happening again.

And Karina had the uncomfortable feeling that he was watching her, even when he didn't seem to be looking. That was probably just paranoia.

At last he announced he'd seen all he could from the vegetable garden. "I'd best check the barn next, to see if there is anything to be learned there." Without warning, he turned towards Karina. "And what about our lovely visitor? Do you have any insights, Karina?"

She did *not* like him using her name, and that quiet twist of fury made it easier to say, "I don't know anything about magic."

"But about the circumstances of these spells in particular?" he persisted.

"No," she said flatly. "Why would I?"

"Just wondering, my dear. Now let me see, there's been the gilded eggs, the talking horse, and now the overgrown garden. Has there been anything else?"

The question might have been asked to the group at large. But he was still looking at Karina.

She stared back at him, refusing to answer, and the moment stretched long and uncomfortable until finally Forrest said, "That's everything we know of so far. Should we go to the barn?"

"Yes, of course," Master Aurum said, turning away. "Please lead the way. I've been charged to deliver a message to your mother as well, so I'd best stop at the house."

Karina let out a breath and slowly got to her feet. He suspected something. She didn't see how he could know anything, but he definitely suspected something.

She trailed behind the rest of the group as they walked towards the house. If she could have thought of somewhere else to go, she would have. But how did a person disappear in a place with no buildings, no narrow alleys or hidden spaces? Especially with people who would notice and come looking.

When they reached the house, Lynette seemed quite taken with Master Aurum too, but Karina refused to see that as any kind of reassurance. Lynette liked everyone. After all, she didn't find Karina threatening.

Karina slipped out of the kitchen as quickly as possible, ducking into the parlor where at least she was out of Master Aurum's sight. She could still hear all of the conversation in the kitchen anyway. She sat down on the couch by the window, drawing her bare feet up under her, and idly pushed the wheel of the spinning wheel sitting nearby while she listened.

"A boat came in from Ronley just before I left this morning," Master Aurum said, "and this letter arrived for you. Apparently quite urgent, so naturally I volunteered to bring it."

"That was kind of you, thank you," Lynette said, to the rustling of paper.

It wasn't that kind. He was coming here anyway. And she'd just bet he read the letter on the way. Prying into things that were none of his concern.

"Oh no, it's from Mariella," Lynette said, in the first really distressed tone Karina had ever heard her use. "That's Richard's youngest sister—she's expecting a baby and the midwife says it could be any day now. We weren't thinking it would be for another month."

"I do hope everything will be all right," Master Aurum said.

"Are you moving up the plan to go down there?" Forrest asked.

"Yes, we'll have to leave immediately," Lynette said, and Karina felt her stomach suddenly drop.

But that was *silly*, hadn't she been wanting to get away from this whole group of people ever since she got here? If they were leaving for a trip, that was very convenient, wasn't it?

A flurry of orders were being delivered in the kitchen. "Clara, run and find your father. He's in the north pasture today. I know Mariella will want him there, and of course it's always good to have an extra pair of hands for the chores and livestock in this sort of chaos. Elena, go start packing; we'll need plenty of warm clothes for the boat ride this time of year. Forrest, you'll need to manage things while we're gone, it will be at least several days—"

"I know, Mother, we planned all this months ago."

Oh. So not everyone was going. Well. That changed things. Or, rather, changed the present circumstance a lot less.

Unless Forrest took advantage of his mother leaving to throw her out. But somehow that didn't seem as likely as it would have that first morning.

"Can I come too?" Rosie's voice piped up. "I want to see the new baby!"

A slight sigh that sounded like Lynette. "Rosie, dear, we talked about this. You're staying here. You shouldn't miss school and—"

"But Clara and Elena get to go!"

"They are older and they will help take care of the other children."

"And I'll need you to help me here," Forrest said quickly. "Especially since we'll need to watch out for any new magic."

That made Karina flinch, but apparently it pacified Rosie. The little girl went happily out to the barn with Forrest, the prince and Master Aurum, while travel plans continued apace. Karina was quickly rousted out of the parlor and set to chopping more vegetables, to go into the stew Lynette wanted to leave behind.

"Perhaps I ought to go with you all," Karina ventured, as she sliced a knife through the first carrot. It was normal-sized, harvested before everything had gone mad in the vegetable garden. "I could catch a boat from this other island—"

"Oh no, dear, it's even more remote than here," Lynette said distractedly, piling bread and other supplies into a bag.

Such a place existed? She would have said it to Forrest, but she kept her mouth shut around Lynette.

After a few seconds, Lynette paused to look at her with a disturbingly direct gaze and say, "I do hope you'll stay until we get back. I'm sure you could help Forrest and Rosie here."

Karina ducked her head, muttered a non-response, and Lynette whirled off too quickly to notice. Which seemed surprising. But if she actually *did* notice, she didn't say anything.

Less surprisingly, she had all of her family marshaled for traveling in extremely short time, hurrying off to the barn to hitch up Millie and depart before the first party to the barn even returned. Apparently an emergency required even the use of a talking horse.

Everything was quiet then, for a while. Karina went on with her vegetables, and tried to work out a plan. Because surely she ought to have one. Only, the discovery that she was causing random magical havoc didn't change the fundamental situation—that she was still stuck on this rock with nowhere else to go but right here.

It was over an hour—not that she was watching the clock or anything—before Forrest came into the kitchen to tell her that Master Aurum had finished and was going back into town too.

"Did he come to any conclusions?" Karina asked, focusing carefully on the turnip she was peeling. She had almost done the whole thing in one spiral, even though it was harder than an apple. More irregular.

"He wants to look at some books he has to find out more," Forrest said, leaning against the table.

Figured. "So he doesn't have any actual, tangible suggestions about what to do?"

"I'm sure he will," Forrest said with a shrug. "He's still thinking about it. For now, he said we shouldn't worry because Good Fairies cast benevolent spells."

Karina snorted in what she knew was an utterly unrefined way. "He's a *magic expert* and he really thinks Good Fairies can't be dangerous? The only people Good Fairies ever help are royalty. Dastan'll be fine, but no Good Fairy is going to care what happens to you or me."

Forrest's eyebrows rose. "So now you're an expert on magic?"

"I've just heard stories, all right?" she snapped. Not that it mattered, since no sparkly little old woman was causing all of this. Just one girl who had no idea how she was doing anything.

Forrest sighed. "Why don't you just admit you don't like Master Aurum and—"

"Who says I'm *hiding* that?"

"—and admit that it's influencing your opinion of his—"

"He's not being helpful, Forrest! It doesn't matter whether I like him or not. He hasn't given one shred of concrete advice on how to deal with this, and no one but me seems to grasp that this is a *dangerous* situation."

He leaned forward towards her over the table. "So why don't you explain to me why you think it's dangerous today, when you didn't think it was yesterday?"

She looked away. "I did think it was dangerous yesterday. I said so."

"But you were a lot calmer about it. Today you're upset about the magic, and you're back to being irritated with everyone—"

"Not everyone," she snapped, "just you."

He leaned back, stepped a pace away from the table. "Well then. You want to tell me what I did?"

"You didn't do anything, I'm just a nasty, unfriendly person, all right?"

He exhaled. "You know what, I have work to do, I don't have time for..." Whatever else he said trailed away into a mutter as he strode out the door.

Karina stared at the turnip peelings curled on the table. The single strip had snapped somewhere in the midst of that argument. She groaned, and rested her forehead on her palm.

She already regretted the whole thing. He didn't deserve any of this. Maybe she should go after him and...but if she was smart, she wouldn't. Because even if she didn't have magic flaring up around her, he didn't deserve her inflicting herself on him anyway. Whatever this dance was they'd been doing, it was going to wind up like this eventually. Better to just leave it be.

Really it would be better if this provoked him to throw her out after all. That ought to be what she wanted. Because really she ought to be leaving. Even if she couldn't get off the island, it didn't do to stay in one place too long. Or to stay around nice people who didn't deserve the disaster her magical flare-ups could cause.

Later, she'd ask him about where else she could stay. He'd probably be very happy to suggest somewhere else, somewhere away from him. That was a reasonable plan.

Then she very calmly, without thinking too hard about anything at all, finished peeling the rest of the turnips. She finally got a complete strip peeled on the second to last one. She chopped them up and dropped them into the stew pot with the other vegetables.

The only problem with finishing that task was that she had nothing else to occupy her attention once she was done. Maybe a walk. A walk was good, now that her ankle was so much better. And as long as she kept her eyes open, she'd be able to see Forrest from far enough away to avoid accidentally crossing paths. She'd have to talk to him again eventually, but maybe not just yet.

That wasn't an awful plan either. It might have worked out all right. As it happened, she had barely stepped out of the house when Rosie came running up, Dastan tagging behind.

"Karina, I'm going to show Dastan my favorite beach," Rosie announced, and seized her hand. "Come with us!"

"Oh…I, um…"

"Come on," Rosie said, and tugged on her hand. "It'll be fun!"

She *knew* this was a bad idea. If she was going to do the smart (and generous and considerate) thing and cut ties with this family before her magic or just herself caused them a whole lot of trouble, spending the day on the beach with Rosie was *not* the way to do that.

But it was just…so hard to say no when Rosie looked up at her all hopeful.

Karina swallowed and managed a smile. "All right. Where's this beach?"

Chapter Thirteen

The chief problem with sheep was that they were boring. They were utterly useless for providing any significant distraction. Forrest spent most of the day watching the sheep in the north pasture and thinking about Karina.

Probably she really was a nasty and unpleasant person. He should just believe her. That would be sensible. She was nasty and unpleasant and didn't like anyone.

Except he'd seen something in her face, when she looked at the stripe of Marileigh Blue, and talked about people being lost.

All right, so that had been a fluke, that was all. She was nasty and unpleasant and he really shouldn't waste any more time thinking about her.

He lost count of how many times he told himself *that*.

He finally turned back towards the house when the sun started to dip towards the horizon. His path took him on a bluff overlooking the water, and when he glanced down towards the beach he saw Rosie, the prince…and Karina, building a sand castle with Rosie.

It would be easier to believe she was a nasty, unpleasant person if she'd stop being nice to his little sister. But everyone was nice to Rosie; that said something about Rosie, not about Karina.

Right, that was a good, reasonable way to look at it, and now he'd just keep walking back to the house…

He only got two paces before Rosie called, "Forrest! Come see our castle!" And he couldn't very well refuse that.

He walked down the path to the beach, watching the scene below. The blue-green waves stretched out to the horizon, starting to turn pink in the far distance as the sun sank towards them. Nearer by, they really did look like Marileigh Blue. The beach was a white ribbon of sand,

and the company formed a small cluster in the center. Dastan was sitting cross-legged, strumming at his lute. Karina was bending over the sand castle, shoulders tight as she sculpted a tower with more attention than might really be called for. And Rosie was standing next to her, waving.

"Come see, isn't it splendid?" Rosie said when he got close.

It was an impressive specimen of a sand castle, with seven towers and a sprawling network of walls and smaller buildings, all liberally decorated with shells and seaweed.

"Karina never built a sand castle before," Rosie announced, "so I had to teach her."

"Obviously you're a wonderful instructor," Forrest said, because that's what the moment called for.

"It's not something we do...back home," Karina said. She looked up at him through strands of hair that had fallen forward, gray eyes looking blue against her dark hair. Her eyes also looked nervous, and was he deluding himself to think they looked apologetic too?

"You must be from a very boring place," Rosie decided, and cheerfully went off to the other end of the castle to work on another tower.

"We should be getting home before it turns dark," Forrest pointed out.

"In a minute, I want to finish this tower," Rosie said, intent on her work.

Forrest turned to look at Dastan. "And shouldn't you..."

"I have permission today," Dastan said with a grin, "so no search parties. You don't mind if I stay for supper, do you?"

"Why not? I'm sure Mother left more food than we can possibly eat, so make yourself at home." Forrest folded his legs, sat down on the sand and shrugged. "Everyone does." Though everyone wasn't as simple as a wayward prince.

"Your mother doesn't give anyone a lot of choice," Karina said quietly, and in spite of himself he found he was meeting her gaze again. The eyes were definitely apologetic and so was the half-smile. "Even when they're nasty and unfriendly."

"Yeah, well," Forrest said, which said absolutely nothing and yet somehow seemed to convey the right idea. "You know," he remarked, continuing not the conversation but the undercurrents, "I already knew you were nasty and unfriendly anyway."

She made a face and threw a sea shell at him, and somehow the world felt much better.

So much better that when Dastan started playing a melody appropriate for dancing, Forrest got to his feet and said, "Hey Rosie, do you remember those dance lessons?"

"Yes!" she said, abandoned her tower, and let him waltz her around on the sand. The height difference made it a little silly, but it was fun.

And he wasn't going to risk Karina's wrath by asking *her*. At least, not until after he'd done quite a few turns with Rosie...and had seen Karina's toes tapping where she sat. Even then, he just offered a hand, easy to refuse if she wanted to—and found himself absurdly pleased when she took his hand and let him pull her to her feet and into the waltz.

Rosie was equally happy spinning about by herself, twirling and kicking up sand.

Karina was easy to dance with, light on her feet, fingers of one hand wound around his and the other resting on his shoulder. Her waist felt warm beneath his other hand as he led her through the steps. It was a funny thing about dancing. Partners faced each other. Karina seemed to have a way of keeping everyone off to one side or the other most of the time, eyes never meeting except in sideways glances. But now they were looking directly at each other, and he was noticing again that her eyes did have hints of blue in them. They seemed gray, unless you looked closely.

They circled and spun and when the tension of their gazes finally became too much, he blinked and asked, "So do they do this back home?"

Her mouth curved into an elusive, maddening smile. "I think they do this everywhere," she said, and he wasn't entirely sure she meant waltzing.

"I don't like dancing," Dastan remarked. "It's more fun playing the music."

"You might like it more when you're older," Forrest said. It had been true in his life.

"I love to dance!" Rosie said, with a twirl so exuberant that she nearly knocked herself sideways. "I wish I could dance forever."

Karina laughed. "I wish you could too." Forrest was still thinking that he hadn't heard her laugh before when he realized her eyes had gone suddenly wide. "No, I don't," she whispered, gaze unfocused. "No, I *don't.*"

"What's wrong?" he asked in a low tone, not wanting to scare the two children. Was Karina scared? He would have said so, except he had never seen her look afraid before, and it was hard to imagine fear as a feeling she could have. "You don't what?"

Karina's attention flashed back to him. "Nothing," she said, and smiled. But the smile looked false and her hand was clenched too tightly around his.

Her gaze went past his shoulder again, and he turned his head to follow its direction—towards Rosie. Involuntarily his own fingers tightened around Karina's, his shoulders going tense too. But this was overreacting, Rosie was fine, still dancing around. Whatever Karina was alarmed about, it wasn't his little sister. It couldn't be.

"I think we should go," Karina said abruptly, pulling her hand free and stepping a pace away. "We should stop dancing and go back."

"Good, I'm hungry," Dastan said, giving a flourish on the lute and then taking his hand away.

The music kept playing. Everyone stared at the lute, strings continuing to sound with no one touching them.

This might have been the most entertaining, most harmless magic yet. But Forrest was already wound up over Karina's inexplicable alarm, and right now even the cheerful waltzing melody seemed sinister.

Not to Rosie, who just said, "This is fun magic!" Grinning, she danced towards the path up from the beach, feet skipping over the sand, arms flourishing wildly.

Forrest looked to Karina again. She was pale, and wouldn't meet his gaze, her glance following Rosie, his own dragged quickly along the same path. *Nothing* was wrong with Rosie, so why was she looking like that? And why had she got upset before they knew more magic was happening?

Dastan picked up his still-sounding lute and ran after Rosie. Karina quickly followed, but Forrest caught up to her easily as they went up the steep path.

"What is it? What's wrong?" he repeated. "You're worried about Rosie."

He wanted her to deny it. But then he didn't believe her when she said, "It's nothing." Her hands in fists at her sides, the intensity of her focus on Rosie, both said otherwise.

He raked back through his memories of the last few minutes, hunting for a clue. What had he missed? What had reared up to threaten his sister while he was distracted by Karina's eyes? Her eyes that had gone wide just after... "You got upset when Rosie said she wished she could dance all the time..."

"Forever," Karina whispered. "She wished she could dance *forever.*"

A cold shiver of horror crawled up his spine. He looked at his sister again, just as she did another twirl. "No. That can't mean—yes, strange magic has been happening, but—"

"I don't *know*." She pulled her cloak tighter. "It's just that…there's a story I've heard. About magical dancing."

Forrest swallowed. "Me too." Maybe it was the same story. Maybe it wasn't. But from the way Karina was reacting, he'd bet the point of it was the same. The story he was thinking of was about a girl cursed to dance and keep on dancing. Until she danced to her death.

That was not going to happen. Maybe Rosie was still just dancing for fun, with no magic affecting her at all. And if it was magic—he would stop it. He would find a way to stop it. She was his sister and he was supposed to take care of her and he would find a way to stop it.

They were at the top of the cliff by now, Forrest's heart pounding harder than it usually did when he climbed this slope. The path through the grass stretched out towards home, pale in the lengthening shadows. He watched Rosie dip and leap and swing her arms as she went along, her shadow dancing a crazy, blurred echo of her movements.

Forrest lengthened his stride, caught up to Rosie and put a hand on her shoulder. "Maybe that's enough dancing for now," he said, words coming fast but mostly steady.

She slipped away beneath his hand, bounded off along the path. "I *like* dancing!"

He opened his mouth to call her again, to insist, to make her stop—but a part of him didn't want to know. Not yet.

He had barely noticed Karina falling into step beside him again, but she was there. "Maybe we should let her keep dancing until we get home," he said softly, watching Rosie dip and turn. "It would be worse if she panics out here. When we get back to the house, we'll try to get her to stop, and then…we'll see."

"And if she can't?" Karina said, voice tight.

"Then we'll think of something." He would have to think of something.

The walk back to the house had never seemed so long. Surely Rosie was going to stop dancing on her own, any moment, maybe right this second...but she just kept on, and he couldn't bring himself to ask her again. Judging from her smile, she didn't think anything was wrong. Not yet.

Finally they reached the yard by the house. Not that it helped much, since the house was empty. He had a family that never gave him any space and now when he needed them—no one.

Forrest took a deep breath. Time to face this, if there was anything to face. "That really is enough dancing for now, honey. It's time for supper." He reached out to catch Rosie's hands, tried not to grasp them too tightly.

She stuck out her lower lip as her small fingers curled around his. "Oh, all right."

He was watching her face, not her feet. So he saw when the mock pout gave way to a puzzled frown. Rosie looked down. "That's funny...my feet don't want to..." A waver of alarm entered her voice. "I can't stop. Forrest, why can't I stop?"

He squeezed Rosie's hands, didn't look at Karina. "It must be more of that silly magic," he said, trying to make his voice light, unconcerned. He was her big brother. She could depend on him. "But it's all right, we'll just figure out how to stop it."

"We haven't stopped any other magic yet!" Rosie protested, still staring down at her tapping, kicking feet.

"Well, we haven't really tried yet," Forrest said with a heartiness he didn't feel. He felt sick, terrified, scrambling for something they could try now.

Suddenly her hands wrenched against his. Surprised, he let them slip from his hold, and she darted away in a leap and a twirl. "I can't *stop*!" she squeaked. "What are you going to *do*?"

"Maybe it's the music!" Dastan suggested, dodging out of Rosie's way as she spun towards him. "It's still playing. Maybe that's why you're still dancing."

"Good, that's a good idea!" Forrest said quickly, pressing his palms together. It made a certain amount of sense, it gave them a place to start. "So we just have to stop the magic lute."

"That's easy," Dastan said, lifting the lute by its neck. "I just need a knife. Can I get one inside—oh, thanks." He took the knife Karina proffered. One quick stroke severed the strings, and the magic music fell silent.

Nothing changed for Rosie, her feet still resolutely dancing on, circling her past the others where they stood. "I still can't stop!" she wailed.

"The wish," Karina said, knuckles white where she gripped the edges of her cloak. "If it was the wish…"

If the wish really had cast the spell, and if Rosie had wished to dance forever…

"Wish to stop dancing," Forrest ordered, moving to intercept Rosie and catch her hands again, trying to hold her in one place. Her feet went on stepping, her hands twitching inside Forrest's grasp, but she stayed in front of him. "You wished you could keep dancing, remember? So now wish to stop."

"I wish to stop dancing, I wish to stop dancing," Rosie chanted, staring up at Forrest. Behind him, he heard Karina murmur too, "I wish Rosie would stop dancing…"

Because she had wished too, hadn't she? Rosie had said it, but Karina had laughed and echoed it—and which wish had cast the spell? He wanted to glance back at Karina, but he couldn't take his gaze off of Rosie's face.

Rosie said the wish a dozen times, eyes widening and voice growing higher and louder with each repetition, before she gave up.

"It's not working, nothing's working!" she said with a rising level of panic. "What if I can't *ever* stop?"

"We'll think of something," Forrest said with all the firmness he could muster, struggling to ignore his own panic roiling in the pit of his stomach. "We could go into town and get Master Aurum—"

"But town's *miles* away!" Rosie protested. Her hands wrenched against Forrest's, her body trying to twist away into another spin or leap.

"And what's Master Aurum going to do anyway?" Karina snapped. "He's a scholar, not a magician."

"Do you have a better idea?" Forrest demanded, glaring at her.

"I don't know," she said, glaring back, "why don't you *knit* something?"

He knew she meant it as an insult, and somewhere behind that he knew she only flung it because she was scared, just the way he had demanded an answer because he was scared too—but in front of all that, a blinding idea hit him. "Yes," he said slowly, "yes, that's it."

Karina blinked, taken aback, off-balance because he wasn't pushing back. "You're going to knit something?"

"No, better than that." He tugged on Rosie's hands, tried to meet her eyes as she looked down in terror at her feet. "Rosie, honey, I'm going to go inside and get something to help you." That brought her gaze up, eyes like saucers and mouth tight. "Stay right here and don't be scared."

"But, Forrest…" she whispered.

"Stay with Dastan and Karina, I will be *right back*." Then he disengaged his hands, fast, before he could feel any guiltier about it. She immediately spun off to the right but he turned around and ran into the house.

Where was it? Where would his mother have put it? He cut through the parlor. The small room off the parlor, that's where things were stored. He pushed the door open, went to the boxes in one corner.

He dug through old clothes and folded blankets. Where was it, where was... After what felt like forever, he uncovered a small blanket, knit with blue and green yarn. He seized it in one hand, dragged it out and turned to go.

Two steps and he tripped over a strangely solid shadow, one that clunked when it hit the floor. He stumbled, caught himself with one palm against the ground, looked automatically to see what he had tripped over.

A glass boot. Knee-high, with a knife in a sheath at the top.

One of Karina's boots. Turned into glass.

But that meant...

He couldn't think about what that meant right now. He picked up the boot in one hand and, blanket in the other, ran back outside.

Nothing had changed out there. Rosie was still dancing, Dastan holding her hand, their joined hands jerking wildly as the magic tried to pull Rosie into another turn. Karina looked on, her arms wrapped around herself and face set.

Forrest thrust the boot at Karina, who barely managed to react quickly enough to take it, and then he strode over to his sister. He shook the blanket out of its folds as he went, and when he reached her he wrapped the blanket and his arms around her.

"It's going to be *all right*," he murmured into her hair, closed his eyes and *wished*.

He could smell the salt air on Rosie's hair, and some soft flowery scent on the blanket that brought their mother sharply to mind and made his throat hurt. It would be so much better, so much easier if she was here. He could feel the tension in Rosie, her shoulders jerking against his arms as he held her tight.

And then she went still. A few, very long seconds ticked by and Rosie whispered, "My feet stopped. My feet *stopped dancing*."

Forrest let out a slow exhale, swallowing against the even sharper tightness of relief, and for a moment silence lay all around.

"What did you *do*?" Dastan asked, sounding fascinated and impressed.

Forrest stepped back from Rosie, keeping his hands—and the blanket—on her shoulders. "I knit something," he said, without looking towards Karina. "Years ago, when Mother was expecting Rosie. Baby blankets are always all about protection, health, family connections. You know. This one was Rosie's, so that makes it even more powerful."

"Oh yeah, I remember this," Rosie said, looking down at the wrap around her shoulders. "But...if the blanket is stopping the dancing spell, what happens when I take it off?"

The new silence was heavy and uncomfortable, and Forrest wracked his brain for another miracle. Could he knit anklets? Socks? Still just a temporary solution though, and unlikely to be as strong as the blanket, so—

"Maybe the spell's on your shoes," Dastan suggested, pointing as though there could be some confusion. "Lots of spells involve shoes."

"That's true," Karina said quickly. Forrest didn't look towards her. "Usually it's enchanted shoes that make people dance."

And usually part of the enchantment was that the shoes wouldn't come off. But if the blanket was halting the spell even temporarily, at least for long enough to pull a pair of shoes off... "We can try it," Forrest said, and was very firm in his own mind that he was replying to Dastan, not Karina.

Rosie sat down on the doorstep, still clutching the blanket around her shoulders, and Forrest successfully tugged first one and then the other shoe off. But that might only prove that the shoes weren't enchanted at all.

Biting her lower lip, Rosie stood up again, unwrapped the blanket from around her shoulders, and handed it to Forrest.

Her feet remained still.

Forrest felt a tension in his body that he'd stopped noticing uncoil. It really was going to be all right.

He might have done well to stay braced for just a minute longer, as Rosie nearly knocked him over then with a hug. "Thank you!" she said into his chest.

"Hey, what's a brother for, right?" he said, because *she* didn't need to know how relieved he actually was. Sooner or later she'd get old enough to find out he wasn't really very amazing, but it didn't need to be today.

She darted off to hug Dastan, who may have blushed although it was hard to tell in the twilight. And then she hugged Karina too, who didn't blush but looked even more uncomfortable. She hugged Rosie back one-armed—the other hiding the glass boot behind her back.

Now that the crisis was over, other thoughts came tiptoeing up again.

Karina hadn't worn her boots to breakfast, and she'd been defensive about it. And unsurprised now. She had known this morning that her boots had turned into glass, but she hadn't told anyone. She also had realized before anyone else did that Rosie might be in trouble with that thoughtless wish.

Karina knew more than anyone else about what was going on, she had chosen not to share that, and a spell gone wrong could have seriously harmed Rosie. Or worse.

He felt an unfamiliar coldness settle over him. This wasn't something he could just shrug off and move on from.

Rosie let go of Karina and turned to head into the house. Dastan followed her. Karina didn't move, and neither did Forrest.

Rosie looked back from the threshold. "Aren't you coming?"

"In a minute. You go ahead and start serving the stew," Forrest said, and waited for the door to close.

The moment the door clicked shut, Karina began, "I swear, I never meant for anything like this—"

"How is the magic happening?" Forrest asked, that new coldness invading his voice too. It didn't matter what she *meant*, all that counted was stopping anything from happening again. Preventing anything from harming his family.

She looked away. "I don't know."

"Why don't you try looking me in the eyes and saying that?"

She laughed, a short and not at all funny laugh. "Trust me, I could look you in the eyes and lie."

She really was nasty and unfriendly. Right now, that seemed all too easy to accept. "What, is that supposed to be *reassuring*?"

"No, I—I *don't* know how it's happening." She pressed one hand to her forehead. "I think…that I'm doing it somehow, but I don't know how, and I don't know why, and I don't know how to stop it!"

It wasn't that he didn't hear the scared tremble in her voice on those last few words. It was just that he couldn't really believe it, and he wasn't sure he could make himself care even if he did. "And how do I know that isn't a lie? How do I know this wasn't all deliberate?"

"Why would I be doing this? Why would I *want* to make your horse talk? In rhymes, no less?"

"I don't know, maybe it seemed funny," he snapped, and nodded his head towards the house, towards the direction Rosie had gone. "Maybe *that* seemed funny."

"No, I would never—"

"I don't know that! I don't know anything about you. Not even what country you're from."

It was a challenge, and they both knew it. She stared back at him, blue eyes wide and shoulders hunched. "I…can't. You don't understand."

"No. I don't understand," he said quietly, and turned away. "I can't trust you if you won't trust me."

He reached for the door handle, but before his fingers touched it, Karina said, "Don't make me tell everyone."

That was, possibly, a step forward from a flat refusal. He hesitated, looked back over his shoulder.

"I can't explain the magic," she said, words all coming in a rush, "because I really don't understand it, but—I'll tell you where I'm from, and who I am, and how I got here, and maybe there'll be an answer in there somewhere that I just can't see and anyway—well, then you can decide whether to trust me or hate me and—and then what to do after that. But don't make me try to tell it in front of everyone."

It was stupid even to be listening to this. She had *told* him that she was nasty, unfriendly and a liar, and he ought to just haul her into the house right now and…and he had no idea how he could make her give any answers anyway. So he ought to just tell her to leave, and if she really was responsible for the magic it would presumably go with her, and everyone else would be safe.

Because it was really no business of his what happened to this frustrating, maddening, mysterious, lost, scared girl. And therefore it shouldn't matter to him. At all.

He gritted his teeth. "I'll make an excuse to Rosie and Dastan about why you're not at supper. And later I'll be in the parlor. Alone."

He reached down to pick up Rosie's discarded shoes, to put out of the way somewhere in the house until he could figure out what to do with them. Then he pushed open the door and went inside. Karina didn't say anything else.

Probably she'd just run away. Probably that's all this was, an excuse to give her a chance to run. And probably that would be best anyway.

Chapter Fourteen

Karina was fairly sure that running would be the smart thing to do. Part of her wished desperately that she could just run and run and never look back. Except there was nowhere to run. She was on an island, with no ships leaving.

Since she had nowhere to go, she slipped back into the barn, tiptoed past the chickens, and climbed up into the loft. She sprawled on her back on the hay, stared up at the roof beams in the moonlight, and waited for the lights to go out in the house. And tried to figure out what she was going to tell Forrest, and why she had ever offered to tell him anything to begin with.

She owed him, where Rosie was concerned. She didn't want a sweet little girl on her conscience.

An image floated through her mind, of Forrest wrapping the blanket around Rosie and holding her protectively.

Karina groaned and dragged an arm over her eyes. She was being *weak*. Part of her, the part of her that didn't want to run, this other part *wanted* to tell Forrest her story. So that maybe, just maybe, he'd decide to trust her, and help her, and she wouldn't have to be scared and lost in a magical mess far too big for her—or at least, she wouldn't have to be in it alone.

And how stupid was that? She was going to make the arbiter of her fate the one person who had been the *most* suspicious, the least willing to simply welcome her in and believe that she was friendly and nice. They only believed that because all of them were that way.

Lynette would probably just cluck and say it couldn't really be that bad and give her something to eat. Rosie...she couldn't tell her story to Rosie, but supposing she told a carefully selective version—no, Rosie would just ignore any unpleasant parts and go right on liking her.

But if Forrest decided to trust her—then it would mean something.

And if he decided not to, then the matter would be settled and done. And she wouldn't have to deal at all with that other part of her, the part that said, yes, a big brother to help solve problems would be a nice thing to have—but a *brother* wasn't what she wanted Forrest to be.

Finally the house went dark, apart from a faint glow at a single window, and Karina left the barn to go reluctantly back inside. The front door, naturally, was unlocked. Maybe Forrest had left it deliberately open, but probably they never locked it. That would about figure.

She slipped into the parlor, automatically catching the door handle and easing it closed silently behind her. The room was dim, lit only by the fire. He was sitting in front of it, metal needles catching an occasional glint of light as they moved. Could he even see what he was doing? Probably didn't matter.

She regretted closing the door silently. Now she had to let him know she was here. She hesitated, eased the door open an inch, and swung it shut again with a thud this time.

The room held just enough light for her to see him look up. "I expected you to disappear." Then he looked down at the probably-invisible knitting again.

"I thought about it." She padded closer and sat down, not in the opposite chair, but on the floor leaning against it. That put the chair between her and the fire, let her hide in even deeper shadows within this already dark room.

"So." She twisted her fingers together in her lap, wishing she had a knife or a lock or anything to occupy her hands, to channel all the nervous tension she was feeling. She did have a knife, but taking it out now would just send the wrong message. "I guess I owe you my story now."

The faint click of needles paused, then resumed again. "Some answers would be appreciated."

The basket of yarn scraps sat on the floor next to her chair. She untangled her hands and reached inside the basket, pulling out a few stray bits. She wrapped one around her finger. "I don't know if I have any answers. All I have is the story."

No pause in the clicking this time. "All right." His voice sounded cautious, wary.

What did he imagine she was going to say? He knew it wouldn't be good. She had told him that much, and whatever else she said now was going to define how he felt about her. Not that she really knew how he felt now.

She flexed her fingers, still tight with nerves, then gathered three strands of yarn together and tied a knot at one end of the cluster.

He must have liked her some. When they were dancing on the beach. When they talked about Marileigh Blue. Or maybe—a horrible thought, but what if she had cast a spell on him during that conversation? She had been thinking about connections, about people belonging to each other, and if that was enough for the magic…

No, that couldn't be right. Every signal he was giving now did *not* suggest any magical compulsion to care about her. Except for his willingness to listen. But that didn't prove anything, didn't mean anything.

And on the off-chance that *was* why he was listening…she couldn't help taking advantage of it anyway. Because even though most of her didn't want to tell this story, she didn't want to be alone even more, and she knew that telling the truth, telling who she was and how she'd got here, was her absolute last chance.

Though just at the moment, she wasn't getting the story told. "I'm not sure…where to start."

"By casting on."

"What?" She really didn't need any more confusion right now. With a nervous twitch she crossed two pieces of the knotted yarn over each other.

A sigh. "Sorry, knitting term. Begin at the beginning."

The beginning. But that was part of the trouble, where did anything in life start?

She chose as far back as was even faintly reasonable, maybe because it was one inch easier than starting more recently. "I was born in Ilsonine, in Giramm, and I never knew who my father was." That was already enough information to upset some people. Not the crowds she ran with back home—it was too common a fact there—but some people. She paused a breath, waiting, crossed the third piece of yarn to start a braid.

No gasp of horror from Forrest, or any change in the rhythm of the knitting. She went on. "My mother died when I was nine. By then I was already a skilled pickpocket, giving me some standing with the kids I landed with. It wasn't great, but it could have been worse. We did low-level stuff, picking pockets, stealing food. It beat starving."

She had the rhythm of the braiding down now, making it easier to get into the rhythm of the story too. Think about the braiding, not the story, and as far as she had to think about the story, think about it as something that had happened a long, long time ago, to someone else.

"I got older, I got better with a knife and a lock pick, and I got in with a better class of criminal. And about a week ago, on an ordinary day when I was just sitting in the Black Lion thinking about getting a new lock open, we had a chance at a job that...went unexpected directions."

When she got to the end of the shortest piece of yarn, she reached for another one, tied it on, went on braiding. And went on talking, about that morning at The Black Lion. Less than a week ago, but it felt like a lifetime.

Book Two

~ ♦ ~

Chapter Fifteen

The Black Lion was quiet in the late morning, and Rin liked it that way. She liked it when it was loud and crowded and friendly too, but right now she was trying to puzzle out the secrets of an especially intricate lock, and preferred the quiet.

There was no lock installed in The Black Lion that she wasn't confident she could pick, and none she would have risked trying. The lock she was working on was attached to a small metal chest, sitting on the thick plank table in front of her, and so far it was standing firm.

With a frown, she set down one small prod and picked up another, narrower one from her leather envelope of tools. If she could tease it in between the tumblers…

Footsteps on the bare wooden stairs announced a new arrival. She tracked the sound without turning her head, recognizing the heavy steps as belonging to Old John and therefore not a threat.

The narrower prod proved no more effective than the previous one, and she threw it down in disgust. She could try the hook, but maybe one of the fake keys would be a better approach.

Old John sank onto the opposite bench, propped his chin on one hand, and stared blearily at her. "Rin, love, how can you be doing something that actually involves thinking this early in the morning?"

"Because unlike you, old man, I didn't drink a barrel of ale last night." She studied her array of false keys, ran her fingertips along the neat line. She knew them better by touch than by sight, because who ever robbed a place in bright light? Even now, in the back corner of

The Black Lion, she was relying mostly on candlelight. Only a smudge of sunshine made it through the small, begrimed windows at the front of the building.

Old John winced. "Don't remind me of my sins of imprudence. Can't we blame it on your youthful vigor?"

"If you'd rather," she said absently, selecting her smallest bit key.

Old John was the oldest and roundest of the Black Lions, the gang Rin had been running with for the last six months. Cleaned up and smiling, Old John looked positively cherubic with his bald head and fringe of white curls, provided you didn't realize how many knives he had hidden on his person. He claimed to have been a great actor in his youth, and was still brilliant for the cons. Haughty nobleman or hapless victim, given the right clothes he could play anything. Even now, in his fitted tan jacket and ruffled shirt, he looked more respectable than most people who frequented The Black Lion.

If he was awake, the rest of the boys couldn't be far behind. The way Old John stomped about, he'd probably awoken the entire upper floor just getting down here.

Old John bellowed across the common room, "Magdala, sweetheart, bring me bread and a drink, I'm perishing of thirst!"

And that surely woke up anyone who had managed to sleep through the stomping.

Magdala poked her head in from the kitchen. "All right, all right, I'll be there in a minute. Though the way you took on last night, you ought to still be floating."

"Everyone has it in for an old man." His face morphed into his most mournful, victimized expression. "Always a harsh word from everyone."

"The truth is cold," Rin said, trying to turn the bit key just a hair farther.

More footsteps on the stairs. The drumbeat of fingers on the railing meant it was Weldon and...yes, a few seconds behind him, taking the steps two at a time, had to be his brother Tyrone. Weldon aimed straight for the kitchens, while Tyrone loped over to Rin's table, giving her braid a tweak as he passed.

"How's our pretty little lioness this morning?" he asked, swinging a leg over the bench beside Old John, and sitting down with his arms folded on the table.

It took only an eyeblink for the knife in Rin's arm sheath to be in her hand, and then embedded point first in the table a quarter inch from Tyrone's black sleeve. "Still clawed, thank you," she said sweetly.

"All right, all right, don't get your fur rumpled," Tyrone protested, lifting his hands defensively.

"Don't tug my hair," she countered, pulling her braid over one shoulder and slipping the knife back into its place.

"So what's in the box?" Tyrone asked, rapping the top with his knuckles.

"Nothing, I'm just practicing on the lock. Or I *was*, until you lot woke up."

"Aw, you know you'd be bored without us," Tyrone said with a grin.

From the kitchen, there came a clatter of pots and a plaintive voice. "But Magdala, my heart, my love!"

"Sweet talk will not get you breakfast faster, Weldon!" the barmaid snapped back.

"Will it be cheaper?"

"I ordered first!" Old John shouted towards the kitchen. "I demand food first. I was here before him!"

"You see?" Tyrone said, raising his hands, palms up. "What would you do without us?"

"Get my lock open," Rin said, but she was smiling too.

Tyrone and Weldon were nearly identical in good looks and love of fun, except that Tyrone was a half-inch taller and never let his brother or anyone else forget it. They were the closest of friends when they weren't the bitterest of enemies. An explosive fight usually occurred about once a week, most consistently about women but sometimes about other matters, generally things too obscure and complicated and largely fabricated for anyone else to make much sense out of. Someday one was going to kill the other in a duel, although since both were deadly with knives, Rin would be hard-pressed to predict the winner.

Magdala eventually returned from the kitchen with bread and cheese and ale, and Rin managed to tickle the lock open before the boys had finished eating. It required a combination of a tension wrench, an s-rake, and a very careful touch.

The boys were finishing up the last crumbles of cheese, and Rin was trying to decide if it would be worth it to dismantle the lock, before she heard another set of footsteps on the stairs. The truth was, she had been half-listening for more steps ever since Tyrone and Weldon came down, leaving just two more members of the Black Lions unaccounted for. These footsteps were firm, decisive, each foot planted in the center of each step on the stair, and they were not the ones she'd been hoping for—just a little. These footsteps belonged to the captain of the Lions. He must have a name, but no one knew what it was.

Everyone straightened up and tried to look more serious and generally competent when he came over to the table.

"At ease," he said lightly, sitting down at one end. He raised one hand, and didn't look to see Magdala's curtsy in response, before she hurried back into the kitchen.

He studied the rest of the table thoughtfully. "You boys awake enough yet to talk sensibly?"

"I'm wide awake," Old John insisted, laying one hand on his chest and flourishing dramatically with the other. "Wide awake and as capable as any man!"

"Hmm." The captain nodded slowly. "If you're swearing you're capable, means you actually will be in another twenty minutes."

"Ah, well…" Old John shrugged, and drained the last of his ale.

The captain glanced around the empty room. "Dimitri not back yet?"

"I didn't know he was out," Rin said, fingers tightening on the lockpick in her hand. So much for the last set of footsteps she'd been expecting.

"He thinks he's found a lead on a job," the captain said. "Mentioned last night he was going to go out early to learn more."

"Must've been early," Tyrone commented, "if our morning lark wasn't here yet. What've you been up for, Rin, two hours?"

"Three." Which had still meant waking up a good hour past sunrise, which seemed like enough of the morning to waste.

Weldon groaned. "When do you *sleep*, Rin? No one should be awake that early."

She raised an eyebrow. "Do I criticize your sleeping habits?"

The speed with which he could morph his expression into a grin was astounding. "Want to find out more about them?"

Rin sighed, and lifted her hand, though she kept her knife in its sheath. "I already pulled a knife on your brother this morning; is it so important to you to stay even?"

She had no intention of getting romantically entangled with anyone right now, and especially not a pair of someones who would start boasting about their conquests as soon as they were into their drinks. It was hard enough already getting the men to treat her as an associate and not as a bit of fluff to be chased, caught and forgotten.

Better to stay aloof, and reinforce the point at knife-edge if needed.

More knife work and possible bloodshed was staved off for the moment by the creaking of the tavern's door, accompanied by no footsteps at all.

And that was how you could recognize Dimitri's footsteps—he didn't make any. He usually didn't bother avoiding the squeaky third step on the stairs, but otherwise he was always a silent arrival.

Rin had known Dimitri for years. They had run together in the same gang as kids, and even after he had moved on and up and ties loosened, they never broke entirely. He'd joined the Lions before she did, and it was no secret he'd recommended her to the captain. Though she wouldn't have stayed long if she hadn't been able to prove her own merit too.

Dimitri joined them at the table, sitting down on the end of Rin's bench and pushing shaggy black hair out of his eyes. "Morning. Or is it later than I thought, if you lot are awake already?"

There were a series of groans, a few jests thrown back and forth, and then the captain brought them to business.

"So what's the word on this rumor of a job you caught?" the captain asked Dimitri.

"So far it's looking like truth," Dimitri said, leaning back against the wall behind them, his tan jacket standing out against the dark wood. Rin always took the bench along the wall. Safer that way. Never sit where someone could come up behind you, unless you deeply trust the person sitting across from you. Dimitri had taught her that trick.

"There *is* a job," Dimitri continued, "the question is whether it's one we want—and if we can get it."

Rin's palms itched. There hadn't been a truly exciting opportunity in over a month. Not that they'd been without work entirely, but she wanted something that would let her properly show her skills. She was still the youngest, newest member of the Black Lions, and she still had plenty to prove.

"I caught a whisper on a possible something from Red Charlie last night," Dimitri began—and then there was a frustrating pause in the story as Magdala arrived with the captain's breakfast and ale.

It wasn't as if Magdala didn't *know* they were thieves. She'd been at The Black Lion tavern for years, and the Black Lion gang had made it their base since long before most of their current members had joined. But it never paid to let any more people than necessary find out details about a job. Loose talk led to a tight noose.

Once Magdala was away to the kitchens again, Dimitri snagged a roll off the tray and resumed. "So Red Charlie thought there was something big going down—a noble who wanted to pay very well for a recovery operation."

Rin smiled as she polished her lock picks. A recovery operation *might* mean stealing back something wrongfully taken—but most often meant stealing something someone else felt ought to be theirs, whether it had ever been theirs or no.

"I went down to see Johnny Vane this morning," Dimitri said, tearing off a chunk of bread. "Figured he'd know if anything important was on. He has it from sources who remain unnamed that there's a noblewoman looking to make a hire, and willing to pay an amount that will have every thief in the city jumping for the chance. But she's not willing to hire just anyone."

"I wouldn't say we're just anyone," the captain said with a frown.

"Of course not," Dimitri agreed, raising his hands in innocence, one of them still holding half the roll. "But the lady is skeptical, and perhaps also not the sort to be acquainted with the reputations of people like us."

"So, you tell Johnny to put in a good word for us?" Tyrone asked.

"It's not that simple. She's got her own ideas. She wants a test." Dimitri leaned in closer, dropping his voice. "The job involves robbing one of those big houses up on Sunrise Hill. The lady wants to talk business with anyone who can get in, steal a glass with the family crest to identify it, and get out again. Produce the glass, then she'll discuss the real score."

Sounded complicated, and Rin never liked complications. But she was intrigued too. If the test run was this elaborate, what would the actual job involve? Something to show off her skills, if she had to bet.

The captain shook his head slightly. "Not sure I like it. It's taking a risk getting into a place like that with no promise of payment for the first entry."

An initial objection didn't mean he was ruling the idea out, just that he wanted them to show they could think by raising pros and cons. Rin settled back on her bench, watching to see which way this was going to tip.

"It's not a large risk," Old John said, "if I play my Lost Nobility from the Next Country role. I'll wander into the wrong house for a cup of tea, palm a glass and be gone again."

"Could work," the captain acknowledged. "Also could make a second trip harder if the household can recognize us."

"With the right disguise, they'll never know me again," Old John proclaimed, with another of his characteristic flourishes. This one narrowly avoided splashing ale on Tyrone. Keeping her back to the wall wasn't the only reason Rin preferred not to sit next to Old John.

"Your lost nobleman can't wander about alone," the captain said with a wry grin, "but you won't need all of us either. We might still keep a few faces unseen, to avoid relying too much on the strength of your disguises."

"There's an advantage to taking an initial trip too," Dimitri pointed out. "If we can get in once, we may be able to get in the same way a second time. And the first trip gives us the chance to study the landscape to prepare for the second."

"Possible, possible," the captain said with a nod.

"Does Johnny know if anyone else has tried this yet?" Rin asked. It paid to consider all your potential foes, not just the obvious ones. "If anyone's managed an entry already, the job may not stay open. And if anyone's been caught, the household will be on the alert."

"Smart point, lass," the captain agreed. "No, I'm not sure I like this whole idea."

"Well, maybe not then," Dimitri said with a shrug. "Though Johnny did say the pay was likely to be upwards of a thousand gold pieces..."

It was all Rin could do not to drop the key she was holding. A *hundred* gold pieces was considered an excellent opportunity. A *thousand*... Even split six ways, that was more money than she'd ever seen. Not more than she'd ever dreamed of, but more than she'd ever expected to have.

The table went very quiet.

"On the other hand," the captain said, "I might yet be talked into the idea."

"And Johnny's reasonably sure no one has made an attempt yet," Dimitri continued. "The word just got out late yesterday, and no one he knows has tried. Yet."

"Right, let's take a gamble," the captain said, slapping the tabletop with one palm. "And if we're doing this, we do it now. As Rin says, this is no time to be second. I think we'll send in...John as the noble, Rin can play his daughter, and Dimitri as a guard. Just one guard ought to keep the house relaxed, and the rest of us will be stationed outside in case of trouble."

Rin held back a sigh. Playing a nobleman's daughter meant an enormous dress that would get in her way, and she'd have to spend a lot of time before the job messing about with hair and face paint. She wished she could still pretend to be a boy, but her body hadn't cooperated on that point in the last couple years. It was still barely a possibility in the dark, but for a daytime run there was no point even suggesting it.

"John, start working out costumes," the captain directed. "Rin, Dimitri, you take a first look at this house, see what you can learn from the outside. Tyrone, Weldon and I will hit the streets, check some contacts, see what kind of rumors are floating about this opportunity and who else might be jumping for it. We meet back here in two hours and if everything still looks good, we move on it. Understood?"

Nods and affirmatives went all around, and soon everyone was scattering to their business. Rin and Dimitri were the last two at the table.

He finished the end of his drink and set the cup aside, reaching out to pick up the chest in front of Rin. "Trying a new lock?"

"Yeah, picked it up this morning at the tinker's," Rin said, folding up her tools and tucking the leather envelope into her belt. "I got it open just before you came in, and was thinking I might take it apart next. Want a try at it first?"

"Nah, that's all right," he said, dropping it back on the table. "You take it apart, learn a new trick and then teach it to me. Provided it isn't one I already know."

She leaned back and tucked her hands behind her head. "I've known more tricks than you for *years*." True, he had taught her lock-picking to begin with—but she'd definitely been as good as he was for a long time. Maybe even better.

He sighed theatrically. "And I very kindly let you have your delusions…"

She threw a leftover crust of bread at him and he ducked, laughing. "Come on, let's get to work before you hunt up something sharper to throw."

"I wouldn't have to search," she said, rising to her feet.

"Then I thank you for your kindness in only throwing bread," he said with a grin, sliding out from behind the table too.

She grimaced at him, picked up her blue cloak where it lay across the bench, and followed him out the door of The Black Lion.

Chapter Sixteen

The boys might think it was still early morning, and it might be too early for many visitors to the tavern, but the city was wide-awake. The narrow street The Black Lion faced on was already busy with passers-by, mostly on foot with the occasional cart. The bakery across the street was crowded with customers, the fish seller on the corner was loudly calling his wares, two women leaning out of nearby windows were shrieking an animated conversation to each other across the street between, and all five of the regular beggars were staked out in their usual spots.

Rin and Dimitri joined easily with the stream of traffic on the road, heading west towards the better part of town. Happily, that also put them upwind from the fish seller.

As they went, the narrow, crooked streets gradually grew wider. The mud road gave way to paved cobblestones, and the crowds grew more diverse. No less busy, but with nicer clothes mixed into the array, and more exotic ones too. Visitors from far away lands weren't likely to choose the neighborhood of The Black Lion as a place to visit. And they didn't last long if they stumbled in by mistake.

The crowds thinned as the ground rose up into the hills. The nobility didn't like rabble in their neighborhoods if they could prevent it. It was a different world, where even the sun shone brighter, the roads wider and the buildings set farther back.

The disappearance of the beggars from the street corners was a sure sign they'd entered the richest part of town. Not to mention the size of the houses, bigger than buildings that housed several dozen families back among the alleys and mud roads.

"Which house would you buy if you could?" Rin asked as they strolled up the hill. Their whole gang used to play this game as kids.

What food would you eat, which house would you choose, what clothes would you wear? None of them had ever had enough money to buy anything, but they had loved coming up with the most elaborate, exotic and expensive ideas.

"Maybe that stone one with the narrow windows," Dimitri said after a moment. "Good defensible design. Hard to break into that one."

Rin rolled her eyes. "Don't be so practical! Which would you choose if you didn't have to worry about things like that?"

"But I *would* worry about that, if I had a house like that," he said with a grin. "I know too much not to. Maybe I'd hire a lot of guards, though. Or even a magician to cast protection spells or something."

Rin shivered, shoulders twitching. "Guards, sure, but you couldn't pay me to put spells on my house. That's more dangerous than thieves."

"Maybe," Dimitri said, typically. He'd never quite agreed with her poor opinion of magic. His gaze drifted back to the houses and his grin faded. "It doesn't really matter. Not like I'll ever have to make that choice anyway."

"Maybe one day," Rin said, sticking her hands into her pockets and studying a white-painted house with a balcony. Balconies were terribly foolish if you had a worry about thieves. "If we really get a thousand gold pieces out of this job…maybe more, if a thousand is just the starting point."

"A thousand split among us."

"It's *still* a good pay. Really good."

"Sure, better than we're likely to see again any time soon. And a house like one of these—it would take a hundred-thousand, easy. We're never going to make that kind of money." He scowled at that stone house with the narrow windows. "You have to be born to a place like that. No one else can get there."

Dimitri got like this sometimes, and Rin usually tried to laugh it off. Getting bitter about things that couldn't change didn't put food in their stomachs, or do them any other good. "Who needs a house that big anyway?" she said lightly. "No one needs that much space. It's only there to make room for lots of things someone else can steal. Something smaller, though—a little house by itself with some breathing room around it so you can't hear the neighbors through the walls, but not so big that someone can get lost in it…a person like you or me might work up to something like that."

He laughed shortly. "Why, Rin, are you saying your fondest ambition is a cute little cottage in the country?"

"That's not what I said at all," she said promptly, lifting her chin higher. It really wasn't and besides, his tone made it clear enough what the only acceptable response was.

Although even if she hadn't meant to talk about a house in the country, even if she'd had in mind something in one of the middling parts of the city—well, the country didn't seem like such a bad place. Maybe. It wasn't like she'd ever been there to find out. But there was a stained glass window in a church near where she grew up—not right in the neighborhood, it was too fine for that neighborhood, but nearby—that showed rolling green hills and an arching blue sky and a scattering of sheep. The point of the window was supposed to be the man sitting in the middle, teaching the crowd of people around him, but Rin's eyes had always been drawn to the background. What would it be like to have that much space around you? Might be nice just to find out.

But Dimitri's contemptuous tone didn't invite that line of thought. "What would I possibly do," she continued, "in a cute little cottage in the country?"

"Raise up cute little babies, of course."

"Oh sure," she scoffed. Not that she didn't kind of like kids—but admitting that would just make her look soft. She couldn't afford it, not even around Dimitri. She put her shoulders back, walked as tall as she could. "That's about as likely as owning one of these fine houses."

Dimitri's glance roved out to the grand manors around them again. "Few things are less likely than *that*," he said, and the bitterness was back in his voice.

"Never mind," she said quickly, regretting bringing the conversation that direction again. "What have we got to complain about anyway? We've already come a long way from when we were kids picking pockets."

"True." He turned his head and studied her as they walked along, and Rin found herself holding her head higher under his gaze. Disappointingly, the corner of his mouth turned down into a frown, making her chest go tight. "You know, you could *look* like you've come farther." He reached out to tweak the edge of her cloak. "When are you going to replace this old thing?"

"When I find one I like better," she said, pulling the cloak defensively around her. True, she'd had it forever, the hem was stained and the clasp only caught if you knew the trick for it, but its dark blue shade was such a good color for blending into the night. But anyway, she didn't want to discuss her clothing with Dimitri. "So where's this house we're supposed to be looking at?"

"Top of the hill," Dimitri said, and pointed.

At the top of the hill stood the biggest house yet by far, a great sprawling stone edifice with diverging wings, sections of varying height, and a wall stretching around a substantial property.

Rin groaned. "There has to be a wall."

"Yeah, but on the counter side, a place that big *can't* be full of people. It should be easy enough to sneak into an unoccupied portion."

"Except then we'll have to find what we need, which could well be in an *occupied* portion. Assuming we can even find it."

Dimitri grinned. "Just means we have to walk soft."

"Hmph." She could do that, but it was nicer to not have to. She frowned, studying the property with an appraising eye. "The house walls look all right. That rough stone should be easy enough to scale."

"What do you think of the roof? Sharp peak."

"It's manageable, if we have to go that way. Take some careful balance, but that's not a problem. Too bad it can't be all one height, but none of the drops look too far." She shook her head. "It's still the outer wall I don't like. It's going to make today's job harder. I was hoping we could land on their doorstep after just being knocked over by a carriage. The wealthy always feel obligated to let other wealthy people inside under those circumstances. But no one would believe we came all the way down the drive and banged on their gate when we might have gone to another house without a wall."

"Looks like we'll have to do Old John's Lost Noble Routine."

Rin sighed, resigned. "I suppose. But I'm making *him* do the fainting."

Chapter Seventeen

Rin and Dimitri circled the house on the hill, studying as much as they could of the layout from the outside, and identifying three windows for likely access, should they need that kind of information later on.

They were the first ones back to The Black Lion, but the captain, Tyrone and Weldon arrived soon after. The word around the neighborhood made it clear they had got in early on this opportunity, but with no time to be wasted. Word was filtering out, though so far it seemed to be more an interested murmur than an indication of definite plans. The nature of the opportunity was causing some reluctance, but that potential reward would eventually draw other thieves. Most troubling, the Dockside Pirates had been to see Johnny Vane late in the morning, with an interest in this same opportunity.

The Black Lions and the Dockside Pirates had been cordial enemies for years. The Lions maintained that you could not legitimately call yourselves pirates if you only robbed ships and sailors while they were *in port*. The Docksiders disagreed. More importantly, perhaps, the Docksiders did not confine themselves to the port, which put the two groups in direct competition too often for friendly relations. If they were sniffing around this new opportunity, that made it a race for who could snatch it first.

Rin made that argument, about the importance of haste, when Magdala plunked her down in front of a mirror and brought out a long array of pots and jars, but the words fell on deaf ears.

"Now, now, you can't rush beauty, I always say," Magdala said firmly, bringing an apparently never-ending supply of cosmetics out from all the drawers and cupboards in her vanity table where they normally resided. Rin liked Magdala's *kitchen*, where she could always find something tasty to eat, but Magdala's bedroom upstairs was a fearful place. It was all full of purple drapery and pink pillows, with heaps of frilly and ruffled clothing all over the place. And so many, many little jars and bottles and metal tools for curling or plucking or who knew what.

"You're not going to use all of these anyway," Rin protested. It was more a fervent hope than definite knowledge.

"I like to have my options in front of me," Magdala said, emptying the last drawer and stacking a half dozen little jars in a precarious tower in the only space remaining on the table top. She leaned down, chin nearly on Rin's shoulder, and studied Rin's face in the mirror. "Oh yes, so many possibilities! I just love it when you lot decide to play nobles. You have such nice features, and you never *do* anything with them."

"They're perfectly good like they are for day to day," Rin muttered, ducking her head. If she were to do up her face every day the way Magdala wanted, not a single one of the Black Lion boys would take her seriously at all. Months and years of effort would be squandered by a little powder and polish.

"Let's start with the eyebrows," Magdala announced, and reached for one of her tweezers.

"Let's not," Rin growled, holding a hand defensively over her brows. "My eyebrows look fine, and we *really* don't have time for that." Besides, it hurt.

Magdala sighed huffily. "You of all people should know, in beauty and disguises, details matter. If you don't let me shape your eyebrows, the whole effect will be wrong." She pulled Rin's hand away and darted in to snatch a couple of hairs and yank them out.

Rin narrowly held in a squeak of pained protest, and kept her lips pressed tightly together until Magdala had finished plucking and pinching and pulling. *Men* didn't have to deal with this.

"There, perfect!" Magdala said happily, studying the effect when she was finally done. Rin studied it too; her face seemed softer, her eyes bigger. It was disconcerting. "Now," Magdala continued, "you have such pale skin, it must be all that night work, I'll use my lightest powder..."

Rin let Magdala's cheerful commentary wash over her and watched in the mirror as the other woman puffed and powdered and painted. She unscrewed little jars, dabbed here and patted there, and transformed Rin into a person she barely recognized.

"And now the hair!" Magdala said, tugging off the leather tie and unwinding Rin's braid.

"Something that will *stay*," Rin interjected. "You can't do something that'll fall to pieces if I turn my head."

"Yes, yes, all right. Now where did I put that blue ribbon—it's just the right shade for those lovely light blue eyes of yours."

"They're gray," Rin muttered. Unless you looked very, very closely. And since scarcely anyone did, they might as well be gray.

Magdala piled Rin's dark hair up into coils and mounds and wove a ribbon through and, when complete, it all held in place when Rin shook her head. She tested to make sure.

Next came the dress. Rin began, "One with—"

"—long sleeves, I know, so that you can hide those knives of yours." Magdala perused the pile of options thoughtfully. Her own clothes were too large for Rin and not the right style for this job anyway, but Old John had boxes and boxes of all sorts of things he had picked up somewhere, much of it supposedly from long ago theater productions. He had dropped off an array of dresses.

"The blue one looks fine," Rin said quickly, hoping to settle the matter.

"Yes...although..."

Magdala spent twenty minutes deciding, changing her mind, and then deciding again, all to finally settle on the blue dress anyway. Rin rolled her eyes dramatically, which Magdala failed utterly to notice. Even when that failure prompted a second eye roll.

When it was all done at last, Magdala insisted Rin stand in front of the mirror 'to see how beautiful she looked.'

Rin studied the elegant girl in the mirror with an uncomfortable knot in her stomach. She agreed that she looked beautiful—but that girl wasn't *her*. That girl was a complete stranger, someone with an altogether different life. She was nothing but a role Rin was briefly assuming, not anything she really was. Not anything she could even look like on her own, if she had wanted to. Even though she'd been watching, she didn't have any very clear idea of how Magdala worked her magic.

It was really this last moment in the mirror that made her hate putting herself into Magdala's hands. All the dabbing and fussing was annoying (and the plucking hurt) but she most hated this last moment. When she had to look at everything that she wasn't.

It wasn't as though she *wanted* to be that girl in the mirror. But she still felt an ache in knowing that she wasn't, and couldn't, and wouldn't ever be.

Maybe that was how Dimitri felt, looking at those grand houses.

She finally escaped from Magdala (with admonishments following her down the hall to try not to touch her face or her hair or anything else if she could avoid it) and went to join the others in the captain's room. Downstairs was busier by this time, and it wouldn't do to be seen down there like this.

She slipped into the room, to be greeted by near simultaneous whistles from Tyrone and Weldon.

"Don't start," she warned them both. "If I have to, I'll apologize to Magdala for spoiling her work with blood stains."

They made no comments, though they did grin at her. Haughty dignity seemed the best response. She stalked over to the empty chair next to Dimitri and sat down, trying not to tangle up her skirts in the process.

"It's an improvement on that old blue cloak," Dimitri remarked.

"Not if I have to climb in a window," she snapped. Even if that had been a compliment, it didn't *count*. He was complimenting the girl she wasn't. She kicked one heel against the leg of her chair, managing not to wince when her thin slipper did nothing to protect her foot from the sharp wooden corner.

It was wildly unfair. Dimitri's guard uniform was, in function, not any different from his usual clothes. Pants, a shirt and a jacket are all more or less the same, even if this jacket was neater, and had strategically-placed gold braid here and there. It looked good on him too. As for Old John, he strolled into the room after her with great flourishes of his silk cloak, demonstrating he was having a wonderful time with his costume.

Rin heartily wished she could still pass for a boy in daylight.

Once Old John arrived, the group slipped down the back stairs and out into the alley behind The Black Lion. Rin wore her blue cloak after all, to hide the fine dress until she was out of this part of town. They went by back ways and less frequented paths until they'd left the immediate neighborhood. Once they reached the wealthier part of town, Rin and Old John took off their concealing cloaks, the captain, Tyrone and Weldon faded off to find places where they could watch the house…and then it was time for the Lost Noble Routine.

Chapter Eighteen

Dimitri rapped sharply at the front gate of the stone house on the hill, while Rin and Old John waited a pace behind. Rin kept her back straight and her head up as she stood with her arm through Old John's, and tried to look as though she wore this sort of dress and this sort of hairstyle every day. *She* couldn't get into a place like this, but that girl in the mirror would consider it a simple matter of course.

The knock was answered promptly by a guard, who opened a panel in the heavy wooden door and looked out at them. "State your business," he said crisply, all perfectly correct. But Rin was pleased to see that he looked barely older than she was. With any luck, he wasn't really as confident as his bearing suggested.

Dimitri cleared his throat. "Lord Fitzwilliam Henry Meritricious Abernathy of Perrelda, and his daughter the Lady Elizabeth Catherine Isadora, here to see the Lord Brownen."

The guard's forehead wrinkled. "You must be mistaken. There is no Lord Brownen here."

"But our directions were most distinct," Dimitri protested sternly.

"And I am very certain that I know my lord's name and—"

"That is the *last* time I let that silly Isabella give me directions," Rin announced, putting her chin in the air and trying to look disdainful. "*She* said we couldn't possibly miss it, and yet here we are and—didn't I tell you, Father, that that girl didn't know what she was talking about?"

"Yes, yes, my dear," Old John rumbled, patting her hand. "Although she was so sweetly trying to help."

"But see where it's brought us now? And I was not easy in my mind about you coming out at all this afternoon. You really don't look well."

"Nonsense, I'm just feeling a little tired," Old John said, raising a handkerchief to his forehead.

"Guard, ask him where Lord Brownen lives," Rin directed in her most imperious tone. She did enjoy, just a little, getting the chance to order Dimitri around. "Father should not be out any longer than necessary. I *told* that silly Isabella that we should take the carriage, but no, she said it was such a short walk. I really don't know why we let that girl express opinions at all."

Dimitri fixed the young guard with a piercing stare. "Can you direct us to Lord Brownen's house?"

"I, uh, don't know of a Lord Brownen," the guard said, with a marked and very encouraging faltering of his assurance.

"It was Brownen, wasn't it?" Rin said, tapping one finger against her chin. "Or was it Bronten? Brinten? I know Isabella told me, but it wouldn't surprise me a bit if she got it wrong and—"

Old John suddenly let out a wrenching groan and sagged against Rin. She braced herself, reaching out with both arms to help hold him up. It was lucky he was largely faking this, still supporting some of his own weight; he had to be three times her size.

"Father? Oh, I *knew* he wasn't well!" Rin prided herself on never having had hysterics in her life, but she pitched as much hysteria as she could into her voice now.

Dimitri rushed to help support Old John, asking, "My lord, can you hear me? Are you well?"

"Fine," Old John rasped, "just a bit dizzy, I—ohhhh, dear..." He went limp again, this time falling towards Dimitri, who was better able to catch him.

"Open this gate at once," Rin demanded of the young guard, whose eyes had by now gone wide with anxiety. "My father must come in immediately."

The guard's eyes went even wider, fairly bulging from his face. "But I—that is, I don't know—"

"Surely you are not going to leave us here in the street! Open this gate right now, my father must sit down, have something to drink, we may need to fetch a doctor—"

"Well, I suppose…" The guard's gaze darted about rather frantically, plainly looking for someone else to take charge of the situation.

Rin caught Dimitri's eye and raised her eyebrows at him. Sometimes what a situation needed was a good firm military command, from a voice that sounded like its owner could be in the military. Hers, unfortunately, did not.

"Open this gate this moment," Dimitri barked, "and be quick about it!"

"Er—yes, sir," the guard said, sounding more relieved than anything else, and hastened to follow orders.

The heavy gates swung ponderously open, and Dimitri and the guard between them supported Old John down the walk to the front door. Rin fluttered about, making anxious queries and directing half-orders and altogether trying to make sure the guard didn't have the opportunity to think.

They made enough commotion that the front door was already open by the time they reached it, with a rather flabbergasted footman and two maids peering out. Perfect. With any luck, they'd get in and out without even dealing with anyone of status or importance in the household.

"Don't just stand there," Rin snapped at the gawking servants, "my father is not well. Where can we take him?"

"Er, the Blue Parlor?" one maid suggested, twisting her hands together.

"Excellent, show us the way," she directed the maid who had spoken, and to the other one she added, "And you, bring something to drink at once!"

They entered through the front door, and Rin noted with a professional eye that it had a solid oak bar on the inside and therefore would not be a possibility for a lockpick. Not that they generally got in by the front door in this sort of house anyway.

The door opened onto an enormous entryway dominated by a sweeping marble staircase. The first maid led them to the left, while the second maid scurried off through a small door on the right. The kitchens were probably that direction then.

They followed the first maid through a room that looked like a parlor to Rin—but the girl kept going, so maybe the room had some other purpose, despite its couch and fireplace. Who could understand the wealthy? The room opened onto a much larger room with blue paneling, two fireplaces and five couches. This, apparently, was the Blue Parlor, because the maid directed them to the nearest couch.

Old John collapsed onto it with a great deal of sighing and creaking—the first from Old John, the second from the couch. Rin dropped to her knees beside him, belatedly realized this would probably wrinkle her skirts, and pushed the thought aside. She could apologize to Magdala later; even though it wasn't Magdala's dress, she'd be personally offended on the subject.

"Father, are you all right?" she asked, leaning solicitously over him, and noting the window behind him. Big enough to get in through but it was too exposed, visible from the street, and besides, it had an internal lock. She couldn't see the details from here, but it looked like a solid one. "Can you hear me?"

"I'm afraid my head is…spinning rather…" Old John said feebly.

Rin turned at once to the remaining house maid. "Quickly, you must fetch a damp cloth for his head. And smelling salts."

The maid bobbed a slight curtsy and hurried off out of the room. The first one wasn't back yet, so that just left the guard.

"Father, how do you feel? Do you need anything else?" She made sure her voice was anxious and tremulous, and that the guard was at the wrong angle to see her face as she tried to urge Old John with raised eyebrows to ask for something more.

"Er, well…" His forehead wrinkled and his eyes darted about, as he plainly tried to come up with something he could need.

She turned her face farther away from the guard and mouthed "the cold" to Old John.

His forehead cleared. "Ah, it is a bit, well, rather chilly in here…"

Rin clasped her hands together. "We must have a better fire!" She turned to the guard. "You, go see about more wood. And perhaps some blankets. Hurry!"

He took a step. And then he stopped. "I…meaning no disrespect, but I think I had best stay here."

Oh well, it had been a long shot that they'd be left alone anyway. Though she would have liked a few moments to see where the two other doors in this room led to.

They kept up a proper flurry and clamor, and kept the maids running in and out, but the sole guard couldn't be enticed into leaving his post. But with one request and another, mostly by rejecting one drink or another, soon half a dozen glasses had been brought into the room and left carelessly on a side table. The only trick now was to get one of them out the door.

Rin was responsible for stealing the glass, and in this there was at least one good thing about her costume. It had a full skirt and, contrary to usual custom, had a pocket sewn into it, well-hidden within the folds. Fashion had to make *some* concessions to the practical needs of a thief, and many of Old John's costumes had been modified in similar ways.

Rin made a great fuss about trying different drinks on her 'father,' and meanwhile eyed the glasses thoughtfully. Every glass was etched with a crest, so on that point any could do. Three were large tumblers she doubted she could hide, and two were long-stemmed goblets that would be almost as awkward to manage. Luckily she'd thought to ask for strong spirits—for reviving purposes, of course—and this had arrived in a small glass only a few inches tall. The obvious choice, except as the only one of its type, its absence would be more easily noticed.

She'd just have to go the dramatic route. The entire production had been ridiculous enough to begin with anyway.

Old John drank down the spirits very happily, and Rin took the small glass back, to return it to the table with the others. She leaned over as though to set it down—and instead palmed the glass, while using her knee, hidden beneath her skirt, to give the table a good shove.

The spindly table went over in a great tumult and crash of glass. Rin leaped backward with a horrified exclamation, whisking her skirts out of the way and slipping the small glass into her hidden pocket.

Renewed flurry arose as the maids rushed forward to tend to the broken shards, and Rin loudly said, "Oh, I *am* sorry, that was so very clumsy of me. I'm just so distressed about Father, and I simply…"

She trailed off at the sound of a door opening, not the one they had entered through. And standing in that doorway was a man far too well-dressed to be another servant.

So much for getting in and out without meeting anyone of importance.

She dipped into a curtsy, not too low, considering her assumed rank. It was her best guess at the appropriate etiquette, and it also gave her a few seconds for observation.

The lord of the house was tall and thin, dressed all in black with iron gray hair. He had a hooked nose and a very, very straight back. Behind him was what might be some sort of art gallery, judging from a display case or two she could just catch glimpses of.

"I do hope there's no trouble here?" the lord asked. His voice was a low purr that made the hair on the back of Rin's neck stand up.

"No," she managed, "not at all. That is…my father was taken ill just at your gate, and your servants kindly let us in and—"

"So I see," the lord interrupted, pacing into the room. He clasped his hands behind his back and turned his attention to Old John. "And are you recovered?"

Out of the corner of her eye, Rin could see Dimitri moving closer. She was glad of it, and of the four knives she had hidden under this silly dress.

"I, ah…" Old John sat up, damp cloth falling from his forehead. "Much better, thank you. The, er, water was very reviving."

"Excellent," the lord said, without sounding in the least pleased. "How fortunate we could be of assistance."

Rin had a terrible sinking feeling in the pit of her stomach, and a suspicion that he knew just how ridiculous their excuse for being here really was. "I'm terribly sorry for the imposition," she said quickly, "it's only that I was so concerned about Father, I simply couldn't think of anything else, and…"

The sentence died away as the lord turned his gaze on her again, and shivers ran down her spine. Closer now, she could see that his eyes were a hard, cold blue. "Your father is fortunate to have such a conscientious daughter. I suppose you take after your mother in looks?"

She could feel the weight of the small glass against her leg, somehow heavier than it had seemed only a moment before. She forced a slight laugh. "Oh, yes, everyone remarks on that!"

"I'm sure." He looked again at Old John. "If you are feeling quite well, perhaps it is time to be going. I am in the midst of some delicate work at present. You understand."

"Of course, of course," Old John blustered, "I hate to be a bother, I never—"

"Very good." The lord turned on his heel and strode back towards the open doorway. "Guard, show them out. Now."

"Yes, sir," the young guard said instantly, back going even straighter.

Old John rose to his feet, and the guard showed them all to the door, down the path and out the gate with a haste that, had Rin really been aristocracy, she no doubt would have found insulting. She barely had time to make note of the second guard who had taken over the post at the front gate. Probably that meant others in strategic places around the rest of the house too.

All that really counted was that, within a few minutes, they were back out on the street, and the small engraved glass was still safely stowed in her pocket.

That was the important thing. The *only* important thing. Yet Rin still found herself glancing over her shoulder, back towards the stone house, and muttering to Dimitri, "I don't think I like that man."

"Just as well," he said easily, "who ever wants to rob someone they like?"

"Yes," she said aloud, but was thinking that she wasn't sure she wanted to rob someone with that much cold power either. Still—a thousand gold pieces. Surely the thought of all that warm gold ought to take the chill off.

Chapter Nineteen

As it turned out, Old John merely thought that the lord of the house had been rather rude, and Dimitri thought he was a typical arrogant noble and what of it, and neither one had the same feeling of deep discomfort that Rin had picked up. Certainly neither one saw any reason to reconsider this job because of the lord's demeanor, and Rin kept her fears to herself. They'd be sure to tell her she was being emotional, and wasn't that typical of a girl?

Everyone arrived safely back at The Black Lion, and the mood was jovial as they compared stories and discussed next steps. Rin was happy to be praised for her role in the deception, happy to get out of the blue dress and back to her usual trousers, and not so happy to have no task in the remaining events of the afternoon.

Dimitri went off to see Johnny Vane, stolen glass in his pack, to arrange a meeting with their potential employer. She would have liked to go with him—but he didn't ask, so she spent the late afternoon dismantling her lock and trying not to remember the chill blue eyes of the lord of the manor.

All the boys seemed to have other occupations for their time, so her only company was Magdala, whenever she passed by in her serving of drinks and food. She came and sat down at Rin's corner table during a slow spell, and watched Rin lay out lock tumblers like so many tiny pieces of a puzzle.

"How you can accomplish anything with just a little metal pick, when you can't even see inside the lock, is just beyond me," Magdala remarked. "It's like magic almost."

"It isn't magic. It's skill."

"I've heard there are spells that can open locks," Magdala continued, apparently cheerfully oblivious to the edge in Rin's voice.

"Or magic keys that'll open any lock. Did you ever think of trying to lay hold of one of those? Might make your work easier."

"Only until I met a lock with a better spell on it," Rin retorted. Her fingers tightened and the tumbler between them dug into her skin. "Besides, I don't trust magic. You can't depend on it and there's too many tricky drawbacks that you don't find out about until it's too late."

"All right, dear, I was just thinking it might be easier."

"But that's the *point*," Rin insisted, "people use magic because they think it will be easier, but then it isn't in the long run."

"All *right*, dear," Magdala said, standing up. "I've got to be getting back to work—and mind, if anyone offers me a magic pot that will cook supper by itself, I'm accepting."

Rin opened her mouth to go on arguing, but Magdala was already walking away. She turned back to her lock pieces with a frown. She had never liked magic. Maybe because the few times she'd seen magicians, they'd given her a prickly, crawly feeling. Some things, people weren't meant to be able to do. Magical power, that was for the rich and the high-born and was just as much out of reach as those fine houses on the hill. So it was better, really, that magic always cost something. She didn't have any opportunity to make the purchase, didn't want to pay the cost, and was altogether much better off staying with her own skills and abilities. She could *rely* on those.

"Don't look so grim. Things are going our way today."

Rin looked up to find that Dimitri had snuck up on her. Irritating, but it was a consolation that he was the only one who could do it. "Good news from Johnny?"

"Excellent news," Dimitri said, sliding into a seat at the table. "I worked the whole business out. It seems the lady in question left directions with Johnny, supposing anyone turned up with the required glass. He'll send word to her, and we're to meet her at midnight tonight at the north tower on the old sea wall."

"Midnight?" Rin repeated. "How dramatic."

"It's as dark a part of the night as any other. Anyway, I told Johnny we'd be there."

"If the captain approves it."

"Of course," Dimitri said, looking faintly surprised. "But you know he will."

"Yes..." He probably would. Still, she didn't feel as easy about it as she'd like. "It is in the Docksiders' territory, though."

"As if they're worth worrying about," Dimitri scoffed.

And that seemed to be the captain's attitude too. At any rate, he agreed to the plan when he heard it, and the moonlight that night saw all six of the Lions climbing the steps of the old sea wall towards the north tower. With luck, *only* the moonlight had seen them on their way here. They had got this far without incident, but Rin found that to be little comfort. It didn't matter if they could get into Docksiders' territory—it was getting *out* again that counted.

But that was a worry to be folded up and put away until later. Right now, they had a potential employer to meet.

It was a strange place to be meeting someone, a thought that recurred to Rin for at least the fifth time as they ascended the stone steps. It was discreet, if the goal was secrecy, but nothing else recommended it. The docks had expanded over a century ago, with magic extending the land's edge and builders stretching their piers farther out, and all of it leaving this old sea wall much less used than it had once been. The area wasn't nice enough for the royalty or anyone else to worry about using it for any purpose of theirs. No doubt the towers would have been used by the criminal elements more often, except that they were so drafty as to be no one's first choice for a regular meeting place. It wasn't the kind of tower that had any rooms in it, just a wider platform at the top of the wall, with only a low partition around it and no roof to offer protection from the elements.

So why would a wealthy woman choose a spot the rich avoided for its bad neighborhood, and the locals avoided for its poor design?

There had to be better places that were just as secret. Conundrums. But intriguing too.

The captain was the first at the top of the stairs, with Tyrone and Weldon just behind, then Dimitri, Rin and Old John last, wheezing loudly as he climbed.

When Rin first stepped out onto the platform, she thought they were the only ones there. Then the deepest shadows moved, and a woman stepped forward from her place against the wall, coming into view in the moonlight.

It was still hard to see anything much about her; she was wearing a long, pale blue cloak with its hood pulled up, hiding her face in shadow. She was tall and slender, and any other description could be nothing but conjecture. And yet, there could be no doubt she was the one they were here to meet. Even muffled in her cloak, she had a regal bearing.

The Lions fanned out into a half circle, an automatic and well-known maneuver. They didn't get too close, both to avoid threatening her and to protect themselves. Rin studied the shadows, eyes adjusting to the reduced light of the tower space, and felt satisfied no one else was lurking.

So the lady had brought no guards. Who was she that she came *here* alone and unafraid?

"You have brought the item I require?" Her voice was like silk, cool and soft, and yet Rin felt a prickle that reminded her very much of her uneasy feeling around the lord of the stone house. This woman might be silk, but a silk scarf can strangle.

"We've brought it," the captain said, drew the small glass from his vest pocket and held it out.

She extended a hand from within her cloak, one covered in a long black glove that reached at least to her elbow. She took the glass and held it up to catch the moonlight, the crest glinting. "Excellent," she breathed. "Then we may do business."

"That was exactly our hope," the captain said, with a slight bow and general air of gallantry. "You will find us very capable for whatever you require."

"Perhaps," the lady said, and then she began to study them each in turn, beginning at one end of the line and moving to the other. It took more than a minute, and she was silent throughout.

She came to Rin second to last, and when that gaze settled on her, Rin had to make an effort not to flinch or look away. She couldn't even see the lady's eyes in the shadows, and yet the gaze seemed to pierce deep into her. Her prickle of discomfort grew. Maybe that was the only reason it felt like the lady stared at her the longest.

The unsettling stare moved at last on to Old John, and Rin concentrated on letting out a held breath slowly, so it wouldn't be audible to everyone around her.

Finally the examination finished, and the lady nodded once. "Yes. I think we can do business." Her hands met in front of her, palms together, and Rin suddenly realized she didn't know what had become of the glass, no longer in the lady's hand. The prickling got worse. "I require the liberation of a certain item," the lady continued, "from the house you already visited today. The item is not mine and never has been. But I want it. Will this concern you?"

"We don't ask about motive," the captain said, with a slight grin that was ample proof he did not feel the same uneasiness as Rin. "Just about payment."

"Very good. The payment for a *successful* endeavor will be one thousand gold pieces." The lady's gaze flicked around the circle again, and her tone did not change as she repeated, "One thousand gold pieces. Each."

Rin couldn't keep her intake of breath inaudible, but it hardly mattered for all the mutterings and shiftings and sudden exhales going on around her. One fine dress might cost three gold pieces, a fine horse twenty—what could she do with a thousand? What *couldn't* she do?

She could buy that house in the country, the one she wasn't sure she actually wanted. Or go traveling. Or buy a tavern—well, maybe a good share in a tavern, anyway. If she wanted one. It was enough money for any of the dreams she might have had on a dark night, the ones that had never seemed possible.

"That will be...acceptable," the captain said in even tones, even though his calm response couldn't hide the obvious excitement of the group.

"I thought it would be," the lady said, inclining her head slightly.

"And what would you have us...liberate?" he asked.

"The matter is a complicated one. The item's owner is clever. It is best not to speak his name, but let us call him..." Here she betrayed a very slight smile, just visible in the shadows of her hood. "...Lord Silver. He is a great collector of rare items, and a possessor of rare skills. It is safe to say that Lord Silver will likely have the item I seek under a disguise, or it may be mixed among worthless duplicates."

"So how do we steal something we can't recognize?" Dimitri asked, earning a glare from the captain for speaking out of turn and making Rin wince. She was always torn between admiring Dimitri's bravado—and wanting to shake him for it.

He earned a long stare from the lady. At last she looked away, turned back to the captain again, and something in her stance made this as clear a dismissal as words could have. Rin saw Dimitri's hand clench into a fist at his side, before the lady's voice claimed her attention again.

"Lord Silver may disguise the item to sight or touch, or create duplicates to fool these senses as well. But there are aspects he will not be able to hide or create falsely. I have something which will enable you to identify the true item." Her hands, held together all this while, parted. She held one out, palm up, and something sparkled against her black glove. "This is similar in feature to the item you will seek. When it comes near the proper item, you will know. Take it."

The captain reached out to do so, and his eyes widened as he looked at the object in his hand. Rin deeply regretted being on the far side of the circle, too far away to see just what was so impressive. "You must be sending us after something very valuable," the captain said.

"That is why I pay very well. And be warned, if you think to run, if you think to steal from me," she said coldly, her gaze landing briefly on Dimitri, "I will find you. And you will regret it."

"We understand perfectly," the captain said, and the rest nodded too.

"Very good." She reached into her cloak, and withdrew a tightly rolled paper. "I have a map of the house, indicating the most likely rooms where the object may be hidden. That is, however, only conjecture. The entry, the search and the necessary secrecy I will leave to your expertise." She handed the paper to the captain, and withdrew both hands within her cloak again. "I expect you to act quickly. If you are successful, meet me here tomorrow at dawn. That gives you a full day and night to accomplish the task. It will be sufficient."

That last wasn't a question, but the captain nodded. "Of course."

"Very good." And then the lady was gone.

Just…gone. No smoke, no bursts of light, certainly no turning around and walking away, or even a leap off the tower. She was just gone.

"That—is not natural," Rin protested, pointing at the empty space. "People should not be able to do that!" Her whole body prickled now, and her stomach was roiling as though the tower had shifted beneath her.

"It explains why she came without guards," the captain remarked.

"What did she give you?" Old John asked, moving closer. "Let us see it too."

"Wish I could vanish like that," Tyrone said, "could be useful sometimes. Get away from some of those girls who get the wrong idea and—"

"No one else is bothered by an employer who can do magic?" Rin demanded. "One we know *nothing* about? Not even her name, or what she looks like under that cloak!"

"I can't guess her name, but I know what we can call her," the captain said, holding up the trinket to sparkle in the moonlight. He smiled as he looked up at it. "Lady Diamond."

Having moved closer now, Rin could see the object better. It was a tiny, perfectly crafted flower, made of diamonds. It was too perfect, and coupled with its owner's very sudden disappearance, it was easy enough to guess that no normal craftsman had ever created it. "That thing's not natural either. Just what do you imagine she's sending us to steal?"

"Something that's worth a thousand gold pieces to each of us," Weldon said, and elbowed his brother. "Maybe you'll finally have enough money to satisfy that blond at The Crown and Candle, eh?"

Tyrone elbowed his brother back, and told Rin, "Calm down, lass, it'll all be fine. No need to get all emotional."

"I am *calm*," Rin said through gritted teeth. Never, not once, had she heard one of them tell another man not to get emotional when he expressed an objection. "And I am *concerned* about this employer and this job."

"It's too late to back out now," Dimitri said, putting a hand on her shoulder, "so we'll just have to be careful. Like we always are."

"Every job carries risks," the captain said, stowing the map and the diamond flower away in his jacket. "But right now, I don't want to risk staying here any longer. Let's get back to The Lion, and start laying some plans for tomorrow night."

He was right about the risk of being in Docksiders' territory, but the caution came too late. They took the stairs down from the wall, descended into the deeper shadows and entered a narrow alley. And that was when a half-dozen figures emerged from the shadows to block their path.

"Well, well, aren't you rather far from home?" the foremost figure drawled, stepping forward. Rin knew his voice, though they hadn't met more than once or twice, and it made her spine crawl in a quite different way than Lady Diamond had. This was Red Hallam, leader of the Dockside Pirates, who liked to fancy himself a mighty pirate lord even though, as far as anyone knew, he had never left shore.

"No drunk sailors for you to rob tonight?" the captain said, tone calm but his shoulders tense. "Or were they not drunk enough to make it easy for you?"

The Lions were already shifting into position. They might talk through this, but they would be ready if not. Rin loosened the knife in her arm sheath, prepared to drop into her hand at an instant's notice. Drawing too soon could provoke an attack unnecessarily, but she wouldn't be caught without a weapon when she needed it. At the same time she shifted a step or two closer to Dimitri, catching his eye as she did. Without looking, she knew Tyrone and Weldon would be having a similar silent conversation, making similar arrangements.

"We thought we'd rather chase us some stray pussy cats tonight," Red Hallam growled. "We caught a rumor you were seen coming this way."

So much for sneaking in.

"We're not looking for trouble tonight," the captain said, raising his hands.

"No, just for a new job," Red Hallam spat. "Or so Johnny Vane tells us."

"Johnny talks too much," the captain said tightly.

"He's been talking about a mighty fine opportunity. One we'd like to get our hands on."

"It's already claimed."

"Yeah, so we heard. But then we got to thinking. If certain people were *unable* to carry out a commission, it's open picking again, isn't it?"

No chance they'd get out of this without a fight. Rin edged another step closer to Dimitri, though by now they had all just about settled into place. She and Dimitri on the right, Weldon and Tyrone on the left, the captain in front and Old John, the admitted weak element in a fight, in the middle.

She glanced around quickly, checking the terrain and the options for a quick exit. And then she glanced back the way they had come, and her throat tightened. Three more figures blocked the way out. They were in a very neat trap.

No more conversation. Red Hallam gestured with one hand, and the Docksiders moved forward from both directions. Rin took another quick step forward and turned, setting her back against Dimitri's, a knife ready in her hand.

She couldn't spare a glance for the others, but she expected Tyrone and Weldon had made the same maneuver. With Old John between the two pairs in the narrow alley, they could offer some cover for him as well. If she had to guess, the captain would probably engage Red Hallam.

The first Docksider to come at her was big, and he smelled like fish. She didn't have time to think beyond that. She never did much thinking once she was into a fight. It was all instinct then, her body responding with long-honed skills. Slashing, twisting, feinting. What she could never afford was to close too tightly with an opponent, since almost anyone she fought was bigger and stronger than she was. The trick was to keep dancing at arms-length, to keep just enough awareness of Dimitri to hold position where they could cover each other's backs, and to stay aware of her peripheries while not getting distracted from her immediate opponent.

He made a slash at her and she ducked under his taller reach to come up and under and score a hit to his shoulder. He cursed and fell back a pace, giving her a fraction of a second to glance to the side, to take in only a confusion of fighting bodies pressed together. Then he was coming at her again, and again she had no room for any thought or observation beyond avoiding the man's flashing knife.

At last she caught another opening, not for a stab this time but to hook a boot around his ankle, wrench him off-balance and send him crashing down against the cobbles. He didn't get up, and after a second or two she turned away.

She turned just in time to see a knife flash down and stab Old John in the chest. He staggered, sank to the ground. The Docksider holding the knife turned to throw himself into the knot around Tyrone and Weldon, and Rin threw herself down next to Old John.

Knife still clutched in her right hand, she reached for his chest with her left and felt warm blood on her hand. She shuddered, a spasm of horror and fear wracking her whole body, and thoughts came back. How bad was it, could she get a bandage somehow, there was no time for anything, not in the middle of a fight still going on overhead, Dimitri was covering her for this brief moment but she had to *do* something and do it now—and she was still trying to grasp at what when Old John's eyes slid closed.

She had a bare instant to stare numbly at his suddenly slack face before another knife came slashing at her and she had to rise to the fight again. And blessedly, the thinking stopped. For now.

More confusion of knives and fists and shoving bodies, a fight that was probably no more than a minute or two seeming to last forever. Then the Docksiders were falling back. As soon as her attention was free, Rin turned towards Old John again—but Dimitri grabbed her arm, tugged her towards the alley's mouth, back the direction they had entered from.

"They're just regrouping," he said, "we have to go *now*."

"But Old John—"

"It's too late. Come on!"

The others were already going, and Dimitri stayed only long enough to see that she was starting in the right direction before he was running for the way out too. Rin began to pick up her stride, to go into a run behind the others.

But after only a step or two something caught at her ankle and she went down, so hard and fast that she had no time even to call out, breath knocked out of her lungs by the impact. She caught a glimpse of the others still retreating, not realizing she wasn't behind them, but couldn't get the air to shout.

She rolled instinctively onto her back, just before the Docksider who had grabbed her ankle landed on top of her. It was the same one she had fought first, the one who had gone down and stayed there, and she cursed herself for a fool for not watching where she stepped when she tried to retreat.

He was twice her weight, had all the advantage of position and held a knife in one hand. Her own knife was still in her right hand, but she instead closed her left into a fist and punched hard towards the shoulder she had wounded before. He flinched away, didn't get off, but it was still enough. The smallest one in any fight, she had learned tricks of leverage and angles. His flinch gave her the opening to shove him over, to reverse their positions.

Now Rin was on top, kneeling above him, and she easily slashed at his right arm when he tried to stab at her with his knife. For the almost haphazard nature of the strike, she was lucky and his knife went clattering to the ground, while her own knife swung back and held poised above his neck.

For the first time she looked into his face, and found him glaring back at her, face pulled into a grimace. "Go ahead," he growled. "Do it, if you dare."

She was suddenly aware of the smell of fish and of sweat, of the slick blood on her hands and her clothes and her knife, of her own labored breathing mixing with the gasping breath of the man whose throat lay just below her blade.

She reversed the knife in her hand and hit him in the side of the head with the hilt. His eyes rolled back and she pushed off, running almost before she was on her feet, pounding down the alley after her friends in the distance.

Chapter Twenty

Rin caught up to Dimitri quickly enough that no one had even noticed her delay. A fight that had seemed very long had really been a matter of seconds. Even as she ran, feet and heart pounding, she knew she was going to spend far more time pinned in that alley in her memory than she ever had in life.

The Black Lions didn't pause for breath until they were many streets away from the scene of the fight, until they had passed the invisible yet indisputable line that marked the edge of the Docksiders' territory. Then the captain finally pulled up in the shadow of a looming stone building, and looked around at his hard-breathing comrades.

"Everyone all right?" the captain asked, voice a rasp.

They responded with murmurs and nods and one or two curse words that still meant yes. Everyone who was *there* was all right.

Rin leaned one hand against the cold stone wall, pushed back her straggled hair with the other, and tried to drag air into her lungs. "Old John, back there..." Even a moment's pause was enough time for the thoughts, and the regrets, to start. "We shouldn't have just left, we should've...we should've..."

Dimitri reached out to grip her shoulder. "There's nothing we can do. There's nothing we could have done. It was too late."

She wrapped her fingers tight around his wrist, looked up at him. "You're sure? You made *sure*?" She heard the wobble in that last word, and knew she was perilously close to being 'that silly girl, who falls apart when things get rough.'

"Yes," Dimitri said. "Of course."

It felt like there should be more to say. But she couldn't say it, not without sacrificing too much. And besides, she had known too, really. She had seen for herself how Old John's face had changed. She had known what it meant.

She let go of Dimitri's arm, stepped a pace away, and for a minute there was silence apart from five breaths.

Then the captain said, "I still have the diamond and the map. So that's all right, at least."

Rin supposed that question would have occurred to her eventually.

They didn't talk much more on the way back to The Black Lion. Rin was mostly trying not to think about that narrow alley back there, and who—what was lying in it. She realized she hadn't even looked to see if any of the Docksiders had been killed. If they had, they weren't in her path on the way out.

That part of the city had just enough law and order that the bodies would be picked up. Not enough that anyone would be hauled into a courthouse to face any consequences.

The Lions could probably figure out where Old John's body would be taken, if they tried. It wasn't their part of town, but they could find out. They couldn't do anything with the knowledge, though. They could walk around the city with a fair amount of impunity, but they could hardly ask the law to ignore them if they showed up trying to claim the obvious victim of a knife fight. The law wasn't *that* willfully blind.

So Dimitri was right. There really was nothing to do. It just didn't feel right, that was all.

Magdala knew what had happened to Old John as soon as they got back to The Black Lion. No one needed to say anything. His absence, the state of their clothes and their faces said enough. She immediately took to murmuring about "the poor man" and "what a shame" and "such a dear, really," and brought drinks for everyone and bandages for those who needed it.

They raised a glass to Old John and drained their cups, but no one went on to a second one. It was only a few hours until dawn, and they had work to do tomorrow, and the next night. A job still had to be done, even if they had lost a member. Proper mourning, a gathering of friends and a proper evening at The Lion to remember, would have to come later. After the job.

Rin was the first to leave the table. She knew they would all be up soon, to go get some sleep before meeting again in the morning to make plans, but she was the first one up.

She said good night and turned to go, but Dimitri caught her wrist. "Are you sure you're all right?" he asked in a low voice, but not too low for the others to hear.

Maybe she would have answered differently if they were alone. Maybe not. As it was, she mustered a half-smile and said, "Of course," because it was the only answer.

His eyes were narrow as he studied her, but he released her wrist. She was pushing open the back door before it occurred to her that Tyrone and Weldon had both passed up an opportunity to offer to keep her company tonight. A sure sign that none of them were really all right.

Rin stepped out into the darkness, let the door swing shut behind her. She leaned against the back wall of The Lion, closed her eyes and let the cold wind blow over her cheek for a moment. The memories, the emotions, were all surging at the back of her mind. She couldn't let them out, not yet.

With a deep breath, she pushed away from the wall and set off through the night. She took a route that was familiar, one of half a dozen she used to make this journey. Alone among the Lions, she didn't make her home in The Black Lion. She trusted the inhabitants of the tavern as much as she trusted anyone, but that said very little and she never felt comfortable sleeping somewhere anyone knew about.

She cut through alleys, climbed over walls and across a handful of rooftops, and finally arrived at the Jacobine Bridge. She climbed over the railing, hung by her hands, and dropped down to land on the narrow ledge beneath, alongside the rushing current of the river. The ledge was maybe two feet wide, invisible from overhead.

The ledge was the only access point to a small space hollowed out of the substructure of the bridge. It was hardly big enough to be called a room, for all that it had a door. She had no idea why it would have been built there, or if it was only a quirk of the architecture and never meant to be a room at all. The bridge was hundreds of years old; someone else, someone like her but with a few more resources, might have added the door at any time. A wooden door but sturdy, it might not have been part of the original plan of the stone bridge.

It hardly mattered why it was here. She had found it once, exploring as a child, and for almost a year it had been one of the several places she stayed, and the most secure.

She checked automatically that the small pebble she had left on the ledge just before the door was still there, and therefore the door had not been opened, then reached into her pocket for her key. She had put a better lock on the door since she had begun staying here.

It opened with a creak, and she didn't bother lighting her candle. She locked the door behind her and threw the bar across it, working mostly by feel in the darkness. A tiny amount of moonlight filtered in through gaps in the stone's mortar, and she could have done this with her eyes shut anyway.

She pulled off her rumpled, blood-stained outer clothes, balled them up and threw them into a corner to be dealt with in the morning. She had cleaned up her hands and face at The Black Lion, so now there was nothing else left to do but take the two steps to her bedroll and sink down onto it. She pulled a blanket up over her head and curled into a tight ball.

And then, finally, she could let go of the hard grip she had kept on her feelings all this while. She could finally let the terrors that had been pressing and fighting for her attention come forward. She could finally stop being brave, could turn her face into her thin pillow, soak it with tears, and trust that no one could hear the sobs.

Chapter Twenty-One

Rin's eyes were dry and her demeanor calm when she returned to The Black Lion the next morning. She had put on clean clothes, her purple shirt, dark pants and leather vest. Her hair was neatly braided back, and she was as ready for business as anyone could expect. She dodged most of Magdala's sympathy and betook herself to a corner table with a hot drink and a loaf of bread to wait for the others to be awake. She tried very hard not to think about the footsteps she *wouldn't* be hearing.

There had to be something else she could think about. Something good.

Not the job. She still thought their employer was unnerving and the job was strange on too many levels for comfort and anything that *began* with someone dying wasn't likely to end well. Which just brought her back to the same thing she *wasn't* thinking about, and it was all pointless anyway because whether she liked the job or not they were doing it, and she wasn't going to be the one to refuse. That would just get her kicked out of the only place where she belonged even a little.

She could think of the money, maybe. The job was a bad thought but the possible reward was another matter. What with one thing and another, she hadn't had the chance to give those thousand gold pieces much more thought since she was talking to Dimitri. It was no good depending on money you didn't have yet—but what was the harm of just imagining a little?

What house would you buy, what food would you eat, what clothes would you choose…a thousand gold pieces would be enough to answer all those questions.

She could buy a new cloak. Her old blue one had survived the previous night's events mostly unscathed. A few new stains weren't much worse than its previous state, which still meant it was probably well due to be replaced. Dimitri thought so, anyway.

She tore off a piece of bread, and tried to think bigger. A cloak was such a tame dream for a thousand gold pieces. It would hardly cost more than one or two, even to buy the nicest cloak she'd ever imagined.

The money wouldn't be enough for one of those fine houses on the hill, but there had to be other wild fantasies she could actually accomplish. She had spent a whole year as a little girl dreaming about beautiful horses…but the truth was she had never had the opportunity to learn how to ride one, so that dream might have some complications. Any fine dresses or jewelry would be equally impractical for her life.

Was a thousand gold pieces enough to change her life? It was certainly enough to take her somewhere else, with plenty left over to start a new life…if she knew what she wanted to *do* in a new life. She didn't know how to do anything except what she was doing now.

Maybe she could go to sea. She had always been curious about those wide blue expanses and crashing waves. What would it be like to go sailing out over them? She had never wanted to be a member of the Dockside Pirates, but she had envied their claim on the harbor and the immediate shore.

Of course, sooner or later she'd have to stop sailing, and land somewhere, and then?

She rested her elbow on the table and her chin in one hand. This was not as much fun as she had hoped it would be. So far, all she could seem to come up with was a lot of nothing, and a frightening feeling that she had not been giving enough thought to what she wanted out of life.

A crash from the kitchen jarred her out of her thoughts, but didn't cause any real alarm. It was the sound of a plate breaking, and that was pretty usual. She wasn't at all surprised when Sam came out of the kitchen in a hurry, broom in one hand and a guilty expression on his face.

"Was that the second plate this week?" Rin called with a slight smile.

Sam sighed. "The third." He began sweeping his way towards her table. "Magdala told me I'd better not come back in her kitchen for at least an hour." The general man-of-all-work at The Black Lion, Sam moved in a perpetual cloud of broken crockery, knocked-over drinks, and spectacular trippings. No new incident ever bothered him for long, though, and Rin watched expectantly for his smile to return. She could use some of Sam's usual cheer right now.

The smile didn't come. He swept along and stopped in front of her table, looking if anything even gloomier. "I heard about Old John. I'm sorry about..."

"Thank you," Rin said, throat suddenly tight.

"He was always a good sort, wasn't he? He used to tell the best stories about when he was in the theater." Sam smiled then, but it was a sad smile. "Not that I ever believed more than half of them, you know, but they were good stories."

This was *not* helping. "Yeah, they were," Rin said, and cast about for a topic change. "Hey Sam, what would you do if you were rich?"

Sam could at least be relied on to take things as they came. He scratched behind one ear and considered. "If I was always rich, or if I got a lot of money now?"

"If you got money now."

"Travel," he said, and made an idle whisk with the broom. "I always wanted to see what life was like in other places. Did you know most people never go more than ten miles from the place they were born in their whole lives? I'd like to go east, see if things are different in Waldisan or Perrelda. Or go a little farther north into Beaumont. I hear there's lots more magic there, that centaurs and dragons are practically ordinary."

"So you'd just set off and leave us all behind?"

"Well...not immediately. And not everyone." It could have been the light, but Sam looked to be blushing. "I'd marry Denae first." He'd been courting the baker's daughter for at least a year, so that was no big surprise. "And then we could go traveling together, you know. It wouldn't be as good, to travel alone."

"No," Rin said. "I suppose it wouldn't be." And affable, pleasant Sam, who never had an unkind word for anyone, couldn't possibly know the pained twist he'd just given her.

The problem, really, wasn't that she didn't have dreams, or that she'd never thought about what she wanted. It was that no amount of gold pieces was going to buy her dreams for her.

Sam talked on a little more about where he'd like to go, if he could, and Rin just nodded a lot. Eventually Sam had to be off to deal with other work, and she was left staring into her cup again.

She jumped when Dimitri dropped into another seat at her table. She *really* had to work on not letting him sneak up on her, and it was only made worse by knowing that he wasn't even trying to do it. He just walked quiet by habit.

"Morning," she said, and hoped he hadn't noticed her start. He just nodded in response as he shrugged out of his coat. If he was wearing his coat, he hadn't come down from upstairs. "Out early two mornings in a row?" she said, with hopefully a light and natural tone. "Must be important business to get you out again."

He stopped, stared at her for a second, then resumed hanging his coat over his chair more slowly. "Not really. I was just out for a walk."

"Oh." He didn't *have* to tell her where he had been. He needn't even think she cared, really. It was his business, wherever he went. Or whoever he had been seeing. Whether it was business or—even if it was that blond over at The Crown and Candle that Tyrone and Weldon went on about, it certainly didn't matter to *her*. "So," Rin said, "what do you think you'll do with that thousand gold pieces?"

"*Not* talk about it before it happens, and neither should you."

He also needn't think he could just push her forever with never a response. "There's no one to hear," she snapped, waving a hand at the room, mostly empty with no one nearby.

"Doesn't matter, it's better to be careful," he said without a hint of apology.

She folded her arms mutinously. "Yes, I know about being careful."

"Good." He traced wood grain in the tabletop for a moment or two, and finally said without looking up, "Might buy a horse."

It was something of a peace offering. "What are you going to do with a horse?" He didn't know how to ride any more than Rin did.

"I don't know." He looked up with a half-smile that was even more of a peace offering. "Might buy a fine carriage to go behind the fine horse."

"Oh, I see. Are you going to buy a fine coachman to drive it? And a fine wife to put in it?"

Something shifted in his eyes, but she couldn't read the expression there. "No. I'd need a lot more than a thousand gold pieces for that," he said quietly, and somehow she didn't think he was talking about the coachman.

Should she ask a serious question? Or laugh it off with a joke? The situation did present a possibility for a range of jokes, some less polite than others. But maybe she should seriously, actually try to find out what he meant, what exactly was making him look like that... She was still staring at him, still trying to work it out, when she heard the captain's footsteps on the stairs. She looked away.

A moment later the captain had joined them, saying, "Good, I'm glad you're both here already. I pounded on Tyrone's and Weldon's doors as I went past. We've got business to discuss."

A day that had begun with more than usual amounts of unease and awkwardness turned into one with a lot of restless energy and nothing to do. It was all right working out a plan for the night, studying the map of the stone house on the hill, deciding who would move where and when and how they would proceed. But then they had very little to do until nightfall. Sharpening knives just didn't take that long, and Rin couldn't muster any interest in any of the things she might have done to pass the time, any of the pursuits, business or pleasure, that usually occupied the day. She had no one she wanted to go see, nothing she wanted to go do.

In the late afternoon, she wound up going for a walk. Just…to walk. A little ironically, since she was pretty sure that wasn't really what Dimitri had been doing in the morning. But she had too much energy and too many thoughts, and at least walking was movement.

Outside The Black Lion, the usual bustle and hubbub went on as normal. She ignored the shouting fight going on between a couple of windows a story or two up, and equally ignored the two or three men who promptly tried to catch her attention. Since they didn't pursue it, she didn't need to do more.

She cut around a group of kids commanding half the street for some game whose rules remained incomprehensible no matter how often she saw them at it. Possibly the game changed from day to day, though the chasing and division into teams and emphasis on only stepping in certain places was consistent in the broad strokes, and it seemed to stay most of the same kids. About a dozen, none over ten years old, and not a clean shirt between them. Maybe some day she'd just ask them about their game but, well, she never had yet.

She passed the bakery, where Sam's pretty Denae would be at work. She passed the fishmonger too, and had to hurry past as the smell brought up memories she'd rather not dwell on.

She wandered along narrow streets and down crooked turns, and eventually, not quite accidentally, wound up back on the street she'd grown up on. The building she'd lived in with her mother was still there, just as sagging and looking as likely to blow over at any minute as ever. She didn't go inside. She didn't recognize any of the faces on the street, though she recognized the expressions—angry or sad or just too worn-down to care much anymore.

Around the corner and up a ways was the marketplace that was prime hunting ground when she was with her first band of very young reprobates. She and Dimitri used to have a good system. Being older and a boy, he had always looked like the more threatening one, and she had been good at playing the saucy, street-wise but well-meaning girl. So for a target who looked too smart to be robbed completely unaware, Dimitri would knock into him first, then dart away. Rin would then be on the spot to help the poor man to his feet, warning him sternly about the dangers of nasty boys like that one—and she could generally palm a coin purse while she did it.

After a moment's thought, she didn't go towards the market, but turned up another street instead. This one led into a slightly better part of town. Not wealthy by any means, but at least the buildings looked like they'd survive the next rainstorm. In this neighborhood sat a little white church with a stained glass window she wanted to visit.

The church door was ajar, which was good since there are some places you just don't pick the locks on. She slipped inside, finding the interior quiet and shadowy, dim except for a few candles here and there, empty except for a few people sitting separately, each intent on his or her own thoughts. That was good too, as she pulled her cloak self-consciously around her. She probably looked worse than she was, but it still didn't feel entirely like the kind of place she ought to be. She hadn't been, for years.

She walked silently around the edges of the room, looking at the windows. It was still bright enough outside that they shone in all their colors.

She stopped in front of the window she had remembered. There was the man teaching. She'd nearly forgotten that there was a cluster of children sitting around him, while the adults looked on. It could be that was what had drawn her eyes to the scene to begin with, when she was a child herself. And then behind the people…there were the green hills and the white dots of sheep and the sparkling blue sky. It was all smaller and simpler than the picture she'd held in her mind, but she could still feel the pull of those wide open spaces.

Maybe that's what she'd do after she got the money. Maybe she'd go find some place like that. Maybe she'd even see who might come with her.

Chapter Twenty-Two

The Black Lions returned to the stone house on the hill an hour before midnight. They didn't take the main road, but swung far around to approach a back corner of the wall, the one they had judged was the most remote from the house.

Dimitri was the first one up the wall, as the tallest and the best at moving silently. He lay flat along the top, looked towards the house for a moment, then reached down one arm to offer a hand to Rin.

She ignored it, setting her boot toes against the rough stone and finding cracks between the blocks for her fingers. Her height could be a disadvantage in climbing, but she liked to think her light weight made up for it. She reached the top unaided, mostly just to prove she could.

She got a leg over the wall, clambered over the edge, and lay on her stomach, minimizing her silhouette. She met Dimitri's glance, then they both looked towards the house.

It stood dark and silent, like a crouching monster, looming even larger in the darkness. A light burned by the front door, probably a lantern by a guard; they hadn't planned to go in that way anyway. No light was visible anywhere else.

Rin and Dimitri looked at each other again, and when he nodded, she did too. They both swung their bodies over to the inside of the wall, held on by their hands, and dropped together.

The wall was maybe twenty feet tall. Easy enough.

Rin twisted around as she fell so that she was facing away from the wall when her feet hit the ground. Her knees were already bent and her palms hit a fraction later. With the ease of long practice she rolled forward, taking the impact on her right shoulder, coming up standing.

A quick glance at Dimitri, and then they both moved forward towards the house, together but a little apart. Some bushes and high grass served as cover, but not enough to be comfortable. Mostly, they had to rely on crouching low and trusting to the darkness. The moon was hardly more than a sliver, and the night was largely black.

Rin let out a near-silent but still relieved breath when she could finally step into the deeper shadows cast by the house, and lean back against the building's wall. They held position for a minute, maybe more. No noise from the house. No sign of anyone stirring.

Rin watched the section of wall they had scaled, but she could still barely see the captain, Tyrone and Weldon when they came over. She and Dimitri had served as a kind of advance guard, a first test. With no reaction from within, the next three attempted it.

She relaxed a little when all of them had gathered in the shadows of the house. First stage accomplished. And even if it was likely more dangerous *inside*, she'd feel better with walls around her. She might be drawn to wide open spaces, but not when she was trying to stay hidden.

While the rest of them remained in the deepest shadow against the house, Dimitri slipped along to a nearby door, to see about affecting an entrance. Rin wished she was close enough to see what he was doing, hunched over the lock. The time crawled interminably when she could only imagine what he might be trying—and what she might be doing differently, if it had been her on this task.

Finally she heard the faintest of clicks, and Dimitri straightened up. He turned the handle—eased the door open an inch—then another—then all the way, and beckoned to the others to come too.

Rin stepped across the threshold just behind Dimitri, entering the stone house for the second time. Even in the near blackness inside, it was easy enough to see they had come in by way of the kitchen this time. Smoldering embers indicated the placement of a large fireplace, providing just a faint illumination.

The kitchen had been the intended plan when they chose this door, after studying the map. The best option, still not an ideal one, considering the possibility of a scullery maid or a hallboy sleeping here.

The captain must have been thinking that too, because with one gesture he directed the others to stay put by the door, and with another indicated to Rin to scout.

She moved forward soundlessly, keeping to the perimeter of the room where she could more easily anticipate obstacles in her path, moving towards the fireplace. If *she* was a scullery maid, she'd sleep near there. Warmest part of the room.

But no one was sleeping there, or anywhere else. Once she was satisfied of that, she turned her head back toward the door and breathed, "Empty." She felt safe enough that no unwanted listener would hear that whisper, which wouldn't carry beyond the immediate walls.

They had all studied the map of the house, and had planned where to go next. Off of the kitchen was a narrow servants' stair, leading all the way up to the attics. The Lions didn't ascend that far, where the servants were sure to be sleeping, but only went up a single flight. This provided easy access to the hallway leading to the second floor gallery, a large room prominently marked on the map as the most likely location of the item they sought.

Again it was Rin and Dimitri who advanced first, while the others held back in the stairwell. It was only a short, albeit tense, walk to the door to the gallery. As expected, it was locked. Rin bent over the lock this time, while Dimitri stood on watch, knife in his hand.

Rin studied the lock visually at first, not that she could see much in the shadows, then drew out a slender pick from the inside pocket of her vest. It did occur to her that the lock could be enhanced with magic, or even that it could be rigged, should someone try to pick it. Someone with a house like this could afford a lock like that. No way to help that though, so she took a deep breath and carefully inserted the pick into the narrow lock.

No explosions, flashes of light or other reaction. She let out her breath and got to work. She had the door unlocked in slightly under a minute, and it swung open without even a squeak.

The others joined them and the Lions entered the gallery, easing the door closed again behind the last one.

Compared to the dark stairwell and hallway, the gallery seemed bright from the moonlight coming through the tall windows. Even a sliver of moon cast something. The room truly was a gallery, each wall lined with paintings, and pedestals scattered throughout displaying sculptures and other items. They still had no details on what they were looking for, so it could have been any of these things.

Tyrone stayed by the door they had entered through, while Weldon crossed the room to cover the door at the far end. Rin and Dimitri both moved near the windows. An attack from that direction was unlikely, but since the windows overlooked the roof of a lower section of the house, it wasn't impossible.

The captain reached into his jacket, and brought out the small diamond flower. Holding it in one hand, he slowly paced around the room, bringing the flower close to each item on display in turn, looking for any sign of a reaction.

While the captain searched, Rin let her eyes wander over the items on display. Mostly sculptures. The bust of a very proud-looking woman over there, a small metal statue of two men wrestling over here, and next to it another bust by a sculptor who had likely been more honest than flattering when he shaped the man's nose. A jewel-encrusted goblet stood next to that bust and was sorely tempting. They could never sell something that distinctive, but pry out the jewels and…no, it was too big, too likely to be encumbering if it came to a quick escape. But the group was already in tacit agreement that if they found something small and valuable, no harm in increasing the expected revenue of this job.

For the moment, best to focus on the task at hand.

The task at hand was not going particularly well. The captain made the entire circuit of the room, held the diamond flower over each object and even by each painting, but it didn't reveal anything. Not that

Lady Diamond had told them exactly how the flower was supposed to react. Not that she'd been terribly clear or informative about *anything*.

Rin was definitely clear that she did not like this job. Not even a little bit. Apart from the reward.

The captain beckoned them together again, by the far door Weldon was guarding. Once they were all closely huddled together, the captain said in a low whisper, "We'll have to try the study."

They had hoped to find the necessary item in the gallery, a relatively removed room. The study was on the first floor, the room right off the Blue Parlor where Rin, Dimitri and Old John had seen Lord Silver before. More importantly, it was just down the hall from Lord Silver's sleeping chamber, making it much more risky to approach.

"Rin and I will go," Dimitri said. "We can get in and out."

Rin felt a tiny flare of pleasure that Dimitri had chosen her for the task with him—and scolded herself for it. They were the quietest and the best at picking locks. She was the logical choice. She had no business getting flattered because he made a logical choice.

The captain nodded, and handed Dimitri the diamond flower. "We'll cut over to the main stair on this level, keep alert for any danger from there." It was a central location, the best for listening for any movement around the house.

They all went out into another hallway, then split in opposite directions. Rin and Dimitri took another servants' stair down a flight. None of the house's obvious wealth was apparent on the narrow wooden stair. Dimitri opened the door at the bottom of the stairs a crack, looked out for a moment, then pushed it open. The hallway beyond was empty, dark and silent. They padded along the soft rugs, and Rin tried to stay alert to all directions. But her gaze kept being drawn to the wooden door at the end of the hall. According to the map, that was Lord Silver's bedroom.

She remembered that cold man staring at her, that shivery feeling she'd had around him, and wished they'd never agreed to this business.

Thankfully, they didn't have to go past his door. The study was closer. It, too, was locked, but Dimitri had it open quickly. The thought occurred to Rin that, for such a formidable-seeming man, Lord Silver didn't have very impressive locks on his doors. Or maybe she should just be proud of Dimitri's and her own skills.

The study was as quiet and empty of life as every other room they'd been through. A fire smoldered in the grate, the only light in the windowless room.

Dimitri nudged her. "Shove your cloak along the bottom of the door," he said softly, "and I'll stir up the fire. We'll never be able to test everything in here without more light."

"All right," she whispered, shrugging out of her blue cloak and rolling it up to cover the crack at the bottom of the door. The last thing they needed was light spilling into the corridor beyond.

Dimitri soon had the fire up to a respectable flame, bringing the room into better view, even if the shadows danced in an unnerving fashion. "Much better," he said, softly but hardly at a whisper.

"Shh!" Rin said with a frantic gesture.

"Wood paneling and books line all the walls," Dimitri said, pointing around the room. "No one will hear, as long as we don't shout or anything stupid like that."

She frowned at him, though it was a fair point. The walls were heavily lined with bookshelves of thick wood, all packed tightly with books. How could there be that much information worth writing down?

The room was almost as cluttered as the shelves. A big wooden desk stood in one corner, covered with papers and quills and other items harder to identify in the dancing shadows. Scattered around the room were small tables, not a single one empty.

"So where's that diamond?" Rin asked. "Let's get this done."

"Here," Dimitri said, holding it up, flickering in the light. "You take it, and I'll guard the door."

Rin hesitated. She didn't want to touch that weird little flower. It was beautiful, but it was…wrong and impossible and unnatural. But she couldn't say that without sounding silly and paranoid. "Yeah, all right."

She held out her hand, and Dimitri dropped the diamond into her palm. She managed not to flinch, and nothing happened when it touched her skin. No humming or burning or anything else. She let out a breath. She really was being silly; it hadn't harmed the captain or Dimitri when they held it.

She headed for the desk first, as good a place to start as any other. Among the papers, she could see a cloudy glass globe, a cluster of dried flowers in a gold vase, and a small chest of some dull metal, maybe lead. No reaction from the diamond flower for any of them.

She turned to start checking the smaller tables when Dimitri said, "Hey, I think I found something."

He had taken a step or two away from the door, to look at something inside the room. He held up a bundle of cloth.

"You think that's what Lady Diamond's looking for?" Rin said doubtfully.

"No, not something for her. Something for you."

He tossed it to her and it unfurled in midair. She reached out her free hand automatically to catch it—a long black cloak. A flash of genuine irritation made her scowl. "This is no time to fool around," she hissed. "And why does my cloak bother you *so much* anyway?"

"Hey, I'm sorry," Dimitri said, spreading hands, "I didn't mean to upset you about it, I just…" He shrugged and looked away. "I just think you deserve better. I think you deserve the best."

She stared at him, taken aback. This was…possibly the most sentimental thing she'd heard him say in…well, in a very long time. She looked down at the black cloak hanging from her hand. She should drop it on the desk, get on with business. But it really would take only a few seconds... Diamond flower tucked in one palm, she swung the cloak around her shoulders, felt for the clasp and clicked it closed.

"What do you think?"

He looked back at her, and smiled. "It looks good on you."

"Right. Well." This time she looked away. "Let's get this done, shall we?" She shrugged the cloak back to free her arms and moved purposefully towards the nearest table.

Three small china bowls sat on this table—one held five withered beans, another held a golden apple, and the third held what appeared to be an ordinary red and green apple with one bite missing, somehow encased in a thin layer of glass.

Lord Silver collected some truly bizarre items.

None of them made the diamond flower react, and she moved on to the next table. This one just held a tea cup with a chip missing in its rim. Maybe it had simply been left there since tea time, but she tried the flower anyway, without effect. The next table held a small mirror rimmed in silver and a red shoe with scuffed soles, the table after that had a large spool of shimmering golden thread, and the third table had a bowl holding four walnuts. No reaction to anything.

She couldn't tell immediately what was on the next table. A velvet cloth draped over something of indeterminate shape. She reached for a corner, and tugged it away.

She stared as the cloth slid down, and whispered, "Dimitri? I think this might be it."

Chapter Twenty-Three

The velvet cloth fell away to reveal a gleaming silver tree. It stood perhaps two feet tall, with a thick twist of trunk and a delicate spread of branches. Even in the firelight, Rin could see the careful, precise beauty of every leaf, of every tiny bud and flower. It was every bit as perfect and impossible as the flower of diamonds, so much in the same style that it was easy to guess a connection.

When she brought the flower in her hand close to the tree, it was no great surprise to see both the flower and the silver tree burst forth with a brilliant light, confirming the connection and the magic in both. The light filled the room and forced her to blink and look away.

It was not a surprise, but it wasn't comfortable either. Before, the diamond flower in her hand had, contrary to what her intellect told her, felt no more strange or alarming than any piece of ordinary jewelry. *Now* it was setting off prickles in her spine, making the hair on the back of her neck stand up, setting off her every instinct that this was terribly, terribly wrong.

She backed away from the glowing silver tree, two paces, three before both the flower and the tree went abruptly dark again. That helped but not enough, and she kept backing up until she could thrust the diamond towards Dimitri. He didn't think there was anything strange about it; let *him* hold the blasted thing.

He took the diamond from her hand and probably put it back in a pocket, though with her gaze fixed on the tree she didn't look to check. "That thing could be difficult to get over the wall," Dimitri said, "but it could have been worse. At least it's not full-size. We should wrap it up again and—"

He broke off as the door of the study slowly opened. Not the door they had come in, but the other one, the one leading to the Blue Parlor. Rin took a step closer to Dimitri, knife already in one hand.

She relaxed a little when the door swung farther and revealed the captain, with Tyrone and Weldon close behind him. Only a little, though—they weren't supposed to be here.

"What's going on?" Dimitri asked, barely above a hiss.

"Guards on the second level," the captain said, pushing the door shut again behind them. "We snuck down the central stair, but they came the same direction and we had to retreat this way."

"So you led them to *us*?" Dimitri said, with an edge of anger that surprised Rin.

From his expression, it surprised the captain too. "It was a strategic retreat with very few available options. They didn't see us so they may not come here at all, and even if they do, strength of numbers is not a bad tactical advantage."

Dimitri didn't say anything to that, and merely looked away.

"Right," the captain said after an uneasy beat. "Two of us can hold this doorway if we need to. Tyrone and I can cover that, and we should put two at the next door to cover a retreat."

"Weldon and I can hold the second door," Dimitri volunteered. "Rin should go into the corridor, keep alert for any threats from that direction if we have to fall back that far."

She didn't love that idea. She hadn't forgotten that Lord Silver's bedroom was off that corridor. And if Lord Silver never emerged, she didn't like the idea of being relegated to the background.

Before she could raise an objection, Tyrone whispered, with one ear pressed to the door, "I can hear them in the next room."

"They still may not come this way," the captain said softly.

And then Rin had a truly terrible thought. "The light," she said, staring at the bottom crack of the door. They had covered the other door. Not expecting anyone to be in the parlor, they hadn't thought of this one.

For a second or two, everyone stared at that door. Then without further discussion or argument, they moved into the positions the captain had dictated. Rin kicked her old blue cloak out of the way and pulled the other door open, stepping out into the darker corridor. There was a closed door nearly opposite the study's door, and she stepped into the shallow niche that provided. Almost idly she tried the handle but it was locked, and this was no time to be fumbling about with lockpicks. Just the doorway would have to do. It wasn't much cover, but it might give her a second or two of advantage, should anyone come down this hall.

As she took up her position, knife in one hand, she remembered about the silver tree. They hadn't said anything about it to the captain or the others. Too late for her to do anything now, but of course Dimitri would tell them. They'd have to find some way to carry it out as they retreated, or this entire operation would all be pointless. The tree would be a handicap, but as Dimitri had said, at least it wasn't full-sized.

Even with the door to the study left open, she couldn't see into the room. She had to mostly rely on sounds to know when the guards came at the far door. That one opened out from the study, making it hard to barricade, but from the sound of crashes, she guessed the captain and Tyrone had pulled a couple tables in front of the door anyway.

Then it was all footsteps, heavy breaths and occasional curses. It was somehow worse to listen to a fight when she wasn't in it. Gave her too much room to think.

The fight was sure to reach her position eventually, and in the meantime she could only wait, muscles tense and throat tight.

Until the door to Lord Silver's bedroom slammed open, and heavy footsteps entered the hall. That prickly, creepy feeling that had overtaken her when she saw him before seemed to precede him this time. She didn't have to see him; just knowing he was there was enough. A tight fist of fear clenched her stomach and she pressed backwards into the doorway. She tried to fight this horror that was sudden and irrational in its intensity, even while her body instinctively tried to shrink back and hide.

It took only seconds for him to come down the hall, and the rush of terror that accompanied his approach grew as he came nearer, until she forgot about fighting it and wished only to hide, to be invisible, to somehow escape his notice.

Her doorway was slightly farther down the corridor from the study's door, but he would come within a foot of her. It was impossible that he wouldn't see her.

And yet—he turned away from her, turned toward the study, and stepped through that doorway instead. The door closed shut behind him.

She exhaled in a rush, staring at the wood paneled door of the study.

And *then* she thought of all the things she should have done. What was the matter with her, she was the look-out! She should have stepped in his way, she should have shouted to warn the others. She should *not* have shrunk away and hidden, she should have *done* something!

She could do something now. She took a step forward, started to reach for the handle of the study door.

A brilliant flash of light showed around the edges of the door, with a crackle of energy that made her leap automatically back. It was an unnatural light, light no candle or lantern could cast, a light that was impossibly, inextricably *black*. She was still blinking at spots in her sight when she heard a low, cold, cruel laugh from within the study.

And then the terror came back. Some part of her recognized now what she hadn't before, recognized that the terror really *was* irrational in its strength. Because Lord Silver was a magician. Lord Silver had cast a spell inside his study, inside the room where all of her friends were gathered. And how would a magician who carried a cloud of terror around him handle a group of people who had come to rob him?

She backed slowly away from that door, the terror telling her to run and run and never stop, and even the more rational shred of her mind was saying that it was too late, she could do nothing against this kind of force, and saving herself was all that was left.

Another blinding flash, and this time there were screams with it.

Rin turned and ran.

She reached the servants' stair at the end of the hall and pounded up it. No worrying about being quiet anymore, it was too late for that. And besides, a magician could surely find another intruder in his house without needing to listen.

She wasn't making too much noise not to hear sounds farther up the stairwell. The disturbance below must be waking the servants who slept on the upper level. She took the first door she came to, coming out on…the second level? The third? No time to worry about it. She turned left at random, too agitated by now to stop and try to remember the floor plan. All she needed was a way *out*.

She halted by the first large window she reached. Probably the third level, hard to tell in the dark how high up she was—but more importantly, this window looked out on a lower rooftop. Good enough.

The window wasn't meant to open, but she was past worrying about niceties. She ran a few steps to pick up a heavy metal vase from a table down the hall, returned to the window. She drew the black cloak around her as a protection, turned her face away, and smashed the vase through the window in a crash of glass. A few more swings of the vase to clear the worst of the jagged shards left in the frame, and she jumped through the opening.

The rooftop was only a few feet down, but it was sharply peaked. She landed with hands and knees spread to absorb the impact, and grabbed for the peak to keep herself from sliding. She caught it, scrambled up, and got to her feet on the narrow ridge of the roof, a flat space perhaps six inches wide.

As easy as running along a wall. Better, even, with the slanted roof right there if she should misstep. She ran to the far edge, hoping to see another, lower roof beyond it.

No luck—she was at the end of this wing of the house, with only empty air beyond. And the ground was far enough away to indicate this was the second level. She turned and slid down the slant of the roof. The bottom edge was at least five feet closer to the ground.

She caught herself in the gutter at the edge, swung her legs over and, similar to climbing over the wall, let herself hang by her hands.

A blinding flash of dark light came from somewhere in the house, illuminating every window at once, and her fingers released their hold on the roof.

Only long instinct let her land safely, her body throwing itself into the customary moves even while her mind was frozen in terror.

She was back on her feet, hardly noticing how she had got there. One step forward, a second, and another flash of light sent her into a run again. She ran to the nearest point on the wall, scrambled over it to land unhurt on the other side, and kept running.

Chapter Twenty-Four

Rin didn't stop running until she could no longer see the stone house, until the hill it stood on was swallowed up by intervening buildings, until she had left the wealthy and elegant part of town behind and was back in the world of dirt streets and slanted buildings. Then finally she stopped in the recessed entry of one such building, leaned over with her hands on her knees, and struggled to catch both her breath and her scattered thoughts.

So she had got away, with no sign of immediate pursuit. Good.

And all the others…Dimitri and the captain and…no, she couldn't think about that right now, about what that dark light and cold laugh signified. Or about the screams.

No, she wasn't thinking about that.

She had to think about what to do now. Where to go.

Back to The Black Lion, that was the only place to go. Magdala had just become her closest remaining friend since all the others— never mind, she'd go to Magdala and do some proper thinking and then…

She hadn't even emerged from the doorway before a shiver down her spine told her that wasn't a good idea.

No *immediate* pursuit. But what if Lord Silver came looking for her?

Maybe that was just paranoia. He didn't even know she existed.

Unless he recognized Dimitri. And remembered the 'noblewoman' Dimitri had come in the house with the day before. And did some investigating. Magicians surely had ways of investigating beyond what was available to ordinary folk, and even someone without magic would probably be able to trace her to the Black Lions, and then to The Black Lion tavern. Would he bother?

She remembered that cold, merciless stare and shivered. That wasn't the kind of man who would let anyone slip through his grasp.

Maybe she could just…pass through The Black Lion. Get some supplies. And see a friendly face. She suddenly longed desperately for Magdala's rough kindness. She could be overpowering, but right now… Only, she'd have to explain to Magdala what had happened to the others.

Explain that she had hidden in the shadows while the magician walked right past her, walked right in on the others who had relied on her to guard their backs and…

No, still not thinking about that.

And she couldn't just pass through The Black Lion anyway. If Lord Silver tracked her there, it would be better for Magdala and Sam and all the others if they hadn't seen her and didn't know where she had gone.

She didn't know where she was going either. It had been one thing to imagine traveling when she thought she'd have a thousand gold pieces in her pocket, and—

She sagged back into the corner of the doorway, a new thought suddenly making her knees go wobbly.

Lady Diamond. Lady Diamond who was going to expect her silver tree at dawn. And not only did Rin *not* have the tree, she didn't even have the diamond flower, and she was the only one left to…no, never mind that.

She had to get away. Very, very far away. Could she steal a horse? But she still didn't know how to ride one. Get a ride on a carriage or a cart? Somehow devise a disguise? Would a disguise even work if people with magic were chasing you, or would they see through disguises?

Or she could get aboard a ship. Surely it would be harder to track someone escaping across the ocean's wide expanses, harder to catch up to anyone too. She could hide aboard a ship. She'd have to get through Docksiders' territory to reach the harbor, but while that would have seemed risky yesterday, today it paled by comparison to the alternatives.

All right. That was, at least, a plan. Not much of a plan, but it gave her a next step. A direction to walk in while she tried to think of what she'd do after that. And while she did not think about anything else.

It was past midnight by the time she crossed into Docksiders' territory. She drew a knife and walked with it in her hand, just in case, though if she encountered a pack of them while she was alone... She'd have to hope that one person wouldn't catch their attention, that she could slip through unseen and onto a ship before dawn. It would be easier to cross Docksiders' territory by daylight, maybe, but much harder to get on a ship. And the thought of Lord Silver, of Lady Diamond, made her want to make no delays.

She got past the old sea wall all right, circling wide to avoid the north tower. Just in case. Lady Diamond wasn't supposed to meet them there until dawn, but...still.

This wasn't an area of town she knew well, so it was lucky the ground sloped down to the harbor. The shore was in sight most of the time. Beyond the wall, she just needed to make it a little farther, find her way onto a ship. That was all.

It was with more fatalism than surprise that she spotted two men turn a corner up the street and walk in her direction. They weren't the first people she had seen tonight, but these two swaggered like they owned the town. They could be Docksiders, or they could be a pair of sailors out looking for fun, and neither were people she wanted to meet tonight.

She was already moving close to the building, hidden in its shadows. She crept forward cautiously, slipped into the side alley to get out of their path. From the mouth of the alley she risked looking back up the street. They didn't seem to have seen her.

While she was looking back at the street, someone within the alley closed a hand around her arm from behind, making her heart jump into double-time. It was her right arm, and her knife was in her right hand, and she'd need a moment to get a weapon into her other hand.

"Hasn't anyone told you little girls shouldn't wander about alone at night?" a man's voice rasped.

If she could buy even a few seconds, distract him enough to use the knife in her right hand, or to wrench free and reach her boot for her other knife... She opened her eyes wide and put on her most innocent expression as she turned to face him. "Oh I know, but my mother is sick and I had to fetch..."

The sentence died away as she saw the man's face. It was familiar. He was big, and he smelled of fish, and she was pretty sure she was the one who had put that mottled bruise by his left eye.

"A doctor?" he suggested, and then his face changed. She tried to turn back away but it was too late. He jerked her arm, pulled her around again. "You," he whispered. "The little lioness from last night's fight."

Could she manage the angle to hit his wounded shoulder again? He'd probably be alert to any trick she might use trying to trip him up. And unless she could incapacitate him almost instantly, any scuffle was going to attract the attention of those other two on the street who, considering she had just met one Docksider, seemed all the more likely to be Docksiders too. She could handle herself with one opponent, but *three* were another story, especially when she was already at a disadvantaged position with just the first one and—

He released her arm, stepped back a pace. Instantly she reached down for her second knife in her boot, had the one in her right hand already raised defensively.

But he was holding up his empty hands and backing another step away. "You let me live last time," he muttered, "and I don't like debts. So consider this as making us even."

Rin hadn't had the slightest idea that any debt existed, but she wasn't going to dispute the question. She just nodded, tucked her left-hand knife into her belt but kept the right one in her grip, and strode past him down the alley. She turned to keep her eyes on him, walking not quite backwards once she had gone past him, her spine and legs stiff all the while with tension.

She didn't run until she had turned a corner, and she was still listening for pursuit for blocks. None came.

As she got closer to the docks, the neighborhood grew busier. The harbor never entirely slept. She skirted around the loudest of the taverns, and tried to blend into the passersby. She pulled the hood of her cloak up, sacrificing some peripheral vision for the hope that it would help hide both her identity and her gender.

It wasn't until her fingers were tugging on the soft cloth of the hood that she remembered that this wasn't *her* cloak. She had left her old blue cloak behind, and this was the black one Dimitri had tossed to her. Because he thought she deserved the best. Just before he…

Still not thinking about that.

Finally she was out among the docks properly, dark hulks of ships looming up out of the water. She had seen ships in the distance before. They seemed much bigger up close, and not as beautiful without their clouds of white sails filled by the wind.

She shook her head, dismissing the thought. This was no time to get nervous about a ship, when there were so many vastly more dangerous things to be worrying about.

So the plan was to sneak aboard a ship. But which one? How could she know which were due to leave soon? Suppose she snuck aboard one that was sitting at port for another week? This was a substantial hole in her flimsy plan.

She wandered slowly along the docks. Maybe she should go back towards one of those taverns, eavesdrop or even strike up a conversation. Might be able to learn something useful.

But that was risky too, to let herself be seen here in Docksiders' territory, and it would leave witnesses should anyone else come looking for her.

What she wanted was to find out what ship was leaving in the morning without needing to talk to anyone.

And maybe that wasn't even what she should be wanting. She *should* want to know just what kind of mess her friends had been drawn into, to find out if there was any way to strike back at Lady Diamond, who had thrown them into danger, at Lord Silver, who had so easily destroyed everyone she cared about.

Throat tight, Rin forced herself to breath evenly. *That* was madness and old stories talking, vainglorious nonsense. There was nothing at all she could do against people like Lord Silver or Lady Diamond with their money and their power and, above all, their magic. Yes, she did want to know more about what their game was, since it had cost her friends their lives, but life was not about getting what you wanted. It was about doing the best you could and settling for what you had to.

"Aren't you coming for a drink tonight?"

The sudden, loud call made Rin jump, but it wasn't directed at her. The speaker wasn't even looking her direction. He was one in a group of three men, shouting up towards another man standing by the side of a large ship, its gangway resting nearby on the dock.

The man in the ship called back, "No, no liberty tonight. We sail at dawn and the captain doesn't want to lose any men to the taverns."

The men on the dock laughed, some good-natured jibes flew back and forth, but none of that was as important as what that man on the ship had said.

Rin took a deep breath, clutching at the knowledge like the gift it was. They sailed at dawn. So that was the ship for her.

She wandered over to a big pile of boxes and barrels opposite the soon-to-sail ship and loitered in their slight cover until the area had emptied. Then she slipped to the side of the dock, crouched down to grip the wooden edge, and slid over into the water.

The water was much colder than the air. She flailed her arms as it closed over her head, forced herself up to get her head above water and dragged in a breath. She caught hold of the wooden piling of the docks, held on for a moment to judge the distance to the side of the ship. She could do that.

She pushed away from the wooden post, struck out towards the ship. One stroke, another, but the cloak was heavy, pulling her down, its clasp pressing against her throat. Kicking in an effort to keep herself up, she reached with one hand to tug on the clasp. She'd just drop it off and—but the clasp was caught and she couldn't deal with it one-handed and after a moment she gave up. She shrugged it into a more comfortable position, wished the wretched thing was lighter, and forced herself forward through the water again.

Within a minute or two she could reach the steep wooden side of the ship, and then she was back to using skills she knew something about. She had climbed wooden walls before, and a ship wasn't so different. She went less than halfway up the side, slipping in at the first porthole she came to.

The dark interior was a confused jumble of shapes at first. She stepped to the side, pressing her back against the wall rather than showing her silhouette at the porthole, pushed wet hair back from her face and waited for her eyes to adjust. When the shapes came clearer, only long discipline kept her from sighing in relief.

She was in the hold, exactly where she had hoped to end up. There had to be food stored down here; she'd find it, steal some supplies, then find a place among the cargo to hide. This wasn't one of the biggest ships in the harbor, it couldn't be going *too* far. She'd only need to stay hidden for a day or two, hopefully. She'd get out at the next port, whatever it was, and set off across country from there.

Going even a couple of days' travel by ship ought to confuse pursuit. At least long enough to get farther away. And then...

She'd worry about "and then" when it came.

Rin was soon settled into a hidden back corner behind a stack of boxes, and by some miracle that could only be accounted to sheer exhaustion, she managed to fall asleep. The rest would be more valuable than keeping a watch; if they found her, they found her, and staying awake to see them coming wouldn't do her any good. She had nowhere else to run.

Rin didn't wake up until the ship was already underway the next morning, a fact she discovered mostly from the way the hold was now rocking, and the way her stomach was protesting that movement. The illness turned out to be a blessing—it was just bad enough to keep her from thinking too much.

After the first day passed with no one coming closer than the far end of the hold, she decided to risk creeping out of hiding during the night, just to look out the porthole to see if she could get any sense of where they might be going. She clambered up to the same porthole she had entered through, and looked out at the moonlit world.

It was a world of tossing waves as far as she could see, and it was not nearly as appealing as it had seemed in her imagination. Mostly it looked like a long, long vista with absolutely nowhere to go.

Maybe she was just on the wrong side of the ship. Maybe land was on the other side.

But when she managed to get to a porthole on the opposite side of the hold, the view was just the same. She slunk back to her hiding place with a growing conviction that she should have found out more about this ship before she boarded it.

It hadn't *looked* big enough to go out across long distances—but what did she know about ships anyway? Maybe they weren't really far out to sea, just far enough that the land was over the horizon? How far could a person see over water anyway?

It had better be something like that, because if this ship was on a long voyage, not putting into port again for weeks or months…she couldn't possibly stay hidden down here that long. And what happened to stowaways on ships?

She could imagine a lot of terrible things, and she didn't want to find out which were true.

She could hear occasional shouted orders from the upper deck, but none of them gave her much in the way of useful information. It wasn't like hearing a conversation, it was just one barked order to do something that usually involved enough nautical words to render it incomprehensible. But she knew what it meant when they started yelling about land in sight near dusk on her second day in the hold.

By then, she'd had enough time to fear being stuck down in the hold indefinitely, until found, that she was willing to take some chances. She risked coming out of hiding as far as the porthole to look for a green smudge in the distance. She watched as it came closer, until she could make out a narrow strip of beach, a not too steep cliff and rolling green land at the top. Maybe more importantly, she could see points of light signifying inhabited land, but they weren't too thickly clustered.

An island, a small one, but an inhabited one. A very small port would make sneaking off much harder, assuming this ship even put into it and she couldn't tell if that was the plan or not. But there was another way off. And the land wasn't very far away by now.

She climbed up onto the narrow wooden lip of the porthole, took one deep breath that was half practical and half emotional, and jumped.

This time, she jumped holding onto a small barrel, hoping it would help her keep afloat. She lost her grip on it when she hit the water, plunging deep beneath the blue green waves, and kicked up until her head just broke the surface. She took a breath, spotted the barrel bobbing nearby, and ducked down again. The last thing she needed was the ship's crew suddenly noticing someone had gone overboard. She had jumped from near the back of the ship, the light was growing fainter as dusk settled into night, and soon more and more waves piled up between the ship and herself, with no outcry from the upper deck.

She caught hold of the barrel, pushed it ahead of her to help her float, and kicked towards shore. It did much to offset the wet weight of her cloak, and the push of the waves helped her along in the right direction.

She was still profoundly grateful when the last wave dumped her on the cold, wet sand of the beach. She scrambled up a few more feet to get beyond the range of the waves, rolled onto her back, and lay staring at the darkening sky for several minutes, chest heaving until she got her breath back.

Land felt wonderfully solid under her, and the empty beach was a relief after the fear of listening to endless bootsteps overhead. Finally she sat up, brushed away sand and wrung out her hair and clothes as best she could. Then she set off up the narrow path on the cliff before it got any darker and harder to navigate. Maybe she could find a barn or shed to spend the night in. She could slip out at dawn, and start finding out about how to get off of this island and back to the mainland.

It wasn't much of a plan, but it was something, and it might have worked. If she hadn't been caught in the morning, and then twisted her ankle when she took a jump out of a hayloft.

Book Three

~ ♦ ~

Chapter Twenty-Five

"And you pretty much know what happened after that." Karina dragged the back of one hand across her wet eyes. She hadn't noticed when the tears had started. They were silent tears that hadn't made her voice catch, so maybe Forrest hadn't realized, hadn't noticed in the shadows. "Your mother made me come in for breakfast and…here we are."

She had lost control of this story somewhere. She had only meant to talk about the magic, because that was the part that might explain what was going on here, now. But once she had opened up her memories of those last few days back home, they had flooded out, beyond her intentions, beyond her conscious control. She had talked and talked until her throat was dry while Forrest sat silently in his chair, clicking through row after row of knitting, never interrupting.

She waited now, sitting on the floor by the big armchair, waited to see what he could possibly say in response to her wild, rambling story. She couldn't even remember clearly now just what details she had put in, whether they were the right ones or whether they would have been better left out, or whether the result had made any sense. She pulled the cloak a little tighter around herself, as though she could hide away from dealing with any aftermath.

She had to wait through a long silence. Maybe he was waiting too, to be sure she really was done now. Finally he cleared his throat and said, "I'm sorry about your friends."

Of course. She should have known. Of course that would be the first thing he said, because he was *nice*. He was the suspicious one in his family, but he was still nice, nice enough that she was sure the twist of guilt the sentence gave her was coming from her, not his intention.

"Yeah, me too," she muttered, wiping at her eyes again. She dropped her tear-wet hand back into her lap, and it fell against her coil of yarn. The braid had spiraled out alongside the story, her hands working with little thought involved, to keep tying on another strand every time she needed one to go on with the braiding.

"You know," Forrest said, voice hesitant, "you talk about them like they're dead, but you don't really—"

"Don't tell me that I don't know, because I *do*. You didn't hear that laugh, you didn't feel that—terror that cloaks him. I did, and I just *know*. They're dead, and they're not coming back, and there's nothing anyone can do about that, and I really don't want to talk about it." She took a breath, and by the time it was filling her lungs she already regretted the words that had emptied them. Not the intent, maybe, but the tone. The poor man said two sentences and she was back to snapping at him.

She exhaled again, another inhale. Some length was still left on the yarn in her hand. She slowly resumed her braiding and tried again to be civil. "I'm sorry I don't have any answers. About the magic, I mean. I don't think I even told the right story. It doesn't explain anything…"

"It was the right story," Forrest said, with all the sureness and conviction that had been in Karina's voice a moment before, so she couldn't help but recognize it. Sometimes, you just know things. Though she wished *she* knew why he knew her story had been worth anything. "The difficulty," he said in a more normal tone, "is to figure out which parts relate to the particular question."

"The question about the magic?"

"Among others," he said, did not explain, and went right on to asking, "So you didn't have anything to do with magic before meeting Lady Diamond, right?"

It felt very odd to hear him use that name. But after all, she had told it to him. "Right. And I didn't have anything to do with magic around her, really. She had magic, but *I* wasn't doing anything then. Not until I got here." She was at the end of all three pieces of yarn in her braid now. She didn't reach for more scraps, just looped all three pieces into a knot at the end.

"That may be the important point," Forrest said, voice thoughtful, as though it was all an interesting puzzle. "When did the magic start happening? That should lead us to the cause."

"It started with your stupid chickens." She toyed with the end of the braid, then began wrapping it around her hand.

"Actually...I don't think it did. It seems to me—you wished Lord Silver wouldn't see you. And he didn't, when he should have. That seems a lot like magic."

Karina swallowed, wrapped another loop of yarn around her hand. It was soft despite all the knots in it, feathery with stray ends. "Or he was just distracted."

"And then on the docks," Forrest persisted, "you wanted to know about a ship that was leaving, and you overheard something that told you exactly that. That sounds like magic too."

"Except those things happened immediately. The magic on Millie, or the vegetable garden, those didn't happen right away."

"Oh. Right..." A pause, then Forrest asked, "Did you actually wish for the chickens to lay golden eggs?"

"No, of course not. And I didn't wish for Millie to start talking. That would be such a stupid wish. I just thought about them and—"

"The magic on Rosie happened immediately," Forrest interrupted. "And you did wish that."

She squeezed her eyes shut. "I didn't mean to," she whispered, maybe too quietly for him to even hear.

Regardless, he ran right along with his thoughts. "Maybe that's the difference, you wished to be invisible and it happened. You only thought about Millie talking, and it took longer. Lots of magic is about mental forces, so that could make sense."

"Maybe," she said, though what he was saying did add together, even if it made her spine prickle too. Was it better or worse to think that she owed her escape to the bizarre, haphazard magic that was suddenly surrounding her? Did it make anything more or less her fault?

But it was stupid to be resisting the idea anyway, hadn't the whole point of telling the story been to piece together why she might now be casting inadvertent, potentially dangerous spells? If it was really something that had started here, on this island, there was no point to telling her story about home at all.

If explaining the magic had been the point. It had been, hadn't it? Everything had got confused somewhere along the line, and she wasn't quite sure that the point hadn't, after all, been to convince Forrest to trust her.

She was even less sure that her story had been any good for that goal.

Comparatively, the magic was the easier question. "Maybe all that back home was magic," she conceded, "but it still doesn't—"

"The cloak," Forrest said suddenly. "You're wearing the new cloak."

So help her, if he said one word about how it looked—Dimitri could comment about her clothes, just barely, but Forrest had no business—*especially* not after this story. "If that's the prelude to a joke—"

"What? No, I don't even know what—no, *think* about it! The cloak's the only thing you took away from Lord Silver's house. And that wish to not be seen, it happened right after you put the cloak on."

More prickles crawled up her spine. She couldn't really have been wearing a magic cloak for days without realizing it, could she? And at the same time—could it be that easy? No curse or magic inside herself, just a cloak that she could take off, just like Rosie's enchanted shoes?

"Where did Dimitri pick it up from?" Forrest asked, and it felt far, far stranger to hear him say Dimitri's name. "Was it just slung over a chair, or was it on a table? Like everything else in there?"

"I don't know, I wasn't looking, I...but it was folded," she said faintly. "Like it had been on a table." She reached up for the clasp, found her fingers hampered by the thick wrapping of braid. "I should have *thought*, I should have known there was something strange about it. It was right there with all those things that looked so ordinary, but why would a magician have them unless they meant something?" She gave up on the clasp and used her yarn-wrapped hand to yank the cloak over her head. She gathered it up, realized she didn't know what to do with it, and just shoved it at the chair seat behind her. "Do you think we should burn it or something?"

"I'm not sure what would happen if we tried. It might be safer to just...put it away for a while. Try to find out about safe methods for disposing of magical items. Besides, we'll have to see if anything else happens, now that you took it off. Shame to ruin a perfectly good cloak if that's not it. But if that *is* it..."

"If that's it, that should solve the problem."

It even solved the question of whether she'd accidentally compelled Forrest to care about her. She hadn't been wearing the cloak when they talked about Marileigh Blue. So that was all right.

And now the magic problem, probably, was solved. The idea held a strange emptiness. She *wanted* the magic solved, of course. But for just a few minutes here, it had served as a kind of…project between the two of them. One piece of unresolved business, now very likely resolved. And now? Now there was silence.

She ran her fingers over the thick wrapping of braid around her other hand. She was surprised by how many, many coils it made, a little taken aback by how long it had grown. She must have been talking for a very long time.

She slipped the fistful of braid off her hand and shoved it in the pocket of her vest, just barely fitting it in. He might not have noticed what she was doing in the dark, and there was no reason to show him how much of his stray yarn she'd wasted on idle fidgeting. Maybe she could untie it later.

And then there really seemed nothing else to do. "I suppose," she said, and rose to her feet, "if the problem is settled, I'd better go. I still can't get off this island for another day or two, but I can at least…go somewhere else…" Where could she go? Not to the inn, to face smiling, acid-sweet Dahlia.

"You don't have to do that," he said, voice soft.

It was not going to help if he was *nice*. "I can't stay here, not anymore."

"Why not?" he asked, as though it really was a question, as though her long, long story hadn't been an answer.

"Because you know who I am now," she said, voice and throat tight. "A thief and a liar."

"Well, yes," he agreed, "but I'm also pretty sure you aren't going to stab anyone in my family."

It was almost a joke. At any other time, when she wasn't so twisted up in emotions, it probably would have been a joke—or maybe it only seemed funny right now, because of those twisted, confused feelings. She couldn't tell. All she knew was that now she laughed— and then stopped because laughing was dangerous. "Well, in that case," she said, and it would have to be enough, because she wasn't sure talking was any safer. She started to move towards the door to the small room she had been staying in, if only because she had to get somewhere else before she started crying again.

"Can I ask you one question?" he asked, as her foot was on the threshold.

"What?" she asked, not looking back, desperately hoping it wasn't going to be something about Dimitri.

"Would you rather we called you Rin?"

She swallowed, whispered, "No," ducked into the next room and shut the door firmly behind her.

Chapter Twenty-Six

Forrest was pretty sure that he disliked Dimitri. It was completely stupid to dislike someone he had never met, and who was in all probability dead, but he still felt it. It wasn't even that he disliked anything *about* Dimitri; he just disliked his existence.

This was hardly the most important point in Karina's story. He knew that. It was just the easiest one to deal with. At least, on a surface level. Getting into *why* he disliked Dimitri might get more complicated. Not that he didn't know why. He knew exactly why. It was just the question of what he was going to do about that.

For right now, he very carefully didn't look at the door Karina had disappeared through, and set about folding up his knitting and putting it away. It wasn't the scarf for Clara. He had been in no frame of mind to work on that tonight; too much of knitting magic was mental, and all the swirling thoughts of tonight shouldn't be spun into his sister's scarf. He had picked up instead a skein of black yarn, the nearest pair of needles, and let his hands go without much conscious input from his brain. Knitting was calming. It had made it easier to not interrupt as Karina's story spilled out.

It was strange. There hadn't really been much in that story to make him trust her. At least, not in the broad strokes, the ones that painted a picture about stealing and lying, about knife fights and picking locks and climbing in windows. Those were exciting, glimpses of a life he had certainly never lived, wouldn't really want to live, except maybe just once in a while. It wasn't a life that should have been reassuring about Karina and her motives. But in the details…about loyalty and friendship, about children playing an incomprehensible game and green hills in a window and not knowing what to do with a fortune…there'd been something in there offering a very different story.

And maybe the point had never been the content of the story. It was the act of telling it that mattered.

Forrest blinked when he realized he had been staring at Karina's balled-up cloak for a good thirty seconds. Right. That was something to deal with. He picked up the cloak from the seat of the chair where she'd pushed it, and shook it out. Nice weight to it, light but solid. He couldn't tell the material, which might be because it was dark—or might not be.

He held the cloak up by the shoulders and tried to get a better look at it in what was left of the dying firelight. And that's when he noticed that the cloak was reaching to within a few inches of the ground. That was too long, much longer than it should be to fit Karina, whose eyes were about on level with his shoulders. In fact, the cloak now looked…about the right length to fit *him*.

Well. If he hadn't been sure that it was magical before, this confirmed it. Maybe this was something Karina should know about. Maybe he should go knock on her door and…

Maybe not. And maybe he should just put this away before anything else happened.

He folded the cloak up quickly (because even magical cloth is still cloth and why create wrinkles if they can be avoided? And some things are just habit) and crossed over to the wardrobe against one wall. It was taller than he was, so pushing the cloak up onto the top ought to keep it well out of everyone's way.

This wasn't a permanent solution, but it would do for now. If no one was touching it and making wishes, that should avoid any trouble. In the morning, they could talk to Master Aurum; he'd know what to do about the cloak.

The cloak, really, was a far simpler question than what to do about the girl who'd been wearing it. The smart thing was probably still to tell her to leave. But he had asked her to trust him and she had—how could he repay that by throwing her out into the night?

Right, he was being thoughtful and considerate and generous. That was it. It wasn't at all that he just wanted her to stay, whatever was in her past.

Or possibly her future, if she was right that there could be a magician or an enchantress chasing after her. If letting her stay here meant putting his family in the path of all that... On the other hand, from the thoughtful and generous perspective, what kind of people would they be if they tossed her out *because* she was in trouble?

That was a rationalization and he knew it. It was even more of a rationalization to argue that, after all, she was only thinking about staying for a few more days anyway. And that she didn't really know if anyone was even chasing her.

It wasn't exactly that he doubted her story, or how dangerous Lord Silver or Lady Diamond might be. But it was hard to *believe* it. To really believe it with the kind of conviction that would justify trying to run from it.

Anyway, he could do nothing about it tonight. He'd think about it in the morning.

In the morning, perhaps not surprisingly, he overslept. By the time he came downstairs again, he could already hear voices. Mostly Rosie's voice. Karina's was much quieter.

"See, I told you it would fit!" Rosie said. "And Clara won't mind if you borrow it."

He followed the sounds into the parlor, and stopped a pace or two away from Karina's room—that is, the one she had been using.

Rosie was kneeling on the bed, while Karina stood in front of the mirror, her back to the open doorway. Karina was wearing a pale blue dress and her unbraided hair fell in dark waves over her shoulders.

He only realized he was staring when her eyes in the mirror met his gaze. "Good morning," he said quickly, and hoped she hadn't noticed how long he'd been standing there.

Karina just nodded and looked away, while Rosie said happily, "Good morning! I thought Karina should have something new to wear, so I found one of Clara's dresses for her. Isn't it pretty?"

"Yes," he said and grinned. "Yes, it is."

Her eyes met his furtively in the mirror, then glanced away again—but she smiled too. She fingered the embroidered flowers along the neckline. "Are you sure Clara won't mind?"

"I told you, she won't," Rosie said. "I promise."

Clara really wouldn't; there were already two cousins she traded clothes with. But that might not be why Karina was asking. "You don't have to wear it," he said. "If you'd rather not."

"But why not?" Rosie demanded. "It's pretty!"

"It's all right," Karina said softly, tilting her head to study herself in the mirror. "It still looks like me."

"Of course it does," Rosie said, plainly with no sense of the import of those words. "Now!" She slid off the bed. "Isn't it time for breakfast?"

It was. Past time, in fact. No porridge today, with Mother away and far fewer people to feed anyway. Forrest cut thick slices of bread off the loaf and skewered them to toast over the fire. Karina and Rosie sat at the table, each one braiding her hair.

This, in Forrest's considered opinion, was absolutely adorable. Probably neither one would appreciate the comment, though, so he concentrated on his toasting and didn't say anything about it.

He was mid-toast when Rosie slid off her chair, one braid clutched in her hand, and darted out of the room. She was back before he'd had proper time to think about whether he should say anything to fill the suddenly weightier silence. She plunked his basket of scraps down on the table.

"I need you to tie off my braid," Rosie announced.

"Oh…right." Forrest looked at the half-browned bread. "I'm sort of…"

"I can do that," Karina said, coming over to take the skewer. She had tied a bit of leather around her own hair, back in its usual single braid pulled over one shoulder.

"Thanks," he said, and went to look in his basket. "What'll it be today, Rosie?"

"Umm…I don't know. You choose!"

He stirred through the mound of scraps. Was there less in here than there had been yesterday? Hard to remember for sure. In the end, he pulled out two white strands and a blue one, braided them quickly together and tied them around Rosie's hair. He pulled out three more while Rosie braided the other side of her hair, and Karina started a new piece of toast.

"You should do one for Karina's hair too," Rosie said, as he tied off her second braid.

He hesitated. "I don't know if—"

"What's good for protection?" Karina asked quietly.

Well, if she wanted him to. It seemed to take longer to find the right strands this time, but he eventually drew out a green strand, a pale blue one, and one of Marileigh Blue. All of those made sense for protection on a theoretical level—and they *felt* right. He braided them together, then handed the strand to Karina. Offering to tie it on her hair might be pushing things.

He took the basket back out to the parlor himself, and on a whim reached into a drawer for something he remembered making a few months back. It was a knit bracelet, made using one of his smallest pair of needles and lightest weight yarns, and cabled to look like a braid. It was a dark blue, and had been knit with a general protection idea in mind, in both the color and the design.

Back in the kitchen, he held it out to Karina. When she raised her eyebrows in query, he said, "It's stronger than anything I might braid out of scraps this morning."

She glanced down at the yarn tied around her hair, then reached out to take the bracelet. "Thank you," she said, and slid it over her hand and onto her wrist.

Somehow, that felt right too.

Rosie did most of the talking at breakfast, but the silence in between her words wasn't an uncomfortable one. After breakfast, she went off to feed the chickens—and to see if they were still laying gilded eggs, and if Millie was still talking, after the horse's trip to town and return by a neighbor after the family had gone. This time, Rosie wasn't going to be back soon enough to keep breaking the silence from becoming necessary.

The silence did linger on, for a minute or two, and then Forrest started to say, "I've been thinking we ought to..." at just the same moment that Karina began, "Today we should probably..." and then they both trailed off.

"Sorry," Forrest said. "Go ahead."

Karina looked down at the table, tracing the wood grain with one finger. "I was just going to say, we should probably—that is, *I* should probably go into town again. To see if there's any news about ships."

He noticed that shift from we to I and didn't altogether like it, but didn't point it out either. "Right. In case that Lord Silver sailed in?"

"Yes," she said, still looking down. She lifted her hand from the table and fiddled with the bracelet around her wrist. "And in case there's one I can sail out on."

Of course. Because that was still the plan, and of course it was the right and practical thing to do, and since he had known that was the plan there was absolutely no reason for the words to make his stomach sink. And anyway, it was up to her, whether she wanted to stay longer or not. "I'll walk in with you," he said, making it a statement and not a question. "I have to handle a few chores, but it won't take long and everything else will keep for a while." He said the words without stopping to think if it was true—then ran a hasty mental checklist and decided it was. True enough.

Karina's forehead puckered slightly. "We can't leave Rosie here—"

"She can come too." Maybe this was ridiculous. Maybe Karina didn't want company. But he had a feeling that if he let her go off on her own, she wouldn't be coming back. And he didn't want that. "Besides, I was about to suggest going into town too. I put that cloak out of the way for now, but that's not a permanent solution."

"What does that have to do with going into town?" she asked, a guarded tone entering her voice.

"I thought we could ask Master Aurum about—"

"No," she said flatly.

Forrest blinked, took a deep breath, and dredged up his voice for calming agitated sheep. "I know you didn't like him very much, but he knows about magic and—"

"I don't want to see him and I don't want him to know anything about me or my cloak or anything else!" She was finally looking up, but she was glaring, so it was no consolation. And when she stopped glaring, she looked away again. "I get the same feeling from him," she continued in a softer tone. "I wasn't sure until I was thinking about it all last night, but I get the *same* feeling. He feels like Lady Diamond and Lord Silver."

The scholar with his piles of books and friendly air felt like the terrifying magician? That seemed hard to believe. "I thought you said Lord Silver walked around with a cloud of terror and—"

"Not *that* feeling. The feeling I had the first time I met him, that there was just…something wrong. I get the same feeling from Master Aurum."

Forrest shook his head. "I don't see how that's different from disliking someone."

"It just is, it *feels* different." The glare was back, and leveled right at him. "And don't tell me I'm being a typical emotional girl."

"I wasn't going to say that," Forrest protested. Why hold him accountable for stupid things people had said to her before? As if he could possibly have lived this long with his mother without learning that women were perfectly capable of managing anything. "But I don't understand why we can't talk to the one person who might actually have answers."

"It's *my* cloak, so it's my decision."

"You didn't even know it was magical until *I* figured it out, and it's currently sitting in *my* family's house."

"That situation can change," she said coldly.

As long as she was still snapping, everything was actually fine. Or if not quite fine, not horribly un-fine either. It was when she got all cold and hard that there was no point in continuing the discussion. That much, he had figured out by now. "All right." He raised his hands in surrender. "We'll try to find another option." Which was not exactly saying that the previous option was entirely out of the question.

But she accepted it. "Good," she said, and looked down to fiddle with the bracelet again. He could imagine how she would have spent a lot of time messing about with locks in the past. It was like knitting. Kept the hands busy.

"So…" Karina said after the silence had stretched out for a while. "I don't suppose Clara has a cloak I can borrow too?"

"We'll see what we can find."

Chapter Twenty-Seven

Karina reflected that a chattering little sister provided certain advantages. Rosie filled up potentially awkward silences so well and so effortlessly, and made what could have been a strained walk into town...really quite pleasant. It made it easy to just stroll along the path next to Forrest, half-listen to Rosie's nearly-independent conversation and think her own thoughts.

The day was sunny, with a breeze that kept it cool enough for walking. Rosie had helped her find both a pair of shoes and a pale lavender cloak that was good for the weather and would be absolutely terrible for hiding in shadows. If a person was doing that sort of thing. It went well with the blue dress, though. Which went surprisingly well with the blue and green braid Forrest had made for her hair, and the blue knit bracelet on her wrist.

Which, starting from the perfectly innocuous topic of the weather, brought her right back around to thinking about Forrest again. At the thought, she managed *not* to look sideways to glance at him—this time. It was very odd, knowing how much he knew, and gave her an almost squeamish feeling to remember it. Why had she included half of the things she'd said last night? About Magdala dressing her up and how strange it felt looking in the mirror, for one. That was not something that had needed saying. Or about Dimitri, for two. She really hadn't needed to ramble on about Dimitri quite so much. It was probably even worse than if she had gone on about Dahlia.

Forrest was almost sure to think that she and Dimitri...and the ridiculous part was that *she* wasn't sure. Yes, part of her had always kind of thought that maybe, someday, the two of them—but it hadn't ever quite happened. And now it wasn't ever going to. And it was too painful to think about Dimitri now to try to figure out exactly what and how much she had ever felt.

Thinking about finding a ship, that was better than thinking about *this*. Even if that made her a little sad too. But this was what she had been wanting ever since she got here, surely. To find a ship, to get back to the continent, to…keep running. Until it felt all right to stop. And when would that be? And who would be there when it did?

She really was being an emotional girl. This was no time to be bothering about any of this, when the important point was to get away before anything else horrible happened.

The town did not feel bigger on a second viewing. Still such a tiny collection of houses. The dock, however, had changed. A ship had come in, one probably big enough to take her back to something like civilization.

Karina stared at the white sails and tried to feel pleased about this.

"Oh look, a new ship!" Rosie announced, Forrest said a very short, "Yes," and Karina said nothing. They headed down the hill into town.

It started out looking as though it would take even longer to get through town on this second trip, because Rosie knew everyone and wanted to talk to all of them. And she was harder to hurry along than Forrest. But on about the fourth house, Rosie encountered a cluster of friends. From the shrieks of excitement, it was hard to believe they had seen each other at school only the day before yesterday. Rosie elected to stay, and Forrest and Karina walked on alone, at a faster pace.

They were nearly to the docks when Forrest remarked, "If you want to go ahead and see about that ship, I think I'll stop by the inn."

Karina stopped walking. "I *said* I didn't want to tell Master Aurum about the cloak, because I don't trust him and—"

"Yes, I know all that," Forrest interrupted. "I was thinking I'd say hello to Dahlia. She'd probably be insulted if I came into town and didn't."

Somehow this explanation didn't make her feel better. She crossed her arms, looked out towards the harbor and said, "Of course. You wouldn't want her to think you forgot where the inn is."

"Exactly." He shoved his hands into his pockets and shrugged. "You're welcome to come too, if you want."

"No, thank you," she said crisply. And she had actually flattered herself that he had come with her because of—well, because of *her*. But if he'd rather run off to see Dahlia, that was perfectly fine too. "I'll just go see about the ship. No sense in wasting time."

"Right. Perfect. So I'll come find you by the docks in a while."

"Fine." They could hardly lose each other in a place this small.

He started off a few paces towards the inn, then stopped and glanced back over his shoulder. "But don't get on a ship and disappear, all right?"

And suddenly she felt just a bit better. "I'll do my best," she said, and continued at a brisker stride towards the docks.

In a way, the docks felt less strange than the rest of the town. Like taverns, docks were docks, more or less, the world over. These were on a much smaller scale than back home in Ilsonine, but they were the same general concept of wooden piers and the piles of barrels and boxes that seemed to grow right up out of the wood. And, of course, there were the boats.

Mostly small ones, fishing boats probably, but there was that one bigger ship, a proper one with two masts. It was similar to the one she had sailed in on—or looked that way to her inexpert eye.

There was some inherent risk in marching boldly up to a ship that might have brought…certain people into town, but if any of those people asked around *at all*, they were going to find her anyway. A town this small, on an island this small, where everyone knew everyone else, offered nowhere to hide. So it wasn't much more of a risk walking into the lion's den, so to speak, and anyway, Clara's dress and cloak felt like a kind of armor. She didn't look like the girl who had been running with the Black Lions in Ilsonine. Not exactly.

And she twitched the hood up, just in case, before she strode up the gangplank to address the man leaning on the railing nearby. His jacket looked nice enough that he was probably of some authority. "Good morning," she called, halting on the gangplank.

The man glanced at her, straightened up, and walked a few paces closer to stand at the end of the plank. "Good morning, miss," he said, lifting a hand to his forehead.

How...unexpectedly polite. It was probably the dress. "I may be looking for passage," she said. "Where are you bound?"

"The capital first. Then on to Gaicaveene."

Karina did some rapid calculations, drawing on a limited knowledge of geography. Gaicaveene, that was at least two countries north of Giramm. Two very small countries, but it would do. Borders counted for a lot. "Good. When do you sail?"

"We were hoping to catch tomorrow evening's tide, miss. It'll be five gold pieces for passage to Gaicaveene, if you're interested."

She was interested. She also had barely two coppers to rub together. "Hmm, yes," she said with a nod, carefully keeping all alarm or worry off her face. "I wonder if we might work out a bargain?"

"Maybe. What did you have in mind?" he asked, and the leer she would have expected to accompany that question back home was entirely absent. It had to be the clothes.

"Well, I can't sail," she said with her very best smile, "but do you need a cook?"

In actual fact, she knew very little about cooking either. It wasn't the kind of thing her life had taught her. But most men seemed to think all women were born knowing how to bake bread, season stew and roast vegetables, and she was perfectly willing to exploit that belief should the need arise. And hopefully she could fake it well enough for just a few days—she had watched Magdala cook.

The man rubbed his chin. "We have a cook...but he could use an assistant."

Even better. "That would be perfect," she said, and gave him the smile again. So that would be that. Tomorrow evening, she'd be on her way. And all the confusing feelings she had around this place, they weren't going to matter anymore. Because she was leaving.

She was already starting down the gangplank when she thought of an abundantly obvious question, a question she should have asked before she made any plans at all. She stopped and looked back, tried to sound casual. "So, where was your last port, by the way?" There were dozens of ports nearby. Surely this was merely a precaution.

"Just came from Ilsonine, over in Giramm," the man said, hooking his thumbs through his belt. "We weren't even supposed to stop here, meant to just go to the capital, but we had a passenger who insisted on being dropped off here. You know how nobles are. Paid plenty for the privilege too, so can't complain. Lucky for you too, it turns out."

"Yeah. Lucky," Karina echoed, and hurried on down the gangplank.

Bad, that was so bad. Why would a noble from back home, from Ilsonine, want to come *here*? To a tiny island with nothing but sheep and knitting? And a girl with a probably magical cloak.

She dug her fingernails into her palms, tried to concentrate on the lines of pain instead of the panic turning her stomach. The important point was to stay *calm*. This could still work out fine, if Lord Silver was looking for her here and she slipped away on the same boat he came in on. Bit poetic, really. Or something. The trick was to elude him until the next evening.

She'd go straight back to the farm and—no, that was no good, she didn't need Forrest and Rosie hunting through town for her. That would be sure to attract attention, draw Lord Silver straight to her.

So she'd go to the inn. Never mind Dahlia, she was the lesser of possible evils—not by a lot, but still the lesser one. She'd find Forrest at the inn, and…and she'd have to tell him that she couldn't go back to the farm. Because how could she, with Lord Silver not just maybe following her, but almost definitely *here*? She couldn't draw him back to Forrest and Rosie and the rest of their family.

She wasn't going to have more people dying because she was scared.

So. The inn. Find Forrest. Figure out where else she could go until tomorrow evening. And then start running again.

As she neared the inn, it occurred to her that maybe she could dodge Dahlia after all. If she circled around to the back, maybe she could find someone else who could get Forrest for her. Dahlia was a comparatively minor problem, but that was still no reason to deal with her if it could be avoided.

A cluster of outbuildings stood at the back of the inn—a stable, a couple of sheds and the like. If she slipped between two of the larger ones, she'd be hardly visible from the windows and could get practically up to the back door before anyone would be likely to see her from inside. No sign of anyone in the yard at the moment.

Until suddenly, as she cut between the buildings, a tall cloaked figure stepped into her path, blocking the far end of the narrow passage.

"Well, well," the figure said. "I thought I sensed something interesting back here, but I didn't expect the Black Lions' little kitten."

Karina froze, heart hammering. Even without the content of the words, the voice and the bearing were unmistakable. Lady Diamond.

Who was maybe a tiny smidge better than Lord Silver, but she wouldn't bet money on it.

"My lady," Karina said, ducking her head. Was it possible to talk her way out of whatever mess this was? "I am…honored that you would—"

"Do not bother with diplomacy," Lady Diamond hissed, stalking a few paces closer. "Didn't I warn you about running? And I really didn't think your little band was stupid enough to try *stealing* from me."

Karina's left hand was at her side, half-hidden in the folds of Clara's cloak, hopefully enough to hide the twitch she needed to get a knife out of her arm sheath and into her hand. People clever enough to watch right hands still didn't always pay as much attention to left hands. "My lady, I swear, I haven't—I would never—"

"My diamond flower," the lady said evenly, and twitched her own wrist, gloved fingers flicking out towards Karina.

A buffet of air slammed into her, knocking her stumbling back and pinning her to the wall, arms stretched out at her sides, invisible forces holding her helpless against the rough wood. She strained to move her left hand, knife clenched in her fingers, and couldn't even ease the pressure digging her knuckles into the planking.

Lady Diamond stepped forward and flipped back her black hood. She had long silver hair—not gray but actually silver, shining even in this shadowed passage. Her face was unlined, her deep blue eyes slanting to an improbable degree. She narrowed those eyes to glare at Karina. "Where is my flower?"

"I don't know," Karina gasped, knowing she wouldn't be believed. "I don't have it." She pushed against the invisible bonds and felt her right wrist shift.

"Do not lie to me." Lady Diamond flicked two fingers, and Karina's head snapped forward and back again to thud against the wall.

"I don't *have* it!" Karina protested again, pain throbbing in the back of her head.

"Hmm. If you don't, then which of your little friends does?"

"None do, Lord Silver killed them all—he must have it!"

She had hoped this would make Lady Diamond go away, to go chase after Lord Silver and leave her alone. Let the two terrifying magicians destroy each other if they wanted to.

This, however, was a tactical mistake. Karina realized that as soon as she saw Lady Diamond's face twist into an expression of rage far beyond what she had shown a moment before. Her voice turned soft, all the more terrifying for that. "You stupid fools let yourselves be seen? You failed in my mission, and revealed yourselves to the man you were meant to rob? You allowed him to discover the plot?"

The wind holding Karina against the wall changed. Now instead of pressing her equally at every point, eddies wrapped around her wrists and neck. And then they lifted, dragging her up the wall until she was dangling a foot from the ground. She twisted and struggled, discovered she could kick against the wall now but that was no good, what she needed was to get her feet on something before she ran out of air and that was happening all too fast…

"Do you have any idea," Lady Diamond growled, "of the magnitude of the *error* you and your little friends have made?"

Sparkles of black were filling the edges of her vision as she struggled uselessly to take a breath.

Her right hand. She'd been able to shift it before. Maybe…

She put all her thought, all her effort into pulling her right arm away from the wall. For a moment, nothing—then it came suddenly free and she reached instinctively for her choking throat, but there was nothing to tear away. All she felt was her own skin, it made no difference at all. She curled her fingers around her neck, no longer thinking clearly, just wanting to breathe, and felt the soft knit of Forrest's bracelet brush against her throat.

And suddenly she was free. The bonds holding her up on the wall vanished and she fell, landing on her hands and knees, dragging air into her lungs, coughing and inhaling again.

She would have believed that Lady Diamond had dropped the spell herself. Except that the lady stepped back a pace and murmured, "Well, well. So the kitten learned a new trick."

Karina coughed again, keeping her gaze lowered, while her fingers tightened on the knife she still held. If Lady Diamond came just a step closer...then they'd find out how magic handled a confrontation with sharp metal.

But Lady Diamond stepped back a pace instead, and Karina risked looking up to calculate how hard it would be to spring forward and get within slashing distance. The lady was looking over her shoulder, back towards the inn. If Karina could just gather herself together enough to take advantage of the momentary distraction—

She was still tensing her muscles to jump when Lady Diamond looked at her again, fixing her in place with a hard stare. "I do not have time to continue with this game right now. But trust me when I say we are *not* finished."

And then she was gone, vanished without any trace, and it was even more disturbing in daylight than it had been on a dark night.

Karina sank back to sit with her legs up and her wrists resting on her knees, gripping the hilt of her knife until her knuckles were white, trying to keep her hands from shaking. She concentrated on breathing, in and out, air rasping in her aching throat. She brought her free hand up to touch her neck. What had just happened? She wasn't wearing the magic cloak, so what had broken Lady Diamond's spell?

Footsteps made her head snap up, raising the knife a few inches before she recognized Forrest's tall shape outlined in the light at the end of the narrow space between buildings. She let her knife hand sag again.

"Karina?" Forrest hurried towards her, knelt down next to her. "What happened? Are you all right?"

"Yes," she said, and coughed again. "Lady Diamond, she's *here*, and..." Her throat was starting to ache in an entirely different way, and his concerned expression was making it worse. "But she disappeared, I don't know—she thinks I stole from her, and I didn't, but—"

"What happened to your neck?" Forrest asked sharply, started to reach a hand out, then apparently thought better of it and let it fall.

She was probably coming out in bruises. Lovely. That would be so helpful for looking inconspicuous. Maybe he'd give her a scarf, that could help... She shook her head, tried to focus. He had asked what happened. "It was sort of—magical wind? She pinned me against the wall, choking..."

"That's horrible," he said, with an intensity that was somehow both comforting and alarming.

"I'm fine," she whispered, closed her eyes and took a deep breath, in and out, then opened her eyes and repeated, "I'm fine. Something broke the spell, I just don't know what. I got my right hand free..." She looked down at her hand, lifted it up. "And then I touched my throat." She stared at the blue knit bracelet wrapped around her wrist.

"Are you sure you feel all right? You should come into the inn; we'll send someone for the doctor. And we can talk to the authorities about—"

"I'm *fine*. Forrest, this bracelet, what is it?" she demanded. "Magically, I mean, what kind of spell did you knit?"

His brow furrowed, confused. "I told you, it's a protection spell. It's not anything special. It's just a standard—"

"The bracelet touched my throat and it broke Lady Diamond's spell." She gathered her legs under her, started to rise. Forrest was quicker, offering her a hand. She took it and let him pull her to her feet. "This must have broken the spell. It's the only thing that makes sense."

He drew her right hand closer, to look down at the bracelet on her wrist. "I guess," he said, but didn't sound convinced. "It's the kind of thing it could do, in theory. But Lady Diamond sounds very powerful, I don't know if—"

"It has to be the bracelet, I didn't do anything." A new thought occurred to her. "What brought you back here anyway?"

"Oh, I was just..." He blinked. Frowned. "I don't know. I just had a kind of feeling, I guess, and I didn't think about it, I just—"

"See, that makes sense!" Karina said, squeezing his hand. "If *your* magical knitting suddenly broke a powerful spell, maybe you sensed that happening, and..." Her gaze traveled from the bracelet to their interlocked hands, and she abruptly let go. "Anyway. Have you got more of these?"

He took a few seconds to answer, shaking his hand out; she hadn't pressed it *that* hard. "Probably, at home. But I still think—"

"Good, you should go home, see what you have. And me, I need to go...where can I go until tomorrow? That boat's leaving tomorrow evening, but until then I—"

"Until then you should come back with us and—"

"But I can't, don't you see? Lady Diamond isn't just going away, she'll be coming back and—"

"*And*," Forrest said, reaching out to catch her wrist, "you shouldn't go haring off alone with some madwoman after you."

"What I shouldn't be doing is leading her back to you and Rosie and everyone else!" Karina said, and wrenched her arm out of his hold. "It's dangerous and I don't want more people getting hurt!"

She watched Forrest do that settling thing he did when he thought she was getting too upset. His chest expanded and his shoulders leveled and his tone got all soothing. "All right. Just slow down for a minute. I still think you should see the doctor—"

"There isn't time for that. And I'm *fine*." Why did he have to worry about her? It was harder to act fine when someone was right there looking concerned and trying to help.

He kept up the soothing tone. "Then at least come back to the house with me and we'll see what else we can use to fight the crazy magic woman. And maybe we can figure out some plans along the way."

She hesitated. She shouldn't do it. She should walk away before it was too late. But she remembered too clearly that hideous feeling of helplessness as Lady Diamond's magic held her pinned against the wall. A scarf, a blanket, something as a shield against the magic was too tempting to resist. That was practical, at least. She tried to ignore the temptation to stay just for the sake of not being alone in this. That wasn't practical. "All right," she said finally. "But Rosie should stay with her friends in town, just in case."

"Obviously," he agreed with a curt nod.

"Good." She never would have guessed that she would start believing in lucky scarves. Or that she'd find herself wanting to rely on Farmboy. "So let's go then." She turned to go out of the narrow alley the same way she had come in, circling around the inn, because she still didn't want to bump into Dahlia if she could avoid it.

"Karina?" Forrest said from a few paces behind her.

She didn't turn. "What?"

"It's just…you don't have to be fine all the time. It's all right if you're not."

Which only showed how little he understood.

Chapter Twenty-Eight

It required no great insight to see that Karina was not fine, whatever she said about it. Forrest wanted to make an eloquent and meaningful declaration about how she could stop pretending to be invulnerable, and how he understood she'd had to put on a fierce front to protect herself before, but it wasn't like that here. *He* wasn't like that.

But considering she completely ignored his first tentative attempt in that direction, apart from her shoulders getting even tenser, it didn't seem wise to push the point.

They didn't say much of anything as they walked back through the town, stopping in to check on Rosie. Karina kept her borrowed cloak pulled closed over her bruised neck, and Rosie considered it a wonderful idea to stay longer with her friends and didn't ask questions.

Once they were out of town and away from idle listeners, Karina started right into the key subject again. "So you understand, right? I'll stop just long enough to pick up anything useful if you have it, but then I need to leave."

"Yes, I know." He understood that *she* thought that. He was less convinced himself that that was the only or best option.

"You know this island—where can I go to hide? Where would be out of sight, where no one would find me?"

"Hardly anywhere. It's not a big island."

She frowned at him as though he was being deliberately unhelpful. Possibly he was. "I don't care if there aren't a *lot* of hiding places, I just need one."

Forrest shoved his hands into his pockets as he strode on. "What kind of hiding place do you need? How did Lady Diamond track you here to begin with?"

Karina's brow furrowed. "Actually…I don't think she did. She said that she didn't expect to see me."

"But that doesn't make sense. If she didn't come here looking for you, why is she here? What's the likelihood she'd just randomly show up where you are?" He liked his home, but he knew perfectly well they were a backwater, not a popular destination for anyone.

Karina shook her head. "I don't know, what does it matter? She *is* here. But if she wasn't trying to find me—she said something about sensing me, I guess because I was nearby."

This sounded like good news. Magic wasn't all-powerful, not even when a practitioner was highly skilled. If Lady Diamond was using a sensing spell instead of a tracking spell, that opened up plenty of possibilities. "So that means you just need to get farther away. There are some secluded islands at the north end of the main island."

"I don't know if that will be enough." Karina bit her lower lip, staring at her feet. "She promised she'd find us if we ran, and now that she knows I'm here, she'll be looking. Have you got anything knitted for concealment?"

"I'll see what I can find," Forrest said, because he wanted to sound positive. Even though it didn't seem likely. Concealment wasn't the kind of thing people typically needed. Not around here. Back in Karina's life before she arrived, it probably would have been very popular.

He tried to mentally run through what he might have around. It was hard—he'd done a *lot* of knitting. Protection, he had knit plenty of items with that in mind, although he'd been thinking more of storms, marauding rams and possibly illness than of crazed magicians. Anything knit for luck might be helpful too, in a general sort of way. But hiding *specifically*, what did he have for that?

Although, they had one garment that was known to provide invisibility when asked. "You could use the magic cloak again."

Karina's shoulders hunched and her jaw tightened. "No. It's too unpredictable."

"But we know it could work, because it did before. It hid you from a magician at close range." His brain raced with the possibilities. This meant she didn't need to go anywhere, she could stay and be perfectly safe. "We should have experimented with it this morning, tried to figure out more about exactly how it—"

"*No.* I won't trust something that casts spells based on passing thoughts, and invents ways to carry out wishes I never even meant to make, and wouldn't have wanted like that even if I did."

He could see her point, and after seeing the way it had all gone wrong with Rosie he was a little leery of that cloak himself. But it *had* been useful before. "We could still experiment with it. Now that we know it's magical, we can be careful and—"

"Knowing only makes it worse!" Karina snapped. "Now that you *know* putting it on means your thoughts could trigger magic, can you really stop yourself from thinking all kinds of things you wouldn't want turned into reality?"

He imagined putting the cloak on, fully knowing the magic involved—and it was true, loads of wishes were springing to mind, some innocuous and some...not. Good weather this season and safe traveling for his family and maybe better bargaining deals when they sold their knitting and even a conveniently-discovered chest of gold, those were all harmless enough, surely. But he didn't *actually* want to wish that Karina would stay, not if it meant she'd be compelled to do it. He didn't want her to stay like that. Not really. But surely he could just not wish that... "With a little discipline," he said slowly, "and focusing—"

She stopped walking, turned to grab his arm and stare into his eyes. "*Don't* think about fire raining from the sky. Go ahead. Try."

Blue. Her eyes really were blue, not gray at all. For a few seconds that was all he was thinking about—then her words got through, and he wasn't just looking at her eyes, he was also picturing sheets of fire falling from the heavens. He frowned, shook his head slightly. He tried to push the image away, to not think of smoke rising up out of the valleys and dips of the island, of his family's house catching ablaze... He'd think of something else, of...anything at all, but the images stayed firmly fixed in his mind. He tried an alternative, imagined water pouring down over the burning island. Now he was just picturing a flooded, smoldering mess... After a few more seconds and a few more circles of thought, he gave up with a loud sigh and grumbled, "Well, now that you put the idea into my head."

"If it wasn't that, it would be something else." She let go of his arm abruptly, took a deep breath. Her hand drifted over to fiddle with the knit bracelet again. "I think I'd rather just use whatever you have," she said in a faint voice.

Even with the darker images still teasing in his mind, he couldn't help a warm glow of pride at that. Hadn't it only been a few days ago that she'd scoffed at his lucky scarf? This was a significant turn-around. At the same time, worry shadowed the pride. Because what if whatever he had wasn't enough? How could his ordinary, simple webs of yarn really stand up to true magicians, masters of their craft, who didn't have any hesitations about using magic far more powerful than he'd ever even thought of?

At least, not ever thought of *seriously*.

If they really were setting the magic cloak aside, then that left them with what he had. Maybe it could work. Especially if Karina was right about the bracelet breaking the spell trying to kill her. Hard to believe, but she had been there.

And there was still one more option to help find another solution. An option he'd just keep to himself for right now.

When they reached the house, Karina went to forage in the kitchen for supplies, still determined that she was going to set off across the hills alone. Forrest went to forage for any useful knitting.

He checked wardrobes and storage shelves and piled anything that might be helpful in the parlor. He didn't notice quite how much it was until Karina came in from the kitchen and looked distinctly taken aback.

"You spend a lot of time doing this, don't you?"

Forrest glanced around at the stacks of sweaters, piles of scarves, and mound of folded blankets. "It's not all mine. Everyone in the family can knit and I just took anything that might help."

A wrinkle appeared between her eyebrows. "Do you know which ones you made?"

"Sure." He didn't see why it mattered, but he did know. He couldn't recite a list of all the things he'd ever made, but put any item in front of him and he'd recognize it.

"All right. Good." Karina knelt next to the couch and lifted up a green blanket. "So what is all this?"

"Basically, most of the blue items have some kind of general protection in them. The green ones are for health, and anything purple is lucky."

"Right. Naturally," she said with a nod. "And what's going to be the most powerful?"

He rubbed the back of his neck. "It's not that simple. There are many variables. One item would be more powerful in one situation and for a particular purpose, while something else would be better for someone else and—"

"What will be best for *me*, right *now*?" she asked, an edge entering her voice.

Right, not the time for theory, even if she was demonstrating a new level of interest. Just, it was a practical interest. He pointed to a dark blue scarf. "To start with—"

Hoof beats outside interrupted. Forrest and Karina looked at each other, and her eyes had gone wider.

"They might just go past," she said in a whisper.

The hoof beats grew louder, and his heartbeat seemed to be speeding up to match time with them. "I think they're in the yard," Forrest said. The window in this room didn't look that direction, an obvious design error he had never previously noticed. "But that doesn't mean—it could be anyone."

The sound of hooves came to a stop, and a moment later came the sound of footsteps as someone dismounted.

"Sure," Karina said flatly. "It could be anyone." She reached for the blue scarf he had started to describe.

This was just silly; he should go see who it was. He started for the door. It opened before he got there, and Rosie bounded in with a smile on her face. "Hello! I got a ride home! I was going to stay longer, but it was *such* a nice day for a ride."

Forrest let out a breath, glanced over at Karina and saw her relax her grip on the scarf. It was just Rosie and a friend who gave her a ride. Everything was still fine.

And then that friend appeared in the doorway too, and Forrest realized with a sinking feeling that things weren't going to be fine after all. They weren't as bad as they could be, but there was definitely about to be trouble.

"Good morning," Master Aurum said with a polite nod. "Since I was coming this way, I thought Rosie would enjoy the ride and it would save you the trouble of coming back for her later."

"That was…very thoughtful, thank you," Forrest said, and snuck a glance at Karina. Her face had gone tight, and she'd pulled the blue scarf into her lap.

Rosie darted past him into the parlor. "Wow, what are you doing with all of this?" she asked. "Did Mother ask you to get rid of old clothes or something?"

No easy way existed to explain what was going on. "Well…" Forrest began, with no idea where to take the sentence.

Master Aurum brushed past him and stepped into the parlor too. "My, you've gathered quite the collection of magical creations here. I'd love to examine them more closely. But I'd best start with that magical cloak that's been causing so much trouble."

That did it.

"You *told* him," Karina said, rising to her feet and glaring at Forrest, scarf still clutched in one hand.

"You have a magical cloak and you didn't tell me about it?" Rosie protested. "That's so exciting! Why do I get left out of everything?"

"I was going to tell you," Forrest tried. "Um, both of you. I just…" He just hadn't expected Master Aurum to come this quickly. He had thought he'd have time to explain to Karina. Later. Because it would have somehow been easier, later. Maybe.

Karina's glare was burning holes into him. "We agreed to keep this a secret, to look for other options."

He'd been prepared for this reaction. He had a defense ready. Only it seemed suddenly flimsier than he'd thought. He spread his hands, tried to look innocent. "Technically, I never actually agreed. I said we'd look for other options; I didn't say we wouldn't tell Master Aurum too."

"But you knew how it sounded," she said in a very small voice. "So you lied to me."

Not *technically*. He had actually said hello to Dahlia at the inn, so that wasn't quite a lie either. "I didn't…" But without even saying it, he knew this defense was going to sound very stupid out loud.

He hadn't noticed moving closer until she took a step back and turned away. And that was when you could tell it was bad. When Karina stopped firing back.

"Don't fight," Rosie said, gaze darting between the two of them. "How can you fight about something as amazing as a magic cloak?"

"I do apologize for creating such strife," Master Aurum said, voice smooth. "However, now that I am here, I think it would be wisest for me to examine the garment in question."

Forrest hesitated, then asked, "Can you tell us how to use it safely?" The damage was already done from speaking to Master Aurum to begin with. It would do no good to not ask him questions now, and they might as well get something useful out of this. Maybe Karina was right, maybe it was just too hard to not think of the wrong things—but maybe they could find a way around that.

"I can certainly try to offer advice," Master Aurum answered. "From the effects we have seen, it seems to be a remarkably powerful object with a great many potential abilities."

"Why should we believe you know anything of use?" Karina said coldly, still keeping a shoulder turned towards Forrest. "It's not like you did before. You kept saying there was a Good Fairy casting spells."

Forrest gritted his teeth; just because she was upset with *him*, that was no reason to be rude to Master Aurum, who was only trying to help.

"And in a sense, I was correct," Master Aurum said with no sign of taking offense. "I have no doubt that a Good Fairy enchanted your cloak. They have been known to do such things quite regularly. Invisibility cloaks are a common gift they grant to heroes, although your particular item seems to be far more diverse. If also less predictable."

"And more dangerous," Karina snapped.

Master Aurum's face stayed calm. "All magic has inherent risks." His gaze drifted to the top of the wardrobe. "I believe that is the cloak in question?"

"Is that it?" Rosie asked, face lighting up at the prospect. She scrambled onto the wicker chair next to the wardrobe. "I'll get it!"

"Rosie, wait," Forrest said, right as Karina said, "Don't do that!"

They had both started towards Rosie, and both stopped when her hands closed around the cloak and she dragged it down. Forrest exchanged a glance with Karina, could tell she was having the same thought. What if Rosie made a wish now? She wasn't wearing the cloak, but was holding it enough? And how badly could things go wrong if an unthinking little girl wished, using a cloak that made its own interpretations on the wisher's intentions?

Fire raining from the sky drifted right through his thoughts again, in sudden, horrifying detail. But Rosie wouldn't think of *that*.

"Rosie, give me the cloak," Karina said, voice too controlled, extending one hand towards her.

"How does it work?" Rosie asked, holding the cloth up, scrunched between her hands. It didn't look like enough cloth suddenly—but it must have shrunk, to be the right size for a little girl. "Will it turn me invisible if I wear it? Is there a magic word to use?"

"Give it to me and I'll show you," Karina coaxed.

"No," Master Aurum said, staring at the bundle of cloth in Rosie's hands. "It's obviously dangerous. Give it to *me*."

Maybe, like everyone else, he just meant to protect Rosie. But the words had a harsh edge that made Forrest look at him in surprise. The magic scholar had never been anything but perfectly genial, but suddenly he remembered again that Karina claimed he made her spine prickle.

Rosie's lower lip pushed out rebelliously. "It's not *your* cloak," she told Master Aurum. "I recognize it. It's Karina's. Maybe I should wish that you can't use it. What would *that* do?"

Master Aurum's voice came a little louder than it should have. "You cannot start making wild wishes. That cloak is a very powerful item which none of you understand. Now *give it to me*."

Forrest stopped edging towards Rosie, and started edging towards Master Aurum instead. He was surely overreacting. But he didn't like that tone or the expression on the man's face, and protecting his sister came instinctively.

It didn't surprise him at all when trying to intimidate Rosie didn't work. Her eyes narrowed, and she pushed the cloak towards Karina. "Here, it belongs to *you*."

Karina took the cloak, gathered it up against her chest, and kept her gaze on Master Aurum all the while. "I don't think anyone who wants this cloak so much should have it."

Master Aurum's gaze seemed locked on the cloth in her arms. "This is not a game! Do you have any idea of the power of that object?"

"I thought you were here to *tell* us about that," Forrest interjected, folding his arms and trying to look imposing. Not that it had ever worked very well with Karina. Not that he was even certain it was necessary now. "To offer recommendations. No one said anything about you taking it." This had to be some kind of misunderstanding. Maybe he was misinterpreting Master Aurum's alarm about the power of the cloak into something threatening—probably because Karina had him expecting villains to come popping up out of nowhere.

Sure enough, his words seemed to puncture the strange tension around the scholar. He could almost see Master Aurum pulling himself together, straightening his back and smoothing his expression into one of calm understanding. "Yes, of course. I certainly didn't mean to create any alarm—but seeing the item now, separate from its wearer, I can see that it is much more powerful than I anticipated. I really think it would be best if you give it to me. To examine." He extended his hand towards Karina.

She backed away, with no softening of her expression. "I didn't trust you to begin with. I'm not going to do it now just because you start smiling again."

"Give me the cloak," Master Aurum repeated, tone gone quiet and not at all reassuring. "It's far too dangerous to fall into the wrong hands."

"Yes," Karina agreed, "that's exactly what I've been thinking." And in a quick movement, she turned and threw the bundled cloak into the fireplace behind her. There were only banked embers there, yet the moment the cloth touched them, it shot up in bright flames.

"You fool!" Master Aurum shouted and lunged towards the fireplace, with Karina standing in the way.

Forrest was faster, catching him by the arm and hauling him backwards. He may have wound up rescuing Master Aurum (not his original intention), considering Karina had her knife out already, raised in one hand.

"I think you'd better sit down," Forrest said carefully. He glanced around the room, at Rosie still crouched on top of the chair, watching it all with wide eyes, at Karina with her knife up, at Master Aurum with his face twisted in rage, arm tense in his grasp. The whole thing felt ridiculous, the kind of hostile confrontation that couldn't possibly be happening in his family's parlor. "I think we'd all better just sit down."

Before anyone could move, the fire belched out an enormous cloud of smoke, setting everyone coughing. Much more disconcertingly, the cloud was pink. Bright pink, shot through with gold sparkles.

Chapter Twenty-Nine

How could a black cloak give off *pink* smoke? Karina coughed and waved her free hand in front of her face, trying to clear the clouds. With her other hand, she held onto her knife. She could still make out the murky shape of Master Aurum through the haze, and if he tried anything in the confusion, he was going to find her ready.

Possibly this was an overreaction. Forrest would say it was. But she had seen the man's face when she threw the cloak in the fire, before Forrest pulled him back. That was a man who was prepared to commit violence. He was going to find out he'd picked the wrong victim if he tried it.

The haze was not too thick for Karina to see when another figure suddenly appeared in the middle of the room. She thought of Lady Diamond, with her sudden appearance trick—but this silhouette seemed too wide. And also... Karina squinted. Was the smoke particularly dense by the floor, or was the new arrival hovering a foot off the ground?

"Oh dear, this is *most* unpleasant!" an unfamiliar voice announced, high-pitched and disapproving. The woman waved a hand, and the smoke spiraled together, whisking in from the corners of the room in puffs and swirls. It condensed down into a small bright ball, and floated spinning above her palm for a few seconds. Then she closed her hand and it vanished.

In the now clean air, there could be no question that the woman was hovering. Probably because of the little wings extending out through her pink dress, flapping madly. A gentle fall of sparkles descended from no particularly clear source, accumulating on the floor beneath her in a pile only slightly more golden than her blond hair.

Karina rubbed the back of her hand over her eyes. Of all the weird magic she'd seen recently, this achieved a new level. Unthinkingly, she glanced at Forrest, ready to ask if *this* was considered normal around here—but he was staring at the woman with an expression that made it clear the answer was no. And she remembered she was angry with him before she actually said anything. She looked away before he intercepted her gaze.

"Are you a fairy?" Rosie asked in tones of hushed awe, breaking the stunned silence.

The sparkling woman smiled at her approvingly. "That is exactly right!" She held out her hands, palms forward, and curtsied slightly. "I am Marjoram, and I am a certified Good Fairy, so there is no reason to be alarmed."

Karina didn't care what the floating lady said, the fact that she was *floating* was sufficient reason to be alarmed. Or at the least, extremely wary. She tightened her grip on her knife, even if it probably wasn't the right weapon for the situation.

"It appears that someone just destroyed one of my gifts," Marjoram said, hands firmly on her hips now, "*accidentally*, I am sure."

If this woman had turned that cloak loose on the world, then Karina felt they could safely skip past wary and go right up to alarmed. All the more so judging from the edge that had entered her voice on 'accidentally.' She shifted her stance, moving a few paces to get her back against the wall next to the fireplace. It probably wouldn't help, but it made her feel better. She glanced at Forrest, who was still staring at the fairy but had also moved to stand between Master Aurum and Rosie. So he wasn't totally unaware.

Marjoram glanced around the room, apparently taking its occupants in fully for the first time, and a frown appeared on her face. "Oh, but I don't know any of you! How did you get one of my magical cloaks? None of you are heroes or princes!"

Karina knew she obviously wasn't one, but how could the fairy know that Forrest wasn't? Irritation joined alarm. "Those are the only people you give magic cloaks to?"

Marjoram flipped golden curls over her shoulder and said, "Well, my dear, I can't just go giving them to anyone! I certainly don't remember giving one to any of you. How ever did you get it?"

"Sort of by accident," Karina answered, because that was probably better than saying, sort of by stealing it. "And I can't imagine it does your heroes or princes much good anyway. All it did for me was cause trouble."

Marjoram sighed loudly, giving off an extra huff of sparkles. "Well, of *course* it did! You weren't the person it was intended for. All my magical cloaks are attuned to their recipients, so it's not at all surprising that it went a bit…off when *you* tried to use it."

That made some sense—but there was too much disdain in that *you* for Karina to forgive the Good Fairy for her wildly unpredictable cloak.

"Not to mention…" Marjoram looked around the room with a puzzled frown. "Interference from other magical power would create complications as well, and I am sensing a *remarkable* amount of power present. You are not the sort of people who ought to have this much magic. I really think it is my duty to investigate further."

Master Aurum, nearly forgotten in the face of this new crisis, reclaimed attention with a sigh and the remark, "I was hoping you wouldn't say that." He lifted one hand, holding up a small glass bottle that Karina was sure he hadn't had before the smoke billowed up.

"Now just a moment there, young man," Marjoram said, sparkles going brighter. "Just what do you think—"

Master Aurum spoke over her in three ringing words that Karina knew she couldn't pronounce. She wouldn't want to try, when just hearing them made her spine prickle and her whole body shiver.

Marjoram's cloud of sparkles started whirling around her in little eddies and spirals, not unlike the pink smoke had a few moments before. Then the cloud began to compress down—and in the center, Marjoram began to shrink.

"I really must protest!" the Good Fairy shrieked, voice already noticeably higher.

She could protest, but she apparently couldn't do anything more than that. She shrank and shrank, and in a spinning whirl of glitter she soared across the room and was dragged down into the bottle. Master Aurum rammed a cork into the bottle neck and for a moment, all was quiet.

"Wow," Rosie said, one arm around the back of the chair she was still crouched on, eyes shining.

"You said you couldn't do magic!" Forrest said, in tones of accusation and betrayal.

"Yes, I know," Master Aurum said with a nod. "And all you trusting people believed me. As if I could possibly *sense* magic without being able to *do* magic."

"That's what I *said*," Karina said, unthinking, turning her head to smirk at Forrest.

"You didn't really know either," he snapped, "you were just guessing."

Rosie piped in with, "What are you going to do to the fairy? Why did you put her into the bottle? Why did you have a bottle to trap a fairy with anyway?"

"She wasn't my intended target," Master Aurum said, possibly answering the third question. "But too good an opportunity to miss." He held up the bottle to look at the sparkling glow within. Karina could just make out the tiny shape of Marjoram inside the pink and gold haze. "Likewise I hadn't intended to reveal my magical ability, but situations arise."

"What are you going to do now?" Karina demanded, still hanging onto her knife as though it was somehow going to help.

Master Aurum smiled at her. It made her skin crawl. "Isn't it funny in stories when people reveal their entire plans just because someone asks? So utterly unrealistic."

"That's not an answer," Forrest said.

"Yes, I know," Master Aurum agreed. And then he took two long strides to his left, neatly stepping around Forrest, and seized Rosie by the wrist.

"Hey!" Rosie protested and Forrest and Karina both lunged forward, but before they could get there Master Aurum had vanished.

And Rosie had vanished too.

Forrest went very pale, stared at the empty chair, and said several words that Karina had only heard in the worst taverns and was surprised he knew. At least, she would have been surprised, if there had been room for that emotion in between the waves of horror and dread and general, unfocused terror.

Don't lose control. It was the first rule, the most important rule. Losing control was how people got killed. Panic didn't help anyone. Don't panic.

"We need a plan." Her voice wasn't shaking, so that was something.

"A plan?" Forrest repeated. "My sister vanishes, and you want to make a *plan*?"

"What else can we do, *not* make a plan?"

"I—no, but—what kind of plan can we possibly make for—" He gave up, gestured inarticulately at the empty chair.

Karina pressed her fingertips and palms together, took a careful deep breath. "First question, can we find them? Where would he go?"

"How should I know?" Forrest growled, and with another curse he kicked the nearest leg of the vacated chair. It wobbled, tipped, fell over with a crash.

Karina stared at the fallen chair for a second, then opted to just ignore the whole thing. "Where were you going to suggest I hide?"

"What? What does that have to do with—"

"You said there weren't that many places to hide, so maybe he's in one of them. Oh wait, Lady Diamond!" The thought struck her, puzzle pieces tumbling together in her mind and a few of them fitting. "She wasn't here looking for me. What are the odds two powerful magicians would be on the same small island at the same time by chance?"

"I don't know, what are the odds you'd land in the same place as Lady Diamond? Maybe none of it's connected, maybe—"

"I wished," Karina said, the idea suddenly falling into place, another corner of the puzzle coming clear. "On the dock, just for a second, I wished I could find out what my friends had gotten mixed up in. So the magic cloak got me on a ship going to the same place as Lady Diamond." She felt a shiver and hunched her shoulders. She didn't like the idea of magic manipulating her actions that way. She didn't like it at all.

Forrest had jumped to something else to not like. "What if Lord Silver shows up too? If he's connected…"

If she thought about Lord Silver, she wasn't going to be able to deal with anything, and they couldn't afford that. "Maybe he will, maybe not, can't do anything about it," Karina said briskly. If only she could get the idea out of her head as easily as she could get it out of the conversation. She started pacing across her corner of the room, nervous energy going into her feet and carrying her nowhere. "What matters is Lady Diamond and Master Aurum are probably connected and they must plan to meet somewhere out of sight. They won't want enact a big magic spell right over Dahlia's head."

Forrest frowned, but looked thoughtful, not disagreeing. "But why would they want *Rosie*?"

"I don't know." But probably it had been planned. She kept pacing while a couple more pieces locked into place. Master Aurum had brought Rosie back from town, suggesting he had planned to abduct her all along. Should she point that out to Forrest? No, it would probably just upset him more. "We can figure that out when we find them. The important thing is where they would have gone and—"

"The old castle on the north island," Forrest said.

"What's that?"

"It's…an old castle." He grimaced, waved a hand. "No one uses it anymore, haven't for centuries. It's the most out of the way place someone might go."

Karina turned on her heel to face him, clapped her hands together once. "Great, brilliant! Can we get there?"

"I guess, if we borrow a boat…" Forrest shook his head. "This is crazy, we can't just—charge off, we should find my parents and—"

"That'll take too long. They were going south, right? Wrong direction."

"Then we should go to the village, talk to the princes, they have guards and—"

"You really think they'd listen to us?"

He stared at her as though this made even less sense than anything else. "Yes. Of course."

Well, if Dastan was a fair representation, maybe they would. "That's not really the point, the village is miles away, and even if they listen it'll take forever to get anything organized and decided." She stepped closer, seized his hands. "*Listen* to me. You and I have clearly led different lives. I don't know anything about going to other people for help, about having other people to trust and rely on. But I know everything about stepping up and dealing with a situation because someone has to and no one else can. And that is what we need to do. Right now."

He stared into her eyes for a long moment. Then he slowly exhaled and said, "All right. All right then." He looked away, gaze roving over the piles of knitting. "There's nothing at all here that can be used as a weapon, unless you want to stab someone with a needle, but some of it might be able to deflect spells. That wasn't what it was intended for, but if the one on your wrist worked, some of these others should too."

"Good," Karina said, and tugged her hands free. "You figure out what to bring, I need to change back into my own clothes." She was not going to storm a castle wearing a dress. "Only pick things you made, all right?" she tossed over her shoulder as she headed for the adjoining room.

"My mother's much better than I am—"

"And I'm not trying to insult your mother, but we haven't tested hers, and we know yours worked." She ducked into the room and pulled the door shut behind her.

Then she took three careful breaths, waiting to see if she was going to crack now that she had the privacy for it.

No—buzzing, terrified energy still ran through her and she had no time for collapsing right now. That would have to wait until later. Right now she had to help a little girl who had never hurt anyone and who didn't deserve to be in the mess she was in now, just because her family had taken in a mysterious stranger with magicians chasing her.

Maybe this wasn't really Karina's fault; Master Aurum had probably planned to abduct Rosie with no influence by Karina at all. But the thought didn't make her feel less responsible.

She shook herself, moved over to the bed where her clothes were folded up at the foot. It only took a moment to slide out of Clara's dress and back into her own shirt and pants. It was an odd feeling, stepping back into something that felt familiar even while it didn't quite fit right anymore. Her boots were still glass (she checked) so she'd have to make do with Clara's shoes. Or barefoot, if necessary. Her knife was in its sheath on her arm, and she was going to pick up a few of Lynette's kitchen knives on the way out; not perfect, maybe useless against magic, but some small comfort.

That just left her leather vest. She pulled it on, smoothed down the front, and felt an unexpected lump in one pocket. What now? She reached in before she remembered what it was, and pulled out the coil of braid she had made the night before, while she talked to Forrest.

She'd just toss that aside, and—instead she frowned suddenly, noticing something as she looked at it for the first time in the light. She let a foot or so unroll from the coil, traced one strand. Marileigh Blue. Of all the random scraps in Forrest's basket, she'd managed to pick up the rare and expensive one. Not just the one piece either—she could see the distinctive blue-green shade all throughout the coil in her hand, even though no single piece was more than a foot long. That was…peculiar. How had she possibly managed to do that, unintentionally, in a room too dark to even see what yarn she was picking up?

"Aren't you ready yet?" Forrest called from the next room.

Karina jumped guiltily, balled up the braid and crammed it back into her pocket. "Yes, coming." She pushed out the door to the parlor.

Forrest was standing by the opposite door, pack over one shoulder, all but twitching with impatience. He had also righted the fallen chair, and in some way she couldn't define, that made her feel better. It was what she would have expected from him.

Chapter Thirty

He should have been faster. Smarter. He should have done *something*. Instead of just letting the crazy magician take his sister.

And he wasn't at all sure that what he was doing now was going to help.

"What if this is the wrong place?" Forrest said, staring up at the old castle as he clambered out of the rowboat onto a narrow strip of sand. The cliff loomed overhead, blocking out most of the light, leaving him cold in its shadow.

They had covered the two miles to the northern end of his island in what he knew objectively was rapid time but had felt agonizingly slow, and 'borrowed' the first rowboat they found unwatched along the shore. And now they were here.

Here was nothing but a craggy pile of rock, maybe half a mile across at any point, and the castle was just another craggy outcropping at the highest point. Moss had grown up the sides, one of the two towers had lost part of its wall, and the whole thing looked like the day after the end of the world.

"If it's the wrong place, we'll come up with a new plan," Karina said, climbing out of the boat behind him. "Maybe we'll go bother the royals about it, like you said." She sounded so calm. Forrest resented and appreciated it in equal measure, too confusing a mix to settle on an appropriate response.

He headed for the cliff, straining to see any movement in the castle above them, feeling a lump in the pit of his stomach as big as the ruined towers. If it was dark, they might have seen lights in the windows, but too much sunlight shone for that. It was fine to say they'd go get help if this was the wrong choice—but there hadn't been enough time to get help *before* they came here. If they needed a second plan, it was already too late.

And nothing said this plan wasn't too late anyway.

"We can get up to the top over here," he said grimly, even though she was already following him.

"No real cover," Karina commented from behind him as they started up the steep and narrow path, "although at least we're in shadow from the cliff..."

"Like that would help with magicians," he muttered. "Besides, we have magical knitting, remember?" Like that was going to help either. He kept his head down, kept trudging, and wasn't surprised when she didn't reply.

Funny, really. Somehow she'd become the believer, while he couldn't convince himself that a couple blue scarves and knitted bracelets were going to do any good against real magicians. Because what he did, that wasn't *real* magic. It was magic, sure, but it was the kind of magic that just...nudged life, made healing happen faster, or helped a little girl remember something she really did know anyway for a test. Sure, the blanket had had a dramatic effect on Rosie's dancing, but that was the most powerful thing he'd ever knit, and it had only been going up against an unthinking, unintentional wish. Not a magician intent on doing harm.

He did have the blanket rolled up and shoved into the pack on his back. It had saved Rosie once already.

By the time they reached the top of the cliff, they'd encountered absolutely no fire raining from the sky, no avalanches, and not even any burst of gold sparkles and pink smoke.

Forrest tried to be glad about that, but right now even hostile magic might have felt reassuring, proof that he wasn't wasting Rosie's only chance by making the wrong choice.

It was only a brief distance across the clifftop to the nearest wall of the castle, and he pushed past the shortness of breath from the climb to keep going forward.

"There's a broken door. This way." He turned left along the wall without looking to see if Karina was coming. The door was where he remembered it, the way he'd got inside the one time he'd been here, when he'd been young and foolish and friends were daring him to spend the night in the haunted castle.

That had seemed frightening at the time, utterly laughable now.

"I should go first," Karina announced, "in case it's a trap." She had a knife in her hand, sitting there casually, as though that was a perfectly natural thing.

Maybe it was a trap. But Rosie was *his* sister, and what was Karina going to do with a knife against a magician anyway? He shoved the decaying wood panels aside and took a long stride across the threshold.

For just an instant, mid-stride, something felt—off. Like the air was thicker, or something was pushing him back. But then his foot came down on the flagstones of the old kitchen and the feeling passed. His gaze darted around the interior, shadowy and dim but apparently empty of everything but dust and cobwebs. At least, no ghosts or guards came jumping out of the corners. Neither did Rosie, but that obviously would have been too easy.

"You *had* to do that?" Karina snapped from outside the door and started to step inside.

"Wait!" Forrest said, turning back. "I felt something…I think some kind of barrier is across the doorway." Finally. Magic. It didn't feel in any way reassuring after all, didn't in any way alleviate his overall fear. In fact, it only made everything feel more real.

Still outside, Karina frowned and reached up her empty hand, palm forward. It moved through the air, then stopped, just on level with the threshold. "I can feel something. It's almost like glass, but…"

Her forehead wrinkled, and her hand moved forward, just a fraction. "…it gives a little. It doesn't feel like I can push through, though."

"It didn't resist that much when I stepped in." He'd have to go on by himself. He couldn't wait for Karina, not with Rosie in danger.

He didn't want to go on alone, but what choice did he have?

"Oh wait, I know!" She dropped her left hand and lifted her right instead, sleeve sliding back far enough to show the knit bracelet. She pushed farther, hand reaching through the doorway. "I can still feel it, but it's not resisting the same way. The scarf probably got you through—so if I just step in…" She did, coming up next to him in two strides. "There!"

He felt more relieved than he wanted to admit, a relief that lasted only a few seconds before the larger fears came crowding back. "So now we know something magical really is going on here," he said, turning away from the doorway, towards the interior, towards whatever was here to be faced.

"And the knitting really is making a difference," Karina pointed out, with a surface cheerfulness that failed to hide the tension beneath it.

"Apparently." So now he *had* to do something. Now it really was up to him.

He made four steps across the kitchen before he realized Karina hadn't moved. He stopped, fighting the instinct to keep moving, to get on with this. "What now?"

She shrugged, looking more uncomfortable than casual. "This feels like the moment when you'd want to tell me I don't really have to do this. I thought we should get that over with before we're farther in and it gets more inconvenient."

It was true that she didn't. Rosie was his sister and he loved her and he *had* to do anything to try to save her, but Karina barely knew Rosie, wasn't responsible at all. He had known that, but— "Why would I point that out to you when I need your help to save my sister?"

She grinned suddenly. "Oh good, self-interest *and* respect, there's hope for you!"

He was too wound up to bother trying to understand that. "Are you even taking this seriously?" he hissed.

The grin vanished and despite the dim room he could see the darker shadow cross her eyes. "Of course I am. And I was going to say that of course I'm not walking away. Now which way are we going to hunt the magician?"

He blinked, shook his head, could not deal with the baffling strange girl right now, and just said, "I thought the great hall. Why come to a castle and not use the biggest room?"

"Makes sense," she said with a nod. "Let's go."

They were out into the narrow corridor beyond the kitchen when Karina said, quietly, "Sorry. Gallows humor, sometimes it helps...but I guess you're not that type."

"Can we just concentrate on rescuing my sister?" he said tightly.

"I *am*."

"Good," he said, occupied with struggling to bring his very hazy memory of the castle's layout into focus. He didn't have *time* to get lost—and he didn't want to get lost in front of Karina either. The great hall should have been easy to find. It was enormous; that was the whole point.

He took two turns he was almost sure were right, and found the foot of a stone staircase. "Let's go up. A gallery wraps around the hall; that should be more discreet than running in on the ground floor."

"Well-done!" Karina said, again with a lighter tone. "You're thinking like a thief." She slipped past him and darted up the stairs two at a time.

He didn't know whether to be complimented or not, but he knew he didn't like her getting ahead of him and made quick work of catching up. "What does your thief wisdom say we should do if we already alerted Aurum by stepping through his magic barrier?"

"Hope we didn't. And since no one's thrown fireballs at us yet, it's probably all right. And if it isn't..." She raised the knife she still had in one hand. "Stay alert."

Right. Fine. He could have come up with *that* plan himself. And magical knitting had to be as effective as a knife against fireballs.

One more turn on the upper level and he felt more certain where they were—right outside the great hall's gallery. And he could hear voices. Forrest took a deep breath, suddenly felt alarm about whether they should be breathing quietly, and tried to let the air out as softly as possible.

Meanwhile Karina was approaching the open doorway onto the gallery, and he grudgingly let her go first. She was better at stealth. The gallery was in deep shadows, but she slipped cautiously around the edge and then dropped into a crouch. After a moment, she beckoned him forward too.

Feeling ridiculous, Forrest dropped to hands and knees. Trying not to let the weight of his pack put him off-balance, he followed Karina to the balustrade lining the gallery. It was only waist-height, if they'd been standing, good enough to crouch behind and peer over.

The gallery was shadowed, but light shone below. Reassuring because it should be harder to see them up here—alarming because he couldn't see any *source* for the light, which was much too bright for the scant windows this deep into the castle.

He blinked against the brilliance, peered down—and saw Rosie.

He swallowed hard, squinting as though it would help him make out any possible detail. She was sitting cross-legged on the floor, hands relaxed in her lap, hair still in its neat braids. Her face was turned away from him, hiding her expression, but nothing he could see indicated that she'd been hurt so far.

Forrest let out a long slow breath, gave himself a few seconds to savor relief before he took in the larger picture...and stopped feeling relieved.

Rosie was sitting at one point of an enormous nine-pointed star drawn on the hall's stone floor. In another point was a huge glass bowl, holding...he had to look twice before he quite believed it. A mermaid. A mermaid with a long blue tail and green hair was floating in the bowl. All right then.

Even a mermaid couldn't distract him indefinitely from the other two people present—both standing well outside the chalked star, a worrisome thing to notice considering where Rosie was sitting.

The man was Aurum, no surprise there, and the sight of him made Forrest's blood pound harder, made him wish he knew anything at all about how magic could be used as a weapon. Aurum was in conversation with a tall, slender woman who missed being the strangest one in the room only because of the mermaid's presence. Something felt distinctly unnatural about the tint of her silver hair.

In a whisper, he asked, "Is that—"

"Yes," Karina breathed, and he noticed that she was rubbing her fingers over the knit bracelet on her wrist.

He turned back to the scene below. He could hear the murmur of conversation, but Aurum and Lady Diamond had their heads together, and he couldn't make out any words.

So they were here. Everyone was here. And now he was right smack up against the point where not having a plan meant he had no idea what to do next. Now was when he was suddenly supposed to be brilliant, to somehow come up with some solution he hadn't been able to see in all this time before, to pull off a miracle and rescue his sister.

Except that, while he really just wanted to strangle Aurum with a scarf, grab Rosie and run, he knew that was not going to work.

His full attention snapped back to Rosie when light flared from her direction. She had one hand raised and as he watched she reached out, poking at the air in front of her—and again the flare of light. She poked again and then repeatedly, fast, and the light shone consistently enough for him to see a column with Rosie at its center. A barrier, similar to the one on the doorway?

"*Stop that* at once!" Aurum snapped, making Forrest's spine stiffen with anger.

Rosie folded her arms and stuck out her tongue at him, and Forrest grinned with a shaky relief. That was a better sign that she was still fine, much better than just the absence of visible injury.

"Can't you control that child?" Lady Diamond said in bored tones.

"Go to sleep," Aurum ordered, and snapped his fingers. At once Rosie's eyes slid closed and her head drooped to one side.

Forrest jerked half-an-inch up and only Karina's hand closing on his arm stopped him from moving farther, halted the instinct to get to his sister immediately, even if it meant jumping off a balcony. He clenched his hands and stared *hard*, and could just see the faint movement of her breathing. Which meant he could breathe too.

A plan. They *had* to decide what they were going to do, and it had to be now.

"So what do we do?" he asked in a low voice, shaking Karina's hand off. She was a thief, let her figure out how to steal a person. "We can probably get through the barrier around Rosie with the scarves, but..."

"But we need to get to her," Karina muttered. "So we need a distraction."

That seemed straight-forward enough. "Split up?" If Karina could attract their attention to a different part of the castle, he could go after Rosie. And run. But then they'd have to find a way to escape from a very small island with no cover to speak of and two magicians after them...

Which would be bad enough without even more people arriving; at that moment two men walked into the hall through a far doorway, with no hesitation or attempt at secrecy. The older man was clearly the leader, the second man walking slightly behind him, probably a bodyguard.

Great. How many people would they have to distract?

"Hello, my friends," the leader called across the hall, a coldness in the tone belying the jovial words. "So pleasant to see you." The man was very thin, with a hooked nose and a perfectly straight back.

Beside Forrest, Karina inhaled sharply. He glanced at her, to see her gaze fixed on the new arrivals. He already had an uneasy guess, and this seemed to confirm it. "Lord Silver?"

"What?" She looked at him, blinked, said, "Yes," and turned back to the hall again.

Of course all three crazy magicians knew each other. It had to be a small social circle, right?

But Karina wasn't looking at the magicians, Forrest suddenly realized. Lord Silver had joined the other two, while the man who had accompanied him stood a little apart. And Karina was looking at *him*.

Glancing again at Rosie, confirming nothing had changed with her, Forrest turned to study the man who had so captured Karina. He seemed unremarkable enough. Young, maybe his own age; wearing a dark cloak, far enough open to show a leather vest and the hilts of at least three knives at his belt; dark hair falling into his eyes. A bodyguard. Nothing exciting.

Except…that was a stone floor out there. And there'd only been the sound of one person's footsteps when the two men walked in.

"You know him?" Forrest asked, though the new sinking in his stomach was already anticipating the answer.

She didn't look away from the hall this time, just nodded tightly. "It's Dimitri."

Well then. That was…interesting.

Chapter Thirty-One

He couldn't be here. He couldn't possibly be here because he was *dead*.

Except that he was here, right there, alive and well and—alive, that was the important point. Karina wanted to be happy about it. She *was* happy about it, her cheeks had gone warm and her palms were damp and a hard knot of pain she'd stopped noticing had evaporated away.

Except… It was a horrible thought, a thought she didn't want to be having. She'd much rather just be happy, only here this other thought was. Except…why was he alive? *How* was he alive? She had seen the dark light, heard the screams. Felt the terror surrounding Lord Silver. How was Dimitri not dead? And why was he *here*?

And how could she find out the answers to those questions or anything else, when he was with Lord Silver? Not to mention Lady Diamond and Master Aurum. And a mermaid. And Forrest's kidnapped little sister.

Which was what she *ought* to be focusing on. They had a job to do here, and Dimitri miraculously turning up didn't change that. Even if she wanted desperately to talk to him.

She wasn't the only one who noticed Dimitri's presence. Lady Diamond looked past Lord Silver with her lip curled in disdain. "What interesting company you're keeping."

Dimitri stiffened. Lord Silver just said, "Yes, I thought so. But we have such a lot to discuss in that area, don't we?"

"If we must," Lady Diamond said in bored tones.

"Go guard the door," Lord Silver ordered, without even looking over his shoulder.

Karina watched Dimitri inhale, exhale again, and say, "Yes, sir." And then he walked on silent footsteps back to the door they had come through.

"Outside and close it behind you," Lord Silver added, keeping his gaze on his fellow magicians.

No response from Dimitri this time, but he stepped through the doorway and pulled the thick wooden door shut behind him.

Which presented an opportunity.

Karina could finally pull her gaze away from the scene below. She turned, sitting with her back to the balustrade, and whispered, "Distraction."

"Yes?" Forrest said.

"I'll go—you stay here—no, go to the stairs in the north corner so you can get down quickly. I'll find some way to make a loud noise or something, and you be ready to get Rosie."

A long pause. "You're going to talk to Dimitri."

He didn't say it like an accusation, or even a question. Just a fact. Which was exactly accurate. "Yes." She looked him in the eye, tried to put honesty into her voice. "I *will* create a distraction. And I'll get Dimitri to help us."

Forrest looked away first, back to the hall below. "You trust him?"

"Yes," she said immediately, instinctively. The thoughts came rushing in after the word. He was with Lord Silver and she didn't understand that and she didn't understand what had happened back in Ilsonine or how he was alive. But she *did* trust him. As much as she had ever trusted anyone which wasn't very much, but surely she trusted him enough. He was Dimitri. There would be an explanation. Of course there would.

"All right," Forrest said, even though his jaw was tight and he clearly wasn't happy with the whole business.

So she went before he had time to change his mind.

She was out into the adjoining corridor before it occurred to her that she didn't actually know how to get to wherever Dimitri was. But they were both on the perimeter of the great hall, so how complicated could it be? She wasn't going to go back and ask Forrest now, if he even knew.

She took the first stairs down that she came to, and walked cautiously once she was on the right level. Not cautious enough, though—she was still moving along what seemed like a parallel corridor to the great hall when a voice around the next corner demanded, "Who's there?"

Because it was Dimitri's voice, she rounded the corner with her hands raised and empty. And there stood Dimitri, only a few paces away in front of a closed door, with a knife in one hand.

He fell back a step, eyes wide and mouth dropping open. *"Rin?"* The knife disappeared back into his sleeve as he strode toward her. "What are you doing here?"

He didn't give her time to answer, enveloping her in a tight hug. She pressed her nose against his shoulder and hugged him back. They used to hug, a long time ago. Not recently, not since joining the Lions had made them both too careful.

"I thought you were dead," she whispered, throat tight, and blinked hard.

"And I didn't know how to find you." He stepped back, holding her shoulders. "You disappeared, no one knew where to. Are you all right?"

She looked up at his face, wanted to be pleased by the concern in his eyes. But wasn't his 'death' more important to discuss than her disappearance? Not to mention… "That last night, what happened? The others…?"

His eyes went distant, and she knew at once that there wouldn't be any more miracles. "I'm sorry, Rin. It was—he caught us in his study and there was nothing we could do."

She took a pace back, his hands dropping from her shoulders. "But *you're* alive. And with him."

"He gave me a chance. I got lucky, I guess. He saw something in me and offered to let me work for him."

Karina's throat was only growing tighter. "But how could you? After he killed all of our friends! How can you possibly promise loyalty to someone who—"

"It's not like that," Dimitri protested. "It wasn't much of a choice to begin with, work for him or die. And I'm not *really* working for him now. I mean, I am, but it's temporary, just until I get a better chance—and who's to say there won't be an opportunity for some vengeance in the process, right?"

He looked her straight in the eyes as he said it, and Rin wanted to be reassured by that. Except she knew the fine art of keeping a steady gaze and an honest face while lying. She had learned the trick from Dimitri.

"Surely you aren't saying I should have nobly died instead?" Dimitri asked, sounding so rational, so reasonable.

It was true, wasn't it? Fine noble sentiments weren't for people like them, people who had to do what was necessary just to stay alive. She had always known that. "No. I just…" But it just didn't *feel* right, even though she didn't know how to say that, never ever would have told Dimitri that her own emotional twinge about something should be a good enough reason for anything.

"But you shouldn't be here right now," he said, without waiting for her to fumble to some sort of explanation. "It's too risky. You should leave, and I'll find you later."

"I can't leave," she said, with a sudden pang of guilt at how much time she'd already spent *not* getting her task done. She had promised Forrest a distraction. "That little girl in there, she was kidnapped by one of the magicians. I have to get her out."

"I'm sure you mean well," Dimitri said, putting a hand on her shoulder and starting to steer her back the way she had come, "but I don't think you understand how dangerous this is. It's too big a risk for a stranger. You have to—"

Karina shook his hand off, held her ground. "I understand the risks. And she's not a stranger, she's a friend."

His eyebrows rose, incredulous. "A friend. Who you met, what, a few days ago?"

"That doesn't matter. She's a friend and she's in trouble and I'm going to help her." Karina squared her shoulders and met his gaze. "So you can either help me, or stay out of my way."

Chapter Thirty-Two

Forrest crept along behind the balustrade toward the stairs, and hoped desperately that he hadn't just made a profound mistake. In theory, if he trusted Karina, and she trusted Dimitri, then it should follow that he should trust Dimitri.

Except that he didn't.

But at the same time, they needed help. And he wasn't certain Karina would have agreed *not* to go to Dimitri if he had asked her, and he didn't want to find out. Which was a vastly less important concern, obviously, than getting Rosie and the two of them out of here safely. Which was what he should be focusing on.

He focused on the magicians' conversation as much for a distraction as to try to learn anything useful.

"I don't suppose there's any point in pretending to be friendly," Lord Silver was saying, and it was hard to imagine a man with that tone ever being friendly to anyone.

"We never pretended to be friends," Lady Diamond purred, "merely colleagues with a common goal."

"Who agreed that we would work together and evenly split the reward," Lord Silver said icily. "An agreement you blatantly flouted."

"I'm sorry, I'm a bit lost here," Master Aurum interjected, and the familiar voice, even the familiar pleasant tone, was much more disturbing than the others' barely-veiled hostility. "Has there been a...disagreement?"

"This *sea snake* sent a pack of thieves to rob me," Lord Silver spat. "And don't pretend you weren't working together on it. I'm sure you would both be happy to cut me out of the plan."

Forrest wished Karina and the Lions had succeeded. Then the magicians wouldn't be here, and neither would Rosie, and neither would he. But then, Karina wouldn't be either.

"I?" Master Aurum said in wounded tones. "Surely you know I am a peace-loving soul, preferring only to live in harmony with all my fellow—"

"Oh do stop that," Lady Diamond drawled. "I can't *stand* hypocrisy, and here I see it before me twice over." She pointed a gloved finger at Lord Silver. "You are no paragon of virtue either, and I hardly see what you have to complain about. You caught the bumbling thieves, who, incidentally, robbed *me*. I fail to comprehend what you lost. You even gained your handsome new guard."

Handsome? Forrest couldn't see it.

Lord Silver glowered at his colleague. "That's supposed to justify casting aside our alliance? You expect me to just ignore two blatant attempts to steal my—"

"Wait." Lady Diamond raised her hand again, finger pointing upwards this time. "Two?"

"Yes, *two*. Once in Ilsonine with those idiot thieves, and again just after I landed here this morning. Which I must say was bold, even for you."

"Not being a hypocrite, I freely admit that the pack of thieves in Ilsonine were mine. But I will not take responsibility for anything that happened today."

"But if you didn't..." Lord Silver swung around towards Aurum. "So! Peace-loving, is it?"

Just now, Forrest didn't feel very peace-loving himself. Let the insane magicians kill each other, that would be fine. Just as long as he could get Rosie out of here.

Aurum shrugged expansively. "Can you blame me for trying to seize an opportunity? Especially when I know for a fact the two of you have met to discuss getting *me* out of the deal." He smiled cheerily. "I have excellent espionage spells, didn't you know?"

"Did you know that cutting you out is still a viable option?" Lady Diamond said, backing away and raising one hand. Forrest ducked back behind the balustrade after glimpsing the ball of blue fire glowing in her palm.

Confronted with an actual fight, his brief hope of a new way out of this suddenly seemed more dangerous than not. How much widespread damage could the magicians inflict while attacking each other?

A flash of blue light filling the hall made him risk a peek over the balustrade again. He was just in time to see Lady Diamond launch a second blast of light. It splattered harmlessly off a wall of white light surrounding Aurum. He looked toward Rosie, trying to calculate angles and distances but he didn't know enough about how the magic worked. She wasn't in the direct line of fire, but was she too close? Although that column around Aurum looked a lot like the one around Rosie; maybe it would protect her too.

Unless it didn't. He rubbed his palms against his pant legs. Could he risk running in to get her? Would he just be throwing away any chance or did he have to move, now, before it was too late?

"You really don't want to do that," Aurum said calmly. "And neither do you," he added, turning to Silver, who had conjured a ball of black flame into one palm. Forrest remembered the black light in Karina's story, his tense shoulders going tighter.

"You really don't want to tell me what *I* want," Lady Diamond, flinging another blast of blue flame, equally ineffective.

"You're just wasting energy this way," Aurum observed.

Aurum and Silver had their back to the stairs, but Lady Diamond would be looking right at them if she turned her head even a fraction. And Rosie was still in Silver's line of sight too. But with all this magic blasting around, how could he risk waiting? Forrest started to edge around the pillar to the first step.

"Cutting me out of the deal is not a viable option," Aurum continued, "because you don't have access to my tree."

So Lord Silver's metal tree wasn't the only one. That would no doubt be very interesting to Forrest if he wasn't in the middle of trying to walk soundlessly down stone steps. He remembered what Karina had said at the cliff and stayed close to the wall for the very slight cover its shadow provided.

"Your tree has to be here somewhere," Silver pointed out, weighing the black flame in his hand as though considering a throw. That angle was going to send his magic terrifyingly close to Rosie.

"Of course," Aurum agreed. "Cloaked by a spell that won't evaporate upon my death."

"You could be lying about that," Silver said.

"Why should he be lying?" Lady Diamond snapped, and the blue flames flickering around her hands went out. "You and I did the same thing when we brought our trees here. We were just hoping he wouldn't think of it."

"Your lack of respect pains me," Aurum remarked.

And suddenly the fight was over, before it had really properly begun, just as Forrest reached the bottom step. No more immediate danger—and no distraction for the magicians either. He froze, heart pounding so loudly he half-believed it would give him away. It was much too far to get back up the stairs and behind the balustrade again. His gaze darted around, saw nowhere to hide—and then he remembered the shadowed niche below the stairs.

He all but dived around the turn of the staircase and into the shadows, was relieved to find the space went back a few feet. It was a flimsy hiding place at best, but it was something. Just until Karina came up with a distraction. He pressed back against the wall, trying to keep his breathing quiet, and waited. Because she was going to come up with a distraction. And in the meantime, he could just barely see Rosie, still peacefully asleep. And the magicians too.

"If we're done playing games," Aurum continued, "can we get on with this? Let's each place our trees in the star. From there we will all be committed to the spell, and we can stop wasting time on these silly confrontations."

"Agreed," Lady Diamond said, and turned to Silver. "But first, let's hear an explanation for your apparent lack of a sacrifice. Or do you have *that* cloaked too?"

"Not at all," Silver said, with a flourish towards the door. "He's simply on guard duty at the moment."

A shudder ran down Forrest spine. A sacrifice. But there were three magicians. Three trees. So odds were it wouldn't be one sacrifice, it would be *three* sacrifices, and that meant that Rosie...

No. He would not allow that, he was not going to let that happen, he was going to...to do...something.

Where was Karina with that distraction?

Lady Diamond appeared to react with equal horror, shoulders drawing back and eyebrows rising. "That bumbling thief? The one I sent to rob you? *That's* who you brought as your contribution to the spell?"

Lord Silver's expression stayed quite calm. "I found him to be the best candidate—"

"I read his aura before I sent him to your house, and he has *no* magic. You brought us someone useless!"

"That's preposterous," Silver shot back. "I read his aura too and he has an immensely strong magical presence. Read it again."

Lady Diamond's eyes shifted sideways, expression distant, and for a moment there was silence.

Was she distracted enough for Forrest to risk approaching Rosie? Should he just attempt it, never mind the risks, because waiting was too dangerous?

Just as he edged one foot forward, Lady Diamond burst into laughter. The laughter echoed and rebounded and sounded more terrifying than angry shouting, making Forrest automatically draw back into the deeper shadows again.

"You idiot!" Lady Diamond said between laughs. "You colossal idiot! You completely misread his magic. He's still carrying around the diamond flower I gave his merry band when I sent them to you. You didn't read *his* magic, you read *my* flower!"

"That's not possible," Silver said, but his voice was less sure. "I'm sure that I... I would have..." His face darkened into a glower, and Forrest could only guess that he had just gained new information magically, since he stopped questioning the idea. "That deceitful liar. I *asked* if he had anything from you and he denied it. I should have known better than to believe a man who could betray all his so-called friends."

Forrest blinked, breath catching in his throat. A man who had done what now? And that was the same man Karina had just gone to get help from?

"No one cares what you should have done," Lady Diamond snapped, momentary levity already gone. "What you *did* do is fail to produce a suitable sacrifice, jeopardizing our entire endeavor."

He had no way to warn Karina, he couldn't even get out from beneath these stairs without revealing himself at once.

"So we'll find someone else," Silver said, and turned to Aurum. "You've been here for months, what are the prospects?"

"I don't see why it should be my job to solve your problem."

"Because it's *our* problem when it halts our spell."

"Hmm, true," Aurum said, with a slight tip of his head. "There are possibilities. Another member of the girl's family, perhaps."

Forrest's face went hot with mingled anger and fear, the mere idea that Aurum might try to drag anyone else he loved into this, that he could so callously view them as nothing but potential sacrifices—but it was all right, no one else was anywhere near, they were all out of reach. Except for Forrest himself, but he was already in this.

"The entire family has some degree of magical talent," Aurum continued, "although of course the youngest of three sisters is the best for our purpose. Or there are the young princes. The heir might be a possibility, though we'd do better to abduct his brother Dastan. He's the seventh son, which has some weight even if he's not the son of a seventh son. Of course, obtaining a prince is always a challenge, but I—"

And then an almighty clatter drowned out the rest of his sentence, making Forrest jump and bump his head against the underside of the stairs. This had to be Karina's distraction. That, or they were being invaded by dragons with clanking scales. Lots of them.

Chapter Thirty-Three

It had seemed like such a definitive ultimatum. Help me or we part ways forever. She should have realized that Dimitri was perfectly capable of negotiating a compromise. He was like that, it occurred to her now. Always good at talking his way around things.

His argument had made sense, though. She didn't need help going off and finding a broken wall to smash, or whatever else she could find to make noise, so really it *was* more helpful if he went on playing the guard, ready to delay pursuit, or to be on hand in case the delay wasn't enough. It was logical, it made sense.

So why did she still feel a cold twist of doubt when she walked away from him?

But she had no time for that now, she had a job to do. And just two rooms away from Dimitri's guard post, she found the ideal distraction. It was so good that she couldn't resist it, even if it wasn't going to give her much head start for running.

But how could anyone pass up a dozen rusting suits of armor, all standing so conveniently just a couple feet apart from each other?

She pushed the endmost suit, watched long enough to see it take down the one next to it in a cacophony of clatters and clanks, and then ran while the rest of the line continued falling.

She didn't want to lead the magicians back to the boat—and she couldn't leave in the boat anyway, without Forrest and Rosie. And with Dimitri? No, don't try to answer *that* question.

She wanted to circle around, lead the magicians on enough of a chase to give Forrest time to get Rosie and get out again. If she could find a place with a view of the beach where they'd left the boat, then she'd know if Forrest and Rosie got there, so she could join them.

She ran up the next flight of stairs she reached, thinking of finding a vantage point, even if her instincts objected to running away *up* stairs. Her foot had just hit the top step, ready to dash down the corridor, when she froze.

Not in emotion. Not even voluntarily. But suddenly her body stopped obeying her.

"Well, well," a soft voice drawled. "You do keep turning up, don't you?"

If she had been able to move, Karina knew she would be shuddering. And supposing she lived long enough to have nightmares again, she knew Lady Diamond's voice would be haunting them.

"You mean we wasted time coming here for one silly girl?"

And just to make the situation *perfect*, there was Lord Silver's voice too.

"Choke her or something," Lord Silver said, "and let's get back to business."

"On the contrary," Lady Diamond said, "I believe she can solve your little problem. You nabbed the wrong thief. Or didn't you bother to read her?"

Karina took a deep breath. At least she could breathe this time. Maybe because she was wearing Forrest's scarf. Would it help with anything more? She tried to shift her shoulders. They raised a little, just a fraction. Not much, but encouraging. She tried her legs, thinking of running. No response.

"Oh yes," Lord Silver said behind her, "I see what you mean."

Karina had lost the thread of the conversation entirely, and had no idea what he was seeing. She concentrated on her right foot. Could she just…?

Behind her came the sound of a single clap and suddenly she was free. Without thinking she launched into a run. In two steps she hit an invisible wall and fell backwards, landing on her back, rolling over instinctively into a crouch.

"Quite the little fighter," Lady Diamond purred. "It's not going to do any good, you know."

Why hadn't the scarf worked? It had worked on the magic barrier around the castle. But maybe *this* magic was stronger than a spell dispersed around an entire castle.

Maybe she had been very, very foolish to convince Forrest that a bit of stitching could stand up against real magic. Real magicians.

Like the two standing at the bottom of the stairs. Her heart sank as she looked at who was there—and at who wasn't. Only two. Had Master Aurum gone a different direction? Or had he stayed behind, stayed on guard? Rendering this whole plan completely useless.

Lady Diamond made a quick gesture with one hand, and a band of blue light wrapped around Karina, jerked her up to her feet, and pinned her arms at her sides. A thin thread of light reached from the coils around Karina, to end in Lady Diamond's hand. Then Lady Diamond and Lord Silver both turned to walk back towards the great hall, the blue light rope pulling Karina along behind them.

She didn't try to resist walking. Likely the magic would just drag her over, and she didn't want to be hauled down a flight of stone steps on her back. She did try to move her right wrist, the one with Forrest's bracelet. It twitched, but that was all.

She didn't meet Dimitri's gaze as she was pulled past him, not even when he said her name. Had he tried at all to stop or delay them? If so, it hadn't worked.

She entered the great hall all prepared to *not* look up at the top of the north stair, to not give Forrest away if he was still hiding there. But it didn't matter, because almost as soon as she entered she saw him, sitting on the floor a couple dozen feet from Rosie, a shimmer of yellow light around him. Karina's shoulders sagged.

"How splendid, we have *choices* now," Master Aurum said. "You see, I caught one too."

"We are fortunate," Lady Diamond said, "that circumstances have made up for *someone's* incompetence."

Lord Silver glowered at her, but said nothing.

"You, over there," Lady Diamond said, pointing at Karina and then towards Forrest. That was lucky, she had wanted to go there anyway. "And you," Lady Diamond said to Dimitri, "go watch them."

He looked at Lord Silver before he moved. Lord Silver nodded, and Dimitri followed a few paces behind Karina.

She sank onto the floor next to Forrest. "What happened?" she asked in a low voice.

"What do you think?" he muttered, gaze fixed on the ground. "I couldn't get through the barrier around Rosie. And then Aurum was there to cast a spell and…"

"Yeah. Me too, more or less."

The three magicians had briefly conferred when they first came into the hall. Now they walked over to Forrest and Karina and stood studying them from a few feet away. Shivers ran up and down Karina's spine.

"Really either one would do," Lady Diamond said.

"Do for what?" Karina demanded. She was ignored.

"I noticed her power before, of course," Lady Diamond told Silver and Aurum. "Unrefined, but a very strong magical talent."

Karina stared at that utterly impassive face and felt a whole new series of prickles run up her back, felt her stomach twist as though she was back on a rocking ship again. She had to be misunderstanding this. Or Lady Diamond was confused—or crazy, that was a possibility. "But I can't—I can't do magic," she said faintly.

Lady Diamond smiled, a thin mocking smile. "Perhaps you have not done any magic, but you certainly *can*. Or didn't you know? It's perfectly obvious to anyone who knows how to look for it."

She *had* to be wrong. Magic wasn't something ordinary people could do, certainly not anything Karina herself had ever thought of doing. She was a pickpocket from Ilsonine, not a magician. And she didn't want to be a magician; she didn't want that kind of world-twisting power.

"I think we should use the brother," Aurum announced. "Equally powerful magical ability, and the connection between siblings may give the spell an added force."

"I don't know," Lady Diamond said, "oldest sons are so unreliable, magically speaking."

"Only the oldest of three sons," Aurum countered. "He's an only son with three sisters. It should work perfectly well. And, of course, there's a great deal of magical talent there, you can see that for yourself."

"Let's just get on with this," Silver said loudly. "If the boy will do, then let's use him for the sacrifice and stop discussing it."

Sacrifice? What did they mean *sacrifice*? Karina tried to turn to look at Forrest, realized magic had her locked immobile in place.

It was all she could do to turn her head just far enough to see what was happening as all three magicians pointed at Forrest, and rays of light wrapped around him, pulling him to his feet. The light dragged him over to one of the unoccupied points of the star drawn on the ground. Karina could tell from Forrest's grim expression that he was trying to fight it—but that was the only evidence, as his efforts had no effect at all. Muscles tensing, she tried to fight against her own magical bonds, to rise to her feet, to do *something*—but all she could manage was to slightly shift her right arm and that wasn't enough to do any good.

The magicians walked towards the star themselves, plainly about to move ahead with whatever spell they were undertaking. The spell that required *sacrifices*, that meant killing Forrest and Rosie.

"We have to *do* something," she hissed frantically at Dimitri, who still stood above her.

"It's going to be all right, Rin," he said, gaze on the star and its inhabitants.

"No, it *isn't!*" Nothing was all right, everything was wrong, wrong, wrong. And it was all her fault, she had got Forrest and Rosie into this—maybe not Rosie, Master Aurum had been planning to kidnap her all along, but that didn't matter, that was beside the point, she had to do *something*, she had to make Dimitri understand—

"After this is all over," Dimitri said, voice relaxed, "I'll talk to Lord Silver about you. He's been very generous to me, and I'm sure he'll be willing to make a deal with you too."

"I will not work for that monster," Karina snapped.

He finally looked down at her, his expression a mixture of annoyed and patronizing. "This is no time to be idealistic, Rin. There are opportunities here, but I can't take care of you if you won't listen to my advice."

Her stomach twisted again and her horror multiplied as she realized that he wasn't thinking about this spell, about what was about to happen at all. "You don't care," she whispered. "People are going to die and you don't even *care*."

He shrugged. "They're no concern of mine." He crouched down next to her, leaned in closer. "I'm concerned about *us*. I know a little about this spell, and it's going to give Lord Silver a great deal of power. That means he'll be able to give even greater rewards. He's already promised me wealth, the kind of wealth I could never make picking pockets or robbing houses with the Lions. And don't you see—with that kind of wealth, we can have a real future. We can do whatever we want. We can even—"

"No, we can't," she interrupted, even though she didn't know what he was going to propose. She turned her head away, blinked suddenly hot eyes. "Because there isn't any *we*. Not now. And there never was."

He leaned in closer, dropped his voice even further. "But I wanted there to be."

"Then you should have said something a lot sooner."

Chapter Thirty-Four

Forrest stood in his point of the star and stared across at the sleeping face of his sister. At least she wouldn't know what was happening. Or know how badly he had failed her.

If he had only been smarter, faster—if this supposed magical talent he possessed had actually been worth anything. But he and Karina had only been fooling themselves.

He looked over at Karina. She was talking to Dimitri.

Fine. Good. Maybe *he'd* be able to get her out of this alive.

The three magicians had spread out, each to a different point of the star. Each one seemed to be studying the other two very intently.

"All together then?" Lady Diamond said.

"Agreed," Aurum said. "Now!"

Each one executed a gesture as though pulling a cloth off an object—even though there were no cloths. But there were objects. Revealed beside each magician, there now stood a metal tree. Each tree was perhaps three feet tall, with a slender trunk and spreading branches. One was of silver, one of gold, and one of diamonds.

Even from his distance, Forrest could see that the trees were impossibly intricate, beyond the skill of any normal craftsman. Only magic could have created such perfect leaves and buds and tiny flowers. This was real magic, so much more than webs of yarn.

It had to take immense time, power and knowledge to create such a thing. And if the magicians were planning to use these three trees in another spell—what were they trying to gain from that spell?

It didn't appear he was going to live long enough to find out.

Still watching each other warily, each magician picked up a tree by its trunk, and all in unison swung the trees into place in separate points of the star. The moment they were in place, a certain tension left the magicians. Forrest himself felt no reassurance, only a renewed dread. Step by step, they were moving forward. How many steps before they got to the bloodshed?

"Now we're all committed," Silver said, "and all required to complete the spell."

So they weren't going to kill each other after all. Forrest had known that was too good to be true. He strained against the spell holding him again. He'd been trying to move his arms in a background kind of way all along, but now he redoubled the effort. It did no good.

Each magician paced counterclockwise around the star, until each had reached one of the remaining three empty points. Again in unison, all three stepped within.

Forrest felt something change immediately. He couldn't say just what sense he was using; it was almost as though the air began to vibrate, or the light to shine more brightly, without being quite either of those things. But he knew that magical power was building in the room, like a ball of yarn unrolling and weaving into a web all around them. Maybe he felt it because he was in the star, part of the spell. Or maybe it was that magical talent the magicians claimed to see in him.

He tried to find any hole in the web, any hope the spell might go wrong, any opening for himself to escape with Rosie—but he didn't even understand what he was sensing.

Silver raised his arms high and intoned, "By the shine of silver, by the light of the moon, by the strength of mountains, I invoke the power of earth."

A shudder ran through that sense Forrest couldn't quite define. The magic took on a new quality, like a deep gray wool, double-thick, stolid and sturdy.

Aurum raised his arms in the same gesture. "By the shine of gold, by the light of the sun, by the strength of lightning, I invoke the power of fire."

A new strand of magic joined the web, scarlet and silk and shining.

Lady Diamond raised her arms now. "By the shine of diamonds, by the light of the stars, by the strength of the ocean, I invoke the power of water."

By now Forrest was anticipating the change in the magical web. This one was like lamb's wool, extra fine, pale blue.

Except it wasn't like *anything*, since this wasn't coming from sound or sight or smell or anything else, but still, the feeling was there.

A feeling that couldn't distract from the fact that he and Rosie were about to die.

The three magicians intoned in unison, arms still raised, "We call down the powers of earth, fire and water, together and separate, balanced and united. We draw them to us by the power of air."

The spell had gone around the circle to each magician, and apparently now was going back the other way. Lady Diamond lowered her arms and pointed at the mermaid in her tank, across the star. "By the breath of the sacrifice," she hissed.

Mermaids breathed? Apparently so, as the mermaid's eyes widened and face contorted in panic. Her hands reached up to her neck, where Forrest could just make out gills. He looked away, feeling nauseous.

Master Aurum would be next. And Rosie was his sacrifice. Forrest struggled again to push against the invisible bonds around him, but if anything they felt stronger than before, like there were extra loops, a thicker, tighter net wrapping around him and holding him in place. He strained against it anyway, trying to push through, trying to tear the magical binding apart.

He only knew that the mermaid had died, that the spell had moved on to its next stage and was somehow delayed when Lady Diamond snapped, "That's *you* next," and Master Aurum lowered his arms.

Every one of Forrest's muscles strained against the invisible bonds holding him in place. A whole pack full of magical knitting on his back, and none of it was doing any good.

But Aurum didn't point at Rosie. He reached into his cloak, and brought out a small bottle that glowed pink and gold. "It's a funny thing," Aurum said conversationally. "In theory, the two of you couldn't be cut out of your share of the power once we started the spell. But when you have enough magical power to draw on, you can override just about any theory."

"You backstabbing traitor," Lady Diamond growled.

Aurum just smiled. "Like you wouldn't have done it if you'd thought of it."

Silver took a more active approach. He strode two steps forward towards Aurum before he hit a wall of shimmering light, outlining the point of the star he stood in. He cursed and slammed a fist against the wall.

Maybe the evil magicians would kill each other after all. Forrest felt a sudden, ridiculous surge of hope. If Aurum got rid of the other two, would he still need two more sacrifices? Maybe there really was something to those lucky scarves.

Or maybe not. Silver had another card to play. He turned to the only person in the room not under magical restraint: Dimitri. "Stop him! If this spell doesn't work for me, there's no reward for you!"

Dimitri hesitated—but only for a second. Then he stepped away from Karina, towards the star. She reached out a hand to stop him (how was she moving that arm? The knit bracelet?) but he brushed her off. Aurum turned as Dimitri approached, but the magician was trapped in his point of the star too. He settled for using his free hand to throw a ball of blazing fire towards Dimitri, who dodged, picked up to a run, stepped over the outer line of the star and crashed into Aurum, carrying him to the ground.

They both smashed into the far edge of the point, and this time the light flared to stop Aurum. Forrest didn't know which one he should be hoping would win. In the struggle and confusion, Dimitri somehow got hold of the small bottle, and threw it across the star— towards Silver, who caught it neatly in one outstretched hand.

With an inarticulate growl, Aurum shoved Dimitri off, orange light crackling in his fingertips. It wasn't a normal shove. Dimitri flew back a dozen feet and landed heavily on his back, chest and one arm seared black.

For just a moment Forrest forgot to keep pushing against his magical bonds as he stared at Dimitri's burns.

"*No!*" Karina screamed, reaching out with one hand, visibly trying and unable to rise from where the magic was holding her.

Dimitri didn't look towards her. He looked at Silver, half-lifted one hand. "Master, help me..."

Silver was intently studying the glowing bottle and only flicked Dimitri a disinterested glance. "Why? This saves me the trouble of killing you later."

Shock crawled across Dimitri's face. "No! You promised me!"

"Oh please, I don't keep promises to my comparative equals," Silver said, nodding at Aurum and Lady Diamond. "And I certainly wasn't going to trust the loyalty of a thief, who sold out all of his friends for a promise of riches. You were quite useful warning me about the plan to rob my house, but I never expected you to be much use beyond that."

In spite of himself, Forrest's gaze darted to Karina's face, to see how she was taking that piece of news so casually dropped by Lord Silver.

Her face, always pale, had gone whiter, eyes enormous. "You betrayed us." Karina had stopped reaching towards Dimitri, looked now as though she'd rather back away if she could. "I *trusted* you, and you got everyone killed—would have got me killed!"

"No," Dimitri gasped, "I wouldn't, not *you*—I protected you, I kept you separate from the rest, remember? Kept you with me—sent you out to the hall…"

A very small, very inconsequential part of Forrest was guiltily glad to see Karina shaking her head, unaccepting of excuses or explanations. No part of him was glad to see the tears in her eyes.

"This is all very dull," Silver said loudly, snapped his fingers and pointed at Dimitri.

Another crackle of flame, Dimitri's head fell back, and he didn't move again. Forrest had been able to see that Rosie was breathing, and he was able to see that Dimitri was not.

Karina didn't scream this time. Just bowed her head, hiding her face from view.

"On to more important things," Silver said briskly, holding up the glowing bottle and giving it a good shake.

An image popped into Forrest's head of the pink and gold fairy careening from side to side within the bottle, shrilling indignant objections.

And then it occurred to him. If the magicians wouldn't kill each other—maybe someone else would do it.

"Don't open that bottle," Forrest said in a rush, words out before he had time to be surprised that the magical binding let him speak. "It holds a monster, one only Aurum can control." If that didn't get a rise from an arrogant magician, nothing would.

Sure enough, Lord Silver leveled a glare that was terrifying even though he'd deliberately provoked it. "There is nothing that fool can do that I can't."

"He's just trying to bait you," Aurum snapped. "I wasn't going to open the bottle either. It's no use to you—"

"So I should just give it back?" Lord Silver said with a nasty laugh. "Yes, because your word is so trustworthy."

"You are all wasting my time *again*," Lady Diamond said loudly.

"Just don't open it," Forrest said, easily putting all his fear and dread and horror into his voice. "Please—the creature inside, it'll kill all of us!"

"No," Lord Silver said, "it will kill only those I command it to destroy." Then he wrenched the stopper out of the bottle, letting a cloud of pink and gold vapor pour out. As it coalesced, Silver pointed at Aurum and Lady Diamond, "And I command you, destroy them both!"

"You *command*?" a voice came from the cloud. The sparkles thinned, and the plump blonde woman came into view, little wings flapping and expression decidedly put out. "What do you think I am, a genie? I'm a Good Fairy. We don't take orders."

Silver gaped at Marjoram, all his confidence of a moment before evaporating. Forrest was never so glad to see someone lose control. "But—I freed you from the bottle, that should mean—"

"It means you have my heartfelt gratitude," Marjoram said warmly, giving off an extra shower of pink sparkles.

Oh great. Forrest hadn't wanted the fairy *grateful*, he had wanted her *vengeful*. "You have to help us," he called to the fairy, "they're going to kill my sister and me!"

"I don't have to do anything," she said, nose in the air, then looked down it to squint at him. "Who are you again? Why should I concern myself with you?"

Forrest's jaw actually dropped. He'd thought that only happened in stories. "But—but you're a Good Fairy, and—they're evil magicians and—"

Across the star, the magicians were still arguing. "You *idiot*," Aurum growled, "I was just going to draw on her power, not free her!"

He shouldn't have spoken. It only attracted the fairy's attention. "*You*! I remember you!" Marjoram whirled to face Aurum, who backed up until he hit the far wall of magic surrounding his point of the star. "You trapped me in that bottle! That was extremely rude and entirely uncalled for and not at all proper behavior!"

That was more promising. Forrest dared to hope she might be some use after all.

Marjoram extended one hand, made a flicking gesture, and a beam of gold sparkles shot out to splash against Aurum. Forrest could feel her magic too, and it was like gold and pink wire, deceptively thin and bright and harmless, but hard as steel.

"No!" Aurum shouted, eyes bulging in horror, trying to brush the sparkles away to no avail. Beneath the wash of gold, his legs turned brown and fused together, feet turning into narrow brown roots that stretched out and dug into the floor of the courtyard. Aurum writhed and twisted, arms raised above his head, as though he could somehow evade the lower half of his own body. The shades of brown crawled up over his body, past his waist and reached his chest. The brown crawled up over his shoulders and out to his upraised arms, turning them into branches which split and multiplied and put out leaves. For one very nauseous-making second, Aurum's head still rested at the top of the trunk, eyes staring out from between the branches—and in the next second, it was nothing but a knot-hole on the tree.

"Much better," Marjoram said, clasping her hands together and beaming happily.

Clearly this was not a woman Forrest *ever* wanted to make angry with him. Assuming he survived long enough for this to be an issue.

But something was shifting in the spell around him. The web was stretching, losing its neat pattern. He tried again to lift his arms from their tight hold at his sides—and for the first time, he felt something give. It was still like pushing against an entangling net, but the net was giving way. He forced his right hand up, and pushed his palm against the wall of magic lining the edge of the star. A flicker, it gave a quarter inch, and stopped. Master Aurum was—had been part of the spell. Maybe his transformation weakened it.

Lady Diamond gave no sign of paying any attention to Forrest, her glare leveled fully on Silver, but her words helpfully clarified his situation. "You fool!" she spat at Silver, "thanks to your meddling, we lost our third focal point of the spell, destabilizing the entire magical structure."

Carefully, praying no one would notice, Forrest reached his hand around to the pack on his back, seized the first piece of knitting his fingers brushed and pulled it free. A purple scarf. Fine, he could use more luck. He wrapped it around his hand, pushed again against the magical barrier and felt it give just a little more.

He looked across at Rosie, still asleep, and at Karina, still with her head bowed, and back at the magicians, still focused on each other.

"You're blaming *me*?" Silver glowered at Lady Diamond. "*He* was going to push us both out of the spell!"

"Yes..." she said, and then swiftly flung a blue web of light towards Silver. His hands were only half-raised, presumably to counter it, when the magic hit him. "But don't think I didn't hear you tell the Good Fairy to 'destroy them *both*.' "

Silver's hands were moving frantically, tracing symbols that had no visible effect on the silver scales sprouting in random patches from his skin. Forrest watched in a kind of morbid fascination, one hand still pushing against the wall of magic, as scales covered more and more of Silver, as his arms shrank down, his legs fused together, and his eyes grew enormous and round. In less than a minute, a silver fish flopped in Silver's point of the star.

Lady Diamond made a circle in the air, and a round globe of sloshing water formed around the fish. She raised her hand, palm up, and the globe and fish rose in the air until they were on a level with her eyes. "Enjoy the rest of your days swimming in my ocean," she said, and Forrest could swear that the fish was, impossibly, glaring at her.

He didn't really have time to figure out how a fish could glare, because his hand, pressed against the restraining wall of magic, suddenly went through it. He stumbled, off-balance, and by the time he had his footing again, he had stepped over the line of the star. If Aurum's transformation had weakened the spell, apparently Silver's transformation had done even more.

"Life-time transformation seems a bit too harsh," Marjoram announced. For a woman surrounded by a cloud of pink sparkles, she had strangely faded in Forrest's awareness, and he didn't have attention to spare for her now. He was too intent on running to the other side of the star to get Rosie, giving a wide berth to both the star and the tree that had been Aurum. Marjoram's voice continued only as a background awareness. "After all, he did release me from that nasty old bottle, and turning him into a fish forever seems a bit...excessive."

"I don't care what *you* think about it," Lady Diamond spat.

Out of the corner of his eye, Forrest saw Marjoram's sparkles brighten up even more. "And *I* do not care for your tone." Maybe the Good Fairy would transform the last magician, and put an end to this whole disaster.

He couldn't be *that* lucky. A haze of gold sparkles surrounded the fish, and Marjoram intoned, "For your crimes against man you've been changed to a fish, but for your kindness to me I will mitigate this wish. For the span of five hundred Sundays as a fish you will swim, after which you may be freed if granted mercy's whim."

Her poetry was about as good as the horse's. Forrest shook his head, and stepped across the line of the star to crouch down next to his sister. He reached out to shake her shoulder, before he could get too worried about why she was still asleep. "Rosie, wake up." Please wake up. He could carry her, but she was getting big, it would be faster if she could run—and he'd feel so much better too.

Her eyes scrunched tighter shut and she muttered, "Don't want to, I have a test today..."

Forrest felt himself grin, and he shook her shoulder again. "Not today, honey. Come on, wake up, we need to go right now."

This time her eyes slid open and she blinked at him sleepily. "Forrest? What's going on?"

"Well…" Forrest glanced at the massive tree, and watched as the sparkling Good Fairy sent the enchanted fish off through a window, presumably towards the ocean. "…that's sort of complicated."

Marjoram clasped her hands together. "I'm sure that one hundred years as a fish will be a good lesson for him."

"Five hundred Sundays," Lady Diamond said, voice dripping venom, "is not one hundred years. That is *ten* years."

"Is it really?" Marjoram said, and shrugged. "Math is so complicated. All those zeroes, you know. Well then, I'm sure *ten* years as a fish will be a good lesson for him. And after all, he can only be turned back after that if he earns mercy from someone, which will surely be a sign that he's reformed."

Even as he pulled Rosie up to her feet, Forrest noted that you don't actually *earn* mercy. That was what made it mercy.

Rosie swayed, steadied, and demanded, "But what's going *on*?"

"We can talk about it after we're out of here," Forrest said, turned to look for Karina and found her only a pace away. She had broken through her magical bonds too.

"Is the plan to run?" Karina asked, voice tight.

"Exactly," Forrest said, and hauled on Rosie's hand to pull her towards the exit. He saw Karina glance once towards Dimitri, then look away, face set, and follow behind Rosie.

"I believe my work here is done," Marjoram announced, clapped her hands once, and vanished in a spray of gold sparkles that scattered all over the room with surprising range.

Even though the star and the magic woven around it was behind him now, Forrest could still 'see' the twisting strands of the magicians' spells. They still pulsed with power, but they were erratic, unstable, loose ends that had been anchored by Aurum and Silver now waving wildly free. In fact… He started moving faster. "We need to go *now*. That spell behind us—we need to get out."

He could feel Lady Diamond too. He, Rosie and Karina got out the door of the main hall and he couldn't physically see Lady Diamond anymore, but he could feel her as the remaining focal point of the tangle of magic in the hall. And he could feel when she tried to gather the strands together, tried to braid them into a workable spell again. He didn't want to think about what kind of power that would give her—but he didn't need to, because he could also feel the strands tearing free of her attempted restraint, of the power building and twisting and growing only more unstable.

"Run," he ordered, and pushed Rosie ahead of him.

"Where are we *going*?" Karina demanded, pulling even with Forrest.

"Straight," he said, which did little to reflect the chaos of thoughts tumbling in his mind. *Was* straight the best option? There was no reason to hide anymore, straight was the fastest to the exit, leading them right to the enormous wooden doors of the front entrance, and more importantly a smaller exit nearby that *should* be easy to force open. Should be. If it wasn't…but if they turned either direction, tried for another door that was more definite it would take longer, and risked getting lost in the maze of rooms and corridors beyond. "Straight," he repeated. Straight or nothing, because if that small door wouldn't open, no other option would be fast enough to save them.

The narrow corridor opened into the wide entrance hall, the enormous wooden doors looming high above them.

"We can't open those," Karina said, not even winded by the run.

"I *know* that," Forrest said, and pointed to the smaller door, off to the left and half-hidden by shadows.

When he got close enough to see through the shadows, it became clear that this door had not held up well against the wind and the rain in the six years since he'd been here. The wood had rotted and torn away from its hinges.

Rosie reached it first and pushed at the unwieldy door. Karina was only half a step behind her, and when she added a shove, the door broke away completely, falling forward with a squishy thump of rotten wood.

As he stepped through the emptied doorway, Forrest felt a new flare in the spell behind him, as if a skein of yarn had suddenly exploded out into a tangle of snarls. The web of magic was expanding and it was not in Lady Diamond's control at all anymore.

"Keep running," he ordered, and had to hope they could get far enough away before the magic reached the crisis point. He hadn't the slightest idea how far away that would be.

The small door—and the enormous double doors—opened onto a narrow stone bridge across a deep crevice. The crevice formed a natural moat, an eddy of water crashing on rocks far below.

The bridge was maybe a dozen yards long. Rosie reached the far side first, stepping onto the overgrown path. Karina was just behind her, was just stepping off of the stone bridge when Forrest felt a kind of snap behind him. The threads of magic broke, tearing apart and falling to pieces and sending out waves of power in the process.

The sense of magical upheaval was enough to make him stumble. It was followed a heartbeat later by a rumbling beneath him, by a crashing of stone as the castle shook from the force of the spell unleashed.

Forrest managed one more step, arms instinctively reaching forward towards the safety of the far side of the crevice, just a few steps away, before he felt the stone blocks of the bridge fall from beneath his feet.

Chapter Thirty-Five

Karina felt the ground shudder and heard rocks crashing behind her. A few paces in front of her, Rosie lost her footing and fell forwards, catching herself on her hands and knees. Karina instinctively flung herself forward too, hitting the ground with her forearms, pulling her body together to present a smaller target and locking her arms over her head.

For a handful of seconds, maybe a minute, the world was a chaos of dust and smoke, a cacophony of crashes and thundering falls of rock that made her clattering suits of armor seem like the tweeting of birds by comparison.

And then the crashing eased, from a continuous tumult to just a few last clunks and thuds, and at last, silence.

Karina waited a few heartbeats more, then unwrapped her arms from over her head, used her hands to push herself up to sitting and took a deep breath.

That was a mistake, with dust still thick in the air, and she exhaled in a hacking cough. But dust was just an annoyance, an irritant, not the kind of danger falling rocks or insane magicians presented. The rocks were done falling, and Lady Diamond *had* to be dead in that mess back there, and so, everything was fine. Everything was going to be all right. Or if not exactly fine, because some things were never going to be fine, at least the worst had to be over.

She really believed that. For a few seconds. Just until Rosie, who had regained her feet faster and with less coughing, who was looking back towards the castle, said in a trembling voice, "Forrest?"

Karina didn't want to turn around. She desperately didn't want to turn around. But the blood was already draining out of her face and fear was uncoiling in her mind and in another few seconds it was going to be worse to go on looking at Rosie's baffled and horrified expression anyway.

She turned her head. Looked back behind her, towards the castle, the bridge and Forrest.

The castle was a smoking heap of rubble, a few walls barely discernible. The bridge was reduced to a few cracked, sheared off stones at either end, great gaping emptiness between them.

Forrest was gone.

The worst was over? She might as well have commented that at least it wasn't raining.

"No," she whispered. "No, no, no, no..." She scrambled for the edge of the gully, even though she didn't want to look—but she had to look, because sometimes it's even worse not knowing, and also she needed to know whether she needed to stop Rosie from looking, because sometimes it's *better* not knowing, especially when you're eight years old and—

"I really hope you have a rope."

Her ears heard the words before her brain managed to understand them, while her eyes were still trying to sort out what she was seeing through the wisps of dust and spray of salt water. Partway down the wall of the rock crevice, Forrest was hanging onto the cliff-face, balanced on the narrowest of ledges, arms outstretched to cling to the rock.

Karina exhaled in a gasp, dizzy with relief. For about three seconds, until the words finally processed.

She didn't have a rope.

Rosie was crouched next to her by now, peering over the edge too. "Forrest?" she said, voice small and scared. "Are you all right?"

"Yeah," he said, "just a little...stuck."

"I don't have a rope," Karina said, mind working frantically, discarding ideas as fast as they came. Her scarf? Not remotely long enough. Her cloak? Same problem. Use her knife to cut the cloak into strips and—no, she was decent with knots, but not good enough to tie fabric so that it would take a grown man's weight. Was there any rope in the boat? She was almost sure there wasn't, and that there wasn't time to go for it anyway. Or maybe… "You have the pack! Is there anything we can use in the pack? You could throw it to us."

Forrest took one hand away from the cliff-face, started to reach to the pack on his back. His hand wasn't even level with his shoulder before he swayed dangerously. He hastily brought his hand back to the rock, presumably seizing onto a finger hold again. "No, that won't work," he said, breath catching. "Ledge isn't wide enough to stand on while I reach around."

"How did you manage to land on a ledge that narrow to begin with?" Karina demanded, not because it mattered but because she was terrified that the only possible idea wasn't possible at all, and blaming him for landing on too narrow of a ledge made some kind of mad sense under the circumstances.

"It wasn't this narrow when I landed," he answered, with an even more maddening patience. "Some of it broke off when the world was shaking."

"Can you climb without a rope?" Karina asked.

"No," was all he said to that, but it was eloquent enough.

"We have to do something," Rosie said. Her voice was too high. "What can we do? Couldn't we go get help, maybe?"

"No time for that," Karina said. And even if there was, she didn't know how to sail the boat. Which meant that if Forrest fell, she and Rosie were very probably stranded. But that was just compounding an already too-big problem and not helping anything at all.

Her hands moved automatically over her clothes, even though she definitely wasn't going to find a coil of rope she'd forgotten about. A few lock picks in one pocket, the knife in her sleeve sheath (for all the good it had done recently), bits of string, a couple copper pieces…useless, all of it completely useless. Her hand slid over her vest—and stopped, feeling a soft lump in her pocket. She reached in, and drew out the fistful of braid.

It was just a few strands of yarn, braided together. None of the individual strands was more than a foot or so long, meaning it was riddled with knots, any of which could come untied. Not that they needed to, anything this flimsy would just break before there was any time for a knot to come undone.

So the idea floating in her head was completely, utterly and entirely ridiculous. Wasn't it?

"I have, um…something that…might work. Maybe. I mean, it's…it's just yarn, really, and it *shouldn't* work, but, well, I braided it last night, when we were talking, you know, and, I mean, the magicians all seemed to think I have magical ability and, I don't know, it sounds crazy but also there's a lot of Marileigh Blue in here and—I didn't mean to do that, it just happened, which is crazy in a different way and…it's long enough, at least, I think it is, probably, and I know that nothing else is." She ran out of words and air at about the same time.

There was a lingering silence.

"But it's just yarn," Rosie said, staring at the bundle in Karina's hand.

"Let me see it," Forrest said, and even though she couldn't imagine what good it would do, Karina held up her hand, visible over the cliff's edge, and let a few coils of braid unwrap and loop down.

He stared up at it, and she braced herself for a scathing comment on what a ridiculous idea this was. She was less prepared for him to say, "Yeah, all right, let's try it."

She stared at him blankly for a moment, then blinked and said, "Right. Um…" Now for the practicalities—if you could describe anything about this idea as practical. She and Rosie between them didn't weigh enough to brace the rope—braid—as it took Forrest's weight.

She looked around, quickly seized a different idea. "I'll tie it up here." The bridge had had posts at either end, and the one on this side had survived, was still firmly planted in the ground beside the gully. At least, it felt firm when she shoved it with one hand. It was only slightly to the side of where Forrest was holding on, so that should do.

She tied one end of the braid around the post, made the knot as tight and strong as she could. Even if this was completely ridiculous, even if the knot up here was completely irrelevant if any of the other knots in this absurd bit of yarn came undone.

She was aware of Rosie watching her, even if the little girl was being uncharacteristically silent.

Karina let the braid unroll, dropping down over the side of the cliff, tumbling down towards Forrest. Against the rough stone, it looked like the thinnest of threads.

Forrest reached out, closed one hand around the braid, and gave it a hard tug. It held, and Karina was almost sorry. If it had broken then, they could have tried something else.

She had absolutely no other ideas about what they could try, but still.

Forrest took hold of the braid with his other hand, reached up with the first and hauled himself maybe a foot up. His feet were braced against the rock face, but the braid was taking most of his weight.

It held.

Rosie's fingers brushed over the back of Karina's hand, and she instinctively turned it palm up, locking her own fingers around Rosie's. The little girl's grip was tight enough that her hand ached by the time Forrest reached the top.

He clambered over the edge of the cliff, rolled onto his back on the ground, and Rosie dived to hug him before he had time to sit up.

Karina looked away before he could meet her gaze, and went to untie the braid from the post. She attended very carefully to rolling up the yarn again, until she was sure enough that she wasn't going to cry.

Chapter Thirty-Six

Forrest didn't know how he knew that the braid would work as a rope. He just knew it. He could see it, in that way of seeing that wasn't exactly seeing. He could *see* that it was just a haphazard thread of yarn, but at the same time he could not-exactly-see that it was solid and thick and blazing with magical power. Physically it was yarn, but magically it was rope.

Still, that climb wasn't something he'd want to do twice.

Once he was on solid ground again, he took stock. Rosie seemed more excited than upset, and while that wasn't going to last forever, it was easier for the moment. Karina was steadily not looking at him, occupied with untying her braid from the post. If that wasn't everything he might have hoped for, it was about what he'd expected.

And there was no one trying to kill them right now. That made this moment better than any that had preceded it for hours.

He wanted to be relieved, he wanted to conclude that the whole crisis was over and they could go home now and everything was going to be fine again. Except he couldn't quite. Because he could feel something from the ruined castle. It was harder than seeing the magic in Karina's yarn, much murkier than that clear shining vision. This was just a sense of…power, as strong and thick as a Fisherman's Rib knit in heavy-weight wool. Lady Diamond could not possibly have survived that explosion, but he wasn't willing to count on it that she hadn't done it anyway.

And under that worry, there was another worry that he could still sense magic, when he wasn't part of the magicians' spell anymore. How was that happening and what did it mean?

But that was a relatively minor worry, and the main point now was just to get out of here before that heavy power coiled in the castle decided to uncoil and take action.

All he said out loud was that they'd better get back to the boat and go home. No one argued.

The fall of the castle hadn't damaged the rock path down to the beach where he and Karina had left the boat. Once they could see the boat below, Rosie bounded on ahead. It gave Forrest an uncomfortable feeling, letting her out of reach, but he let that go, just keeping a careful eye on her. He wouldn't let her get too far. Just far enough that he could talk to Karina without Rosie hearing.

Once he had that space, he still had no good way to say this. Maybe best to just launch into it. "You should know, I think Lady Diamond might still be alive back in the ruins of the castle." He didn't want that news pushing Rosie from excited to scared.

Karina's stride didn't falter, and she didn't turn her head to look at him. Her hand curled into a fist at her side though. "That's not possible. The castle isn't even standing anymore."

"I know, but I sort of have a…feeling."

"You mean paranoia?"

"No, not that kind of feeling." Although maybe that was part of it. "When I was in that star, it was like I could…see magic. And I still can, and I think I can feel that she's still there."

She didn't comment on this new and rather strange ability. Just said, "If that's true, we should be walking faster."

After a few more slightly longer strides, she added, "You saw something in the yarn braid?"

"Yes." He could see something in her too. She was a complicated twist of cables and braids that you could try to trace for days and never understand how it all fit together, and it all shone out bright and beautiful and strong. Part of him wanted to tell her that, but didn't know how to explain it out loud. Even in his head, it only half made sense.

They kept walking in silence.

Rosie had already climbed into the boat by the time Forrest and Karina stepped off the rocky path onto the narrow beach. Karina, a few steps ahead, was almost up to Rosie when Forrest felt something shift up in the castle.

He only got as far as "Get in the—" before it was too late for a warning to be of any use at all.

Chapter Thirty-Seven

Karina was reaching one hand to the boat when she heard Forrest start to shout something—and before she could make it out, a buffet of wind caught her up, twisted her around, and threw her down to land on her back on the sand.

She instinctively tried to rise, pushing up with her elbows, and another buffet of air flattened her again, pressing her down and holding her. She gave up struggling for the moment, to look for her attacker. Even though she knew who it would be.

She could lift her head just far enough to see more than only blue sky, to look along the beach. And of course, Lady Diamond was stalking across the sand, gray cloak billowing behind her and expression murderous. For a woman who had just been in an explosion that destroyed a castle, she was in a remarkably good state. Her silver hair tumbled over her shoulders and she'd discarded her elbow-length gloves, but there was no other sign she'd been through any disaster.

Except possibly the fury on her face. "I am having a *very* bad day," Lady Diamond announced, glaring down at Karina.

She wasn't the only one. It did not make Karina feel sympathetic. She stared up at the madwoman towering over her, and noticed suddenly that Lady Diamond had small blue fins on her wrists. Well, that was odd.

And not a helpful observation. Her gaze darted frantically around, not sure what *could* be a helpful observation under these horrible circumstances.

"The people I'd really like to retaliate against are no longer within reach," Lady Diamond snarled, "so I'm afraid that just leaves *you*."

Karina could see Forrest, behind Lady Diamond. The woman must have appeared on the beach in between them. He was looking towards the boat, making a flattening gesture with one hand. Karina's gaze darted that direction just long enough to see Rosie ducking down out of sight. She snapped her gaze back towards Lady Diamond, hoping that one glance wouldn't draw attention to Rosie.

"Do you know how many *years* I spent preparing for today's spell? It was to be the culmination of a life's work. And now—ruined, all of it!"

Behind Lady Diamond, Forrest had shrugged his pack off, was reaching into it for something. What did he think he was going to do, throw a scarf at the magician? Whatever he took out, he had it bunched in his fist and Karina couldn't tell what it was.

"It wasn't *mostly* your fault, of course," Lady Diamond said, "but it all might have gone differently if your happy little crew had actually accomplished the task I set you. All you had to do was steal that tree, and it all could have been so different."

Maybe. Maybe Karina would still be back in Ilsonine with a thousand gold pieces and her friends still alive. Or maybe Lady Diamond would have killed them all anyway, as soon as she had what she wanted. And either way, Karina never would have come here, never would have met Forrest or Rosie or... But none of that mattered, what mattered was what *did* happen, what was happening right now, not what might have been. There had to be something she could *do*, some way to fight back...

"I put much more blame on your idiot friend, whatever his name was—"

"Dimitri," Karina whispered, the name pushed out against the tightness of her throat and the air pressing against her neck. She wasn't sure anymore that 'friend' was the right term. Somehow, they had been both more and less than that.

Lady Diamond waved one finned hand. "I don't care. Especially since he's dead, and the only one left to blame, my dear, is *you*." She waved her hand again, not a dismissive gesture this time, but a slow circle. "If our spell had succeeded, I would be able to drown this entire country with barely a thought. But as it is, I still have enough magical power to drown one foolish girl."

Karina felt a sudden coldness at the top of her head. She had fallen with her head lying towards the ocean, and as her gaze darted from side to side, she could just barely see rivulets of water seeping up closer, coming towards her.

She could still breathe and yet the air caught in her throat as though she was already drowning, a panicked instinct took over and she kicked and thrashed against the magic holding her down—or tried to, the spell keeping her nearly motionless. *Nearly*—this time, for the first time, the binding gave just a little. Her thoughts cleared, slightly, enough to realize that commanding the water had to be straining Lady Diamond's magic.

She remembered suddenly the knit bracelet on her right wrist, the way that arm had been resisting magic better all along. She tried that hand, and—yes, she could feel the spell was even weaker there.

So that was it, then. One effort to break free, to get her knife out, to throw herself at Lady Diamond. If she was fast enough... Most likely, almost definitely, she was just going to end up blasted and killed. Like Dimitri. But it was still better to go out fighting.

She focused her gaze on Lady Diamond, who was still ranting on about blame and retribution. But as she looked at the enchantress, she could see Forrest too. And he was looking at her, shaking his head and making that flattening gesture again. From the direction of his gaze, he couldn't mean Rosie this time. So *she* was supposed to just lie here? She could feel water at her ears now, pooling under her neck. It was rising.

Then Forrest pointed at himself. Clear enough message: stay still, let him do something. She was supposed to, what, just trust him?

Well. Yes, probably that was exactly what he wanted.

But she didn't *do* that, she never left her survival up to someone else.

And how well, exactly, had that been going for her?

She bit her lip, forced her muscles to relax, and waited, as the water rose, as Lady Diamond went on with her melodramatic speech and as Forrest edged ever closer up behind Lady Diamond, right hand and whatever he'd taken from his pack hidden behind his back.

He was within three paces when Lady Diamond turned to face him. "Isn't this cute?" she drawled. "The shepherd coming to rescue his lady love."

Even with cold water creeping up towards her chin, Karina felt her cheeks flush hot.

And Forrest...shrugged. "Well, I'd hardly call her that," he said easily. "I mean, we barely met a few days ago. But you're right I'm a shepherd, and I've been stuck on this backwater island my whole life. I'm not stupid though, and you're obviously the most powerful person I'm ever going to meet. You and the others, you all said I have magical ability. Couldn't I work for you? An apprentice or something?"

Lady Diamond stared at him for a moment. "Me, waste time with someone like you?" She threw back her head and laughed.

And that was when Forrest took advantage of the extra step gained while he was talking, brought his right hand out from behind his back, and threw a net over Lady Diamond's head.

Chapter Thirty-Eight

The net settled over Lady Diamond's head and shoulders, and an expression of rage settled over her face, so fierce that Forrest was momentarily sure he'd just hastened everyone's deaths. She reached up with one hand to claw the net away, reached out with the other, poised to throw some blasting spell at him—and neither happened. She couldn't shift the net, and no magic came from her throwing hand.

Forrest exhaled in a rush, relief flooding through him. In the boat, Rosie cautiously lifted her head to watch the scene with wide eyes, and on the sand, Karina pushed herself up to sitting, water streaming from her hair, and wiped her face on one sleeve.

And Lady Diamond glowered at Forrest. "What did you do? What is this?"

"Just a simple fishing net," he said. "But it was woven to hold things." And in his mind's eye, he had been able to see the thick, twisted knots of magic in it, and seen too that Lady Diamond's magic was stretching ever thinner, a loose and warped web full of holes.

"I'll release you," he said, "if you swear you'll leave, and not seek any revenge now or later."

"You'd better make it broader than that," Karina murmured.

"And…swear not to inflict harm against Marileigh or anyone in it, ever again." That should be broad enough, covering the entire country.

Lady Diamond's eyes narrowed. "I will not forfeit the right to defend myself. I will only swear not to inflict first harm. Your precious country is safe, provided none of you cause harm to *me*."

Forrest nodded slowly. It wasn't unreasonable—and more importantly, he didn't know how long that net could hold her, so he'd better make this fast. "Swear it by the Stone of the Great Magician." Legend said the greatest of all magicians had been sleeping for centuries beneath an enormous stone in some far away land, and whether it was legend or truth, it was a binding vow for anyone who practiced magic.

Her eyes narrowed further, but she nodded. "I so swear it. But be warned, should anyone in this country ever threaten me again, ever do anything to cause harm to me or mine, nothing will stop me from enacting vengeance." Her voice dropped to a low hiss as she glared out between the lines of the net. "I will remember this day, and I will bring a curse upon this entire nation, a curse that no farmboy with a fishing net will be able to break. I will trap you all in a dance you'll never escape."

Forrest swallowed uneasily—but they were just empty words, surely. She couldn't act unless someone caused her harm first, and no one would do that. She had sworn to go away. It was safe now.

He reached out, pulled the net away and quickly stepped back—because there was no point being stupid.

Lady Diamond folded her hands together and vanished, leaving only empty air behind her.

Forrest stared at the space she had been occupying. It seemed somehow emptier than the other emptiness around it. He hadn't exactly understood the sheer eeriness of that disappearing trick when Karina described it. It was the *lack* of drama that made it so…dramatic.

From the boat, Rosie asked in a small voice, "Is she really gone? Is everything all right now?"

This was no time to get unnerved, now that it was all over and they'd actually *won*. "Yes," Forrest said firmly. "To both."

Rosie scrambled out of the boat, darted over and crashed into him in a hug. "Good. Because that was *scary*."

He stroked a hand over her hair, tugged one braid. "It's all over now. We're going home. And then the scariest thing left to do will be to explain all this to Mother."

"That could be scary too," Rosie said in doubtful tones. "It wasn't our fault but…"

"…but she'll say we should have been more careful, and then won't let us out of her sight for a month." Though compared to recent events, that seemed pretty harmless. "Come on, let's go home."

Rosie went back to the boat, and Forrest walked the few paces to Karina, who was still sitting on the wet sand, staring down. He extended a hand. "Are you all right?"

Predictably she said, "Yes," immediately. But she reached up to take his hand, let him haul her to her feet. Standing, she finally met his gaze. Then she blinked, and tears spilled over to trickle down her cheeks. "No, of course I'm not all right," she whispered, stepped forward and hugged him, hard.

He was almost too surprised to remember to hug her back. But not quite.

Chapter Thirty-Nine

Karina had thought everything might be quiet for a while, now that all the magic was done and gone. But when they got back home, they found the rest of the family had already returned. The message calling them away had turned out to be completely false; considering it had been delivered by Master Aurum, it wasn't hard to guess that this had been part of his larger plan to abduct Rosie.

The family's return meant plunging straight into relating recent events. Despite the predictions of her children, telling Lynette about the adventures with the mad magicians was not nearly as terrifying as living them. Even though Karina felt she deserved a much bigger share of blame in the situation than Forrest or Rosie deserved, no one else seemed to think so. She had meant to slip off to bed as early as possible, but somehow found herself staying up late as the story was told and retold, quietly surprised to find herself an accepted member of the circle.

She overslept the next day, finally dressed and wandered out into the kitchen when the sun was already bright. She found Forrest alone at the table, knitting something out of black yarn.

He looked up with a smile when she came in. "Good morning."

"Is it still morning?" she asked, peering out the nearest window at the bright sunlight.

"Just barely. There's toast if you want it."

She nodded, took a piece from the stack on the table, and listened for a moment to the chatter of voices through the half-open door to the back stoop.

"And that's when the whole castle came crashing down!" Rosie was saying.

"I can't believe I missed *everything*." That sounded like the prince, Dastan. "It sounds so exciting!"

"At least you saw Millie talking, before that spell ended. And maybe there'll be other magic things happening, some other time. If the evil enchantress lady comes back, maybe you'll get to fight her next time!"

Karina shook her head. She never, ever wanted to be involved in any magic like Lady Diamond's or Master Aurum's or that magic cloak ever again. Although…she didn't feel quite that way about *all* magic anymore. Almost without thinking about it, she touched the pocket of the dress she'd borrowed from Clara, felt the soft lump of the rolled-up yarn braid.

She took a second piece of toast and sat down across the table from Forrest. "What are you making?"

"I think it's going to be a shawl," he said. "But I also thought it was going to be black, so who knows?" He held up the knitted portion, displaying mostly black but with splashes of bright blues, reds and oranges at irregular intervals.

"Black yarn knitted into something with colors?" Not that it was any stranger than plenty of other things that had happened in the last few days. She checked for the prickle magic usually gave her, but didn't feel it. Just curiosity.

"Exactly. I kind of think it fits the story." He glanced up from the knitting. "I started it when you were telling me about your past."

"Oh." She looked down at the toast in her hand, looked at his knitting out of the corner of her eye. Black, with splashes of color. Darkness and knife fights and betrayals, but also stained glass windows. Maybe it did fit. "So does the number of stitches make it magical?"

"I'm not sure…" Forrest said slowly, rubbing a piece of the knit cloth between his fingers. "It's not designed to be magical, but it sort of…feels magical. I can still feel magic. Somehow."

Karina checked to see if this was going to make her spine prickle either, but it didn't. "Maybe it's a sense you always had, you just didn't know it. It might be useful. Especially if Lady Diamond ever comes back."

"She's not coming back," he said quickly. "She swore not to."

Unless anyone harmed her first. And in an entire country, something could happen. There was Lord Silver to think about too, only condemned to be a fish for ten years. After that, if he was shown mercy, he could come back too. If he sought revenge on Lady Diamond, if the two of them started a magical war with this country caught in the middle of it...

But that was at least ten years away, if it ever even happened, and today the sun was shining and she had good company and plenty to eat and, for the first time in what felt like a lifetime, no one to run from.

"If she does come back," Karina said lightly, not really able to work up much worry, "let's let someone else deal with her. Maybe those dozen princes you have. Magic is usually a royal problem anyway."

"Some of the time," Forrest said, knit a few more stitches, then very casually said, "So will you be wanting to find a ship soon? To go back to Ilsonine, or...or somewhere else?"

It *would* have sounded casual, if he hadn't stumbled over the last phrase. Somehow that just added to the general good feeling of the morning. And she had been thinking about this, while she was sitting up late. "I don't think so," she said, carefully brushing a crumb off the table. "I mean, I'm not running from anyone now. So maybe I'll just...stay around a while." She couldn't help peeking to see how he was taking that.

His grin was enough confirmation that it was the right decision. Even if the smile then turned a little wicked as he said, "Maybe Dahlia can find you a job at the inn."

"Don't make me throw toast at you," she warned, fighting a smile herself.

"Or we can help you find something else," he said, expression entirely unrepentant.

"Good." Then she hesitated, resisted the urge to touch her lump of braid again, and with her own best effort at casualness said, "I was also wondering...if you might...teach me how to knit."

He blinked in obvious surprise. "Really?"

She shrugged. "You know. Could be useful. Especially if those magicians were right that I can work magic. I ought to do something with it."

The grin, the genuine, non-wicked one, was back. "I'd be happy to teach you how to knit." He held up a knitting needle. "On one condition."

"What is it?"

"Teach me some of those tricks you know about fighting."

"Could be useful?"

"Exactly."

She grinned back at him. "Agreed."

He pushed his knitting needles into the bundle of black yarn, and rose to his feet. "This'll keep until later. If you're done eating, I can start a knitting lesson right now."

She swallowed the last bite of toast. "Done."

They went into the parlor, where he handed her a ball of pale blue yarn and two smooth wooden needles, and directed her to sit on a footstool.

"I could demonstrate," he said, "but then you'd be watching it backwards and it's hard to see what someone else is doing when they knit and...well, there's an easier way."

He knelt down behind her, bringing his head to a level with hers, and reached around so his arms encircled her and his hands covered hers where they held up the two knitting needles.

"I swear this is the best way to teach someone knitting," he said softly.

She felt a giggle deep in her throat. "Really?"

"Really." He lightly squeezed her hands, then reached down for the ball of yarn. "We begin," he said, breath warm across her cheek, "with casting-on..."

That felt right. That black history with its few splashes of color was still close behind her; her tangles of feelings about the last few days, about her friends, about Dimitri, were still too tightly knotted for her to say yet exactly what she would do next, what color or shape the next part of her life was going to be.

But beginning something new, casting-on a new life...she was ready for that.

Looking for More Tales?

Now available in paperback and ebook:

The Storyteller and Her Sisters

Read how events unfold after Prince Dastan grows up, when Lady Diamond finds a loophole to place a curse on Marileigh. Now twelve princesses must dance every night to rescue the twelve princes from her spell, while keeping an enchanted forest from falling into the hands of their mad father.

The Wanderers

Come journey with Jasper, a wandering adventurer, and Tom, a snarky talking cat, as they fight monsters and wander through familiar—but slightly slanted—fairy tales. When they rescue Julie, a witch's daughter, it sets off conflict with her very sparkly Fairy Godmother.

The People
the Fairies Forget

An unusual fairy named Tarragon clashes with Good Fairy Marjoram, by championing the people who live on the edges of fairy tales. See the stories from the perspective of a goatherd trying to rescue his kitchen maid true love from Sleeping Beauty's castle, or a girl who fits Cinderella's slipper and is now expected to marry the prince whether she wants to or not. Find out if Tarry can rescue them from Marjoram's good intentions!

More Books from Stonehenge Circle Press

Secrets in the Dark
by K. D. Blakely

Hiding from bullies in the town cemetery
seemed like a good idea. Right up until we
fell through a creepy secret doorway into
a magic land called Chimera. My friends
and I promised to keep Chimera a secret,
but that's hard when we go there every
month. Who knew being born in THE
STRANGEST YEAR EVER could change...everything!

Pucker Up
by R. A. Gates

Ivy always thought that breaking a curse
with True Love's Kiss was the ultimate
romantic gesture in fairy tales. But when
she has to plant one on a prince who's
been dead for 200 years, it's just gross.

Find more of Cheryl's favorite books:
http://marveloustales.com/recommendedread

Acknowledgements

This book would not have been possible without the support of friends, family, and everyone who enjoyed the last three books and wanted to read more. Thank you to early readers Karen, Dennis, Lynn, Ruth, Meaghan and Kelly for their excellent feedback. As always, thank you to the entire writing group at Stonehenge—you continue to make me a better writer every week!

This book owes more unusual debts as well: to Emi, who taught me how to knit; to Lynn, who made a very significant remark once about the peculiar magic of looping yarn together and having it *become* something; and to Tom Baker and his magical scarf, as re-creating it immersed me in patterns and numbers and varying shades of yarn.

About the Author

Cheryl Mahoney can't remember when she began her love affair with stories. She never goes anywhere (including the grocery store) without a book and a pen. She enjoys knitting but can't claim to have ever made anything with magical properties.

Cheryl also writes a book review blog, Tales of the Marvelous (http://marveloustales.com), and is on Goodreads (MarvelousTales). She has written three previous books in the Beyond the Tales series, and has completed NaNoWriMo four times.